By Tom Piccirilli

The Last Whisper in the Dark

THE
LAST
WHISPER
IN THE
DARK

A Novel

Tom
Piccirilli

Bantam Books   New York

Copyright © 2013 by Tom Piccirilli

All rights reserved.
Published in the United States by Bantam Books,
an imprint of The Random House Publishing Group,
a division of Random House, Inc., New York.

BANTAM BOOKS and the rooster colophon are registered trademarks of Random House, Inc.

Library of Congress Cataloging-in-Publication Data

Piccirilli, Tom.
The Last Whisper in the Dark: a novel / Tom Piccirilli.
pages cm
ISBN: 978-0-345-52900-8 (acid-free paper) —
ISBN: 978-0-345-52901-5 (eBook)
1. Criminals—Fiction. 2. Families—Fiction. I. Title.
PS3566.I266L39 2013
813'.54—dc23
2012043223

Printed in the United States of America on acid-free paper

www.bantamdell.com

2 4 6 8 9 7 5 3 1

First Edition

Book design by Donna Sinisgalli

For everyone with a sin that can't be laid aside, a shadow that won't lift, a haunting moonlit love, an unfixable mistake, a hook they've hung you on, a missing old man, a heart of noir, a cold storm of history, a splinter of unforgettable shame, a secret desire you flee from, a dreaded song In the skull, a figure behind you in the mirror, a story unfinished, a costly lesson finally learned, a well-chosen name that will go unused, *The Last Whisper in the Dark* is for you.

A secret is not something unrevealed, but something told privately, in a whisper.

—MARCEL PAGNOL

We cannot be kind to each other here for even an hour. We whisper, and hint, and chuckle and grin at our brother's shame; however you take it we men are a little breed.

—ALFRED LORD TENNYSON

Part I

THE LAST
DOG
WENT BAD

The first whisper in the dark.

Terrier, I'm pregnant.

I dreamed a desperate dream of Kimmy. It was a vivid memory fueled by my own unhinged fantasies. When I was on the ranch the other hands gave me a wide berth and made me sleep in a fruit cellar converted to a one-man bunk room. I had a habit of lashing out. I talked and shouted in my sleep. I heard myself speaking and tried to answer. I saw her sitting on the edge of my bed, crying, her face turned away from me. I'd reach for her and snap awake covered in sweat, my head ringing.

Terrier, I'm—

I had the dream and the dream had me for the fourth night in a row.

We were in the Commack Motor Inn, one of the pay-by-the-hour motels we used to stop into for a little alone time. Intimacy and privacy weren't among the benefits of living in a large house with a criminal family. My father had retired from the bent life by then but never went anywhere. My mother watched over my baby sister Dale, and Old Shep, my grandfather, who was starting to lose himself to Alzheimer's, his personality seeping out an old gunshot wound in the back of his head. My uncles Mal and Grey stuck close to home with their schemes and grifts. My brother Collie was the only one with enough respect to work his bad deeds day and night elsewhere. And Kimmy's parents hated my guts and kept watch for me like retirees guarding the So Cal coastline from the Japanese in '42.

We were catching our breath, lying back in each other's arms, holding tight. Her wet hair raked my cheek. I lit a cigarette and took a long drag. I blew out a stream of smoke and offered the butt to her. She took it and ground it out against the side of the scarred nightstand. She pressed her lips to my ear.

"Terrier, I'm pregnant."

The blinds had been drawn halfway against the parking lot lights. The air conditioner cranked away on high doing a shitty job. It was dark in our room and I couldn't quite make out the expression on her face. A couple of sparks still clung to the nightstand, glowing red. Her voice was steady, but I couldn't tell if she was happy or anxious or both. Neither of us had hit twenty yet.

I said, "We're not naming her after a fucking dog."

It made Kimmy laugh, a sound that eased the tension that was always inside me. I never knew it was there until she relieved me of it, and then I let out a breath and my muscles loosened and ached.

"Her?" she said. "So you want a girl?"

"I suppose I do."

"Why?"

I didn't even have to think about it. "I like the idea of saying, 'I'm going home to my girls.'"

My ghosts caught up to me again. I couldn't move without inviting them along. They came and went and judged. My eyes opened in the pale dawn and they were with me. My dead brother, my dead uncles, they stood nearby, ready to resume their action. My best friend Chub was there too. He was going to die if I didn't help him. A part of me wanted it to happen. The rest knew that he and I were bound by our shared history. If I couldn't save him I wouldn't be able to save myself. He watched me steadily. Blood bubbled from his lips as he said, *I'm still alive, you prick.*

We were on death watch again. My brother Collie's had lasted more than five years before he'd been walked down that insanely white prison corridor. After a brief inevitable show of defiance, kicking and brawling with the screws, he'd forgone his last words, been strapped down to a table and given the needle.

I watched as his blood turned to poison, hoping he might try to connect with me in those final seconds and explain why he'd gone on his killing spree. But his hateful gaze said nothing and showed no remorse. He sneered right up to the moment that the second plunger depressed and his lungs grew paralyzed. His eyes were stone but I could forgive him that. He was taking his last breath in front of an audience of witnesses who all wanted him in hell.

When he went down he left the rest of the family reeling, and despite all our stoic resolve we were unable to take any more loss. My uncle Mal had been murdered a few days beforehand, knifed in the backyard. My uncle Grey, so far as my parents knew, had gone on the long grift and was living the sweet life somewhere full of sex and satin, maybe in A.C. or Reno.

My father had lost three of the most significant people in his life within a matter of a week, and now his best friend lay dying under the kitchen table.

It had been three days since JFK had eaten or sipped any water. He was ten and his muzzle was thick with gray fur. He was still massive and muscular, with a flat broad forehead and fierce features that hadn't lost any of their intensity.

He didn't seem to be in any serious pain as he continued to grow weaker. We huddled around him on the kitchen floor like our ancestors squatting in front of a fire trying to keep the terrors of the night away.

JFK would occasionally look around the room, his glance landing on each of us in turn. Every time his eyes settled on my mother she whispered his name and stroked him between the ears. My father, a reticent man at best, tried to keep up a stream of buoyant chatter for JFK's sake. I barely recognized his contrived, cheerful voice. My sister Airedale kept petting JFK's haunches, saying, "That's our boy, that's our boy." His dry tongue fell from his mouth as he struggled to lift his head in an effort to kiss each of us. He let out a sigh every now and again, his nubby tail wagging once or twice, before settling back to try to sleep.

"That's our boy."

It was time to put him down. We all knew it. Even my old man knew it. But my father, always a cool realist in all other matters, refused to discuss bringing JFK to the vet. My mother argued softly and begged him to change his mind. He wouldn't. I sided with him at first because like him I was weak when it mattered most.

It was the cruelty of love. Dale, with a tight resolution marring her beauty, said, "Daddy, it's time." She gripped his stubbled cheek roughly, trying to snap him from his daze. He was short and wiry and Dale towered over him now, but his terrible staunchness made itself known. It was the thing inside him that couldn't be moved or persuaded.

My father's thousand-yard stare looked through all of us. Every muscle in his body stood out rigid and straining. His silence brought a barometric pressure to the room, like the hushed anxious period before a storm hit.

Old Shepherd sat in his wheelchair in the corner of the living room, in front of the television watching cartoons. JFK's slow dying had managed to reach through his cognitive fog where almost everything else had failed. He now had odd moments of lucidity where he called to the dog, asking if he wanted to go for a walk in the park. Gramp sounded childlike, overly eager, and a little frightened.

By the fourth day JFK's breathing had grown much rougher. He wheezed all morning long and about noon let out a little puddle of urine with blood in it. I went to the shed and got a shovel and dug a hole under the apple tree where JFK sometimes lay out in the sun. When I stepped back inside my mother was on her knees cleaning the floor with a towel. My old man was pretending he was somewhere else.

She said, "Pinscher, this has to stop." She stood and put her hand to his powerful arm and I saw the tendons and veins in her wrist bulging as she squeezed and squeezed harder to try to gain his attention. "You can't let it go on. He's in pain. He's in terrible pain."

My father wouldn't look at her. He stood in the front door with a chill autumn breeze blowing in through the screen. He seemed to be admiring the veranda. He'd spent a few thousand nights out there staring into the neighboring woods, looking over the arch of his life, with JFK curled at his feet.

I had to travel deep to discover what remained of my courage and mercy. There didn't seem to be a whole lot left anymore. "We have to take him in."

"Pinscher?"

"I'm not putting him down. We . . . we don't have the right. I wouldn't want anyone to steal my last remaining hours. Not even a minute. I won't rob him of his."

Anyone else might have found that ironic, my father being a career thief and an excellent second-story man before he retired to sit on his porch and drink beer, bored out of his fucking head.

But he wasn't talking about himself or the dog. He was thinking of Collie's victims, especially the kids.

"You think that's wrong?" he asked me.

"Yes."

He nodded once, his expression shifting from stonewall to slightly annoyed and back again. He sat at the table directly above JFK and looked everywhere except at the dog.

My mother tried one last time to make him see reason. Her anger was beginning to break through. "Pinscher, he's in agony. Let's give him a little peace and respect."

"You think that'll make any difference?"

"Yes, I do."

"I don't think so."

"I know you don't, but you're wrong."

My old man shrugged at that. I noticed how his hair swung back and forth into his eyes as he lifted his shoulders. He'd always worn a crew cut but he'd been letting his hair grow out the last couple of months. It was a small sign that he was changing inside and it worried me.

He asked me to get him a beer. I pulled one from the fridge and sat the bottle in front of him. He emptied half of it in one pull.

My mother shot me a look. I knew what it meant. We were going to have to buck him. I was going to have to carry JFK to the backseat of my car and take him to the vet on my own. I knew my father wouldn't try to stop me. His conscience was already in a frenzy and I wondered if he'd hold it against me forever. We Rands didn't forgive easily. We Rands had long memories until Alzheimer's turned our brains to tapioca.

JFK moaned groggily as I lifted him. I shouldered through the screen door and carried him down the walk to my car. My mother followed. She sat in back with him, using her thumbs to clear her tears away. After a few seconds my father climbed into the passenger seat. He stared ahead through the windshield, arms crossed over his chest, the black veins crawling across the backs of his powerful hands.

My mother said, "If you're going with Terry then I'll stay here with Gramp."

"I'm going with Terry," my father said.

"All right."

JFK slept the entire ride to the vet's. I found myself hoping he would die before we arrived. I wanted him to go naturally without losing a minute of his allotted time. I didn't want him to struggle to his very last breath. I didn't want him to have to get the hot shot like Collie had.

When we arrived at the vet's office JFK's eyes were open and he was peering at me. His tail thumped twice, tongue hanging. My father led the way inside the place. He looked like he was about to knock over a bank.

I carried JFK in, hugging him to me, his face turned against my chest and bloody urine leaking over my shirt. I didn't sign anything or talk to anyone at the front counter, I just lugged him directly into the examining room and told the lady vet tech that it was time to put him down. Her name tag read *Missy*. She asked questions about his age, eating habits, stool density, vomiting, and pet insurance. I wondered why any of that shit mattered now. My father said nothing. Missy started to slowly back out of the room with a patronizing smile smeared across her face. I finally managed to explain the situation.

Missy repeated her questions and I answered as best I could. She said the vet would be in to see us soon. JFK weakened further while we waited.

I patted his side and wished him an easier death. I said, "It's okay, boy, it's all right." My father knew what I really meant and covered my hand with his, forcing me to stop.

The vet had an even bigger name tag the size of a sheriff's badge. Dr. George Augustyn. It was authoritative, a name to impress. I'd met him before but hadn't seen him in over five years. Dr. George had the beefcake good looks of a B actor who'd made it in the biz on the strength of his smile and chin dimple.

He kept calling JFK "Johnny" and tried to get him to sit up. JFK was always eager to please and made a hell of an effort, whining as he attempted to clamber to his feet on the slippery metal counter surface. He couldn't make it. Dr. George made notations and listened to the dog's chest and belly. I kept a hand on JFK's front paw, rubbing my thumb back and forth across the pad of his sole. It felt like I stood there doing that for hours. I couldn't stop.

George had a code of ethics to follow. He refused to give JFK the shot without giving him a full examination first.

I noticed that on the paperwork in JFK's folder they had his breed down as "pit bull." I almost corrected them by explaining that he was an American Staffordshire terrier. I realized how stupid it was to care about something like that right now and kept my mouth shut. But a moment later it seemed like the most important thing in the world.

I squawked, "You've got it wrong. He's an American Stafford-shire." I wagged my chin as if to clear my head, but it wasn't helping. Luckily, everyone ignored me anyway.

My thumb kept sliding back and forth across JFK's paw. Dr. George told Missy that they needed to do X-rays. The two of them, wearing scrubs covered in dancing kittens, managed to heft JFK into their arms. My father and I began to file out and follow them. The vet said "Stay here" with a commanding note.

We hovered in the doorway shoulder to shoulder. I felt closer to my father now than I had in weeks. I had secrets he'd want to hear and many he wouldn't. I wanted to talk and had no idea what to say.

In twenty minutes Missy returned. She said they'd found a block-age. It wasn't anything serious. The operation would last a half hour. The girl asked us if it was all right to proceed. My old man sputtered for a second. I said, "Of course, yes." He and I finally looked each other in the face.

It took closer to an hour, and then another hour until the anesthe-sia wore off. We sat in the waiting area like expectant fathers. Folks brought their pets in and out. An old sheepdog lumbered past and nosed at my crotch. A pair of beagle puppies ran up and down the length of the room, wrestling and rolling on top of one another. They barked playfully at us. I stuck my foot out and they both came over and gnawed at my toe for a while.

A door opened and Missy told us, "You can see him now."

JFK was in a kennel cage with the gate raised, just waking up. The front paw I'd been rubbing was shaved and had an IV drip in it. His belly was bandaged. His eyes cleared and when he saw us his tail started to go whump. He tried twice to get to his feet before he managed it. He stood shakily on his legs and yawned, then made a noise like he was clearing his throat for a profound soliloquy.

My old man was unable to contain his smile, which kept breaking through and animating his face. He put his nose up to JFK's and the dog gave him a savage kiss.

Dr. George chilled us with the angle of his chiseled chin dimple. His voice ran thick with irritation. He told us what kind of a diet JFK would be allowed for the next few weeks. Bland wet dog food high in protein so he could recover quicker.

I waited for what was coming next. So did my father. Our heads were lowered as we prepared for the lash.

Dr. George let us have it. "As soon as your pets start exhibiting signs of illness," he said, pausing. The pause lengthened. The pause stretched like razor wire. "*As soon* as they exhibit signs of *any* kind of trauma or disease you should bring them immediately into the office. Right? *Immediately.* Why did you wait so long?"

"That's my fault," my father said. "I didn't want him put to sleep."

"Getting a checkup isn't the equivalent of being put down."

A hard, mean diamond glint entered my old man's gaze. How could you explain what a hot shot might mean to us? He wet his lips. "I realize that now."

"John F. Kennedy could have died."

"Yes."

"And you could have saved him a great deal of suffering."

"Yes."

George shook his handsome head. "And when the time comes, it's more humane to put him down than to let him endure such agony."

"I see that now."

"*Good*. You can stay here with him until he's awake enough to walk out on his own."

Two days later I filled in the hole under the apple tree while JFK sat beside me, thumping his tail against the frosty morning earth.

We were about a hundred yards away from my uncle Grey's unmarked grave in the woods, a man I had loved, admired, and eventually been forced to kill.

JFK made that throat-clearing sound again and I turned and said, "What?"

He raised his paw and put it over my heart.

I took it as a sign of forgiveness. I would take anything as a sign of forgiveness.

I'd been watching my former best friend Chub Wright's garage almost every night for two months, keeping an eye on him as he met with various crews and helped them plan their getaway routes. Chub sold souped-up muscle cars and offered information on radar traps, state trooper activity, police routes, the best way out of town, and potential hole-up spots.

Chub had conferred with three different strings since I'd started eyeing the garage. I didn't recognize any of them. All of them paid him off the way he required. A certain amount of cash before the boost and a small percentage of the total take after the heat died down. So far, one of the crews had returned to give him his cut. Nobody in the bent life would rip him off. Chub had a name for himself and still threw weight, partly because he knew the right people but mostly because he'd run with my family for so many years.

There was no reason at all why he should continue to take these kinds of risks. He had a legitimate business making good money. I knew all about his aboveboard finances. I'd crept his office and found both sets of books. They were both way in the black.

My dreams were getting worse. In them, Kimmy begged me to watch over her husband. I woke with her taste on my lips. I woke with Chub's blood on my hands. I showered for hours and still imagined I saw them red.

I checked the time. It was nudging past ten. The garage remained dark. Chub was at home with his wife and daughter, watching television or snacking on chips or making love to Kimmy. The freezing wind shaved my throat.

Chub showed up at ten-fifteen. His luck would eventually play out. It had to happen. He'd keep pushing the odds until one of the crews turned on him or the cops pulled a sting operation. There was no place for him to go except into the bin or the grave.

I watched him park and head inside, flip on the lights in the bays, and step into his office. I thought about crossing the lot, saying hello, and trying to shake his hand. I'd made the attempt before but it had ended badly.

I sat back and lit a cigarette and smoked in the dark staring through the windows of the garage.

Headlights flashed across the lot. I threw down the butt and edged back into shadow.

This latest crew was a tight-knit four-guy unit. The wheelman drove a blue-black GTO with extra muscle under the hood. They carried a lot of hardware. They dressed the same, in black clothing with black jackets, black shoes, wearing black wool hats, with hair dyed the same shade of black. It was something crews sometimes did during heists to confuse witnesses and keep the onlookers from getting a good description. I'd never heard of a string doing it before a job. It proved they were keeping Chub on the outside. They didn't entirely trust him. That might be natural wariness on their part or they might seriously be leery of him. It made me a little nervous.

They talked quietly in clipped, terse voices. Three of them went inside with Chub while the fourth kept a lookout, patrolling the area.

He never stopped moving, never ducked back inside for a few minutes to warm up. The frigid temperature didn't seem to bother him. He wove an impressive pattern all around the junkers and restored classic cars Chub kept on the lot. He glanced through windshields and checked backseats. He doubled back along his own path. He kept his hands close to his sides, a compact .32 hidden against his right leg. I knew how to use the dark but still had trouble keeping ahead of him as we worked our way around. Twice he came within arm's length. If I wasn't a burglar with a practiced step he would've nabbed me for certain.

They were a sharp and professional crew, but I didn't like all the iron. Even the driver packed. So far as I knew, drivers never carried weapons. Their sole function was to stay steely and wait for their string to finish the heist and then get everyone out of there. All a gun did was add five years to the bill if you got caught at the scene. A driver needed horsepower, not firepower.

The fourth guy and I continued to play tag. The others were inside with Chub for half an hour. He would have a well-planned escape route already mapped out, along with contingencies. They'd run the route at least a half-dozen times before pulling the holdup to grind off any edges and make sure it went smooth as ice.

Chub stepped outside and led the others to a dark green '69 Mustang fastback pulled into the corner by the far fence. It was parked beside a second option, a 1970 Challenger. Both muscle cars were unseen from the street, hidden by a number of wrecks. The vehicles would be clean, one hundred percent legal with all the correct paperwork. It was one of the reasons why the strings came to Chub. He never dealt with hot items. The cops had no reason to keep an eye on him because everything in his garage was legit.

The driver checked under the hood of the Mustang and seemed impressed with what he found. The breeze carried their voices to me. They talked engine torque, shift points, speed climbs, and maximum acceleration. They slid in and out of the two-door car with the tight rear bench. It seemed an odd choice for four guys pulling a job. I thought they would have gone for the roomier Dodge. But even that seemed strange to me. I figured you'd want a four-door so everyone could have his own entrance and exit point. But I wasn't a heist man.

The fourth guy kept his .32 in his hand. Chub didn't appear worried. I knew he would be. He didn't like guns any more than I did. He had a wrench in his back pocket. He could cave in somebody's head with it. He kept his body half turned so that the fourth guy was always in front of him. The driver chuckled about something and stuck out his hand to shake. Chub only grinned and nodded. He was being smart. He wasn't going to compromise his hands.

The crew climbed into the Mustang. The car they came in was probably stolen and Chub would have it driven off his lot by an associate for a small cash fee.

The driver couldn't help but goose the Mustang's engine a couple of times before he threw it into drive. But when he got it into the street he drove the speed limit.

When they hit their first turn I hopped in my car and followed.

On the grift it was occasionally important to tail a mark. I gave the crew a significant lead and kept changing lanes. We headed west toward the city. There was still traffic on the Long Island Expressway. There was always traffic on the LIE. I'd forgotten that during the years I hid out in big sky country. When I got back to New York it took a little getting used to. Eating exhaust again, bumper to bumper no matter what time of day you hit the road.

The driver took the Wantagh Parkway exit and then played around on some side streets and access roads.

I did everything right but the driver still lost me. It was slippery and perfectly done. He was there one second and gone the next. He shook me easily. I didn't even think he knew he was being followed. He just pulled the intermittent maneuver to drop a tail in case he ever picked one up. Some guys were just paranoid enough.

If they were on to me I'd know it soon. They wouldn't run. They'd either brace me hard to find out who I was or they'd try to turn the tables and follow me home.

I stood on the gas and got back onto the parkway, heading south. The LIE would have more traffic, but I burned toward Sunrise Highway. There were more exit ramps that bled into strip malls and suburban neighborhoods. It would be easier to spot anyone on my ass and I'd have a better chance of giving them the slip.

Traffic eased up. I didn't spot the driver in my rearview, but I doubled back and figure-eighted myself into minor whiplash. I decided not to head home.

Instead I cruised over to the Elbow Room. It's where Collie went before doing what he did, and it's where he returned to relax after he'd finished. He'd been drawn down into what my family called the underneath. It was that place of panic and despair that made you do stupid things when you were breaking the law. It's what made a punk knocking over a liquor store take hostages and start icing innocent folks.

But I still thought there had to be a reason for Collie to have lost it. When I'd visited him on death row he kept telling me there wasn't. He explained that I'd have to learn to live with that fact, but I wasn't doing a very good job of it so far.

The Elbow Room was where I went to ask the questions that had no answer. It's where I went to think of my brother and to forget about my brother. It's where I went when I needed to take a breath and line up the next move.

I pulled into the lot, parked, and waited five minutes. The crew didn't drive past. I felt more secure that the driver had shaken me without even realizing I was there. It made me wonder what he could do when he really put his mind to it.

I got out and stepped into the bar. It was the lowest dive around. It had gotten even worse since the last time I'd had a drink here months ago.

Desperate men sat in the back corners muttering about their worst mistakes. A few halfhearted games of pool were being shot. The whores worked the losers a little more brazenly than was usual. They didn't bother with subtlety. It was all out front.

The jukebox pounded out a heavy bass riff. It was something designed to kick college girl strippers into high gear, except this wasn't a strip club. I didn't know what the music was supposed to do for the rest of us. The drunk mooks eyed the hookers, the burnt lady barflies, and each other. Everybody seemed to want to throw themselves on the floor. Men wanted to beat their wives, children, and bosses. They wanted to sink their teeth into one another's throats. They wanted to blow up their mortgage service centers. They wanted to shit on the White House lawn. Getting laid by roadhouse chicks couldn't ease that kind of pain. Everyone knew it. Nobody was plying much trade. The whores needed affection nearly as much as cash. The whole placed vibed tension and brittleness.

The speakers beat at my back. I glanced at the register. I always checked the register, wherever I went. It was instinct.

The room was forties film-noir dim and smoky. I didn't want to walk around looking for a booth so I split for the corner of the bar, the darkest spot in the entire room.

I didn't see her sitting beside me until my eyes adjusted to the darkness. Then it seemed bright as noon and I realized most of the mooks were looking this way. I'd sat in a holy place of honor.

She waited there on her stool just out of arm's reach, drawing as much attention as if she posed in a spotlight. Every other man in the room looked on mournfully. They stared, none of them canny enough to use the bar mirror to watch her. Their murmurs underscored the music like backup singers coming in on the chorus. Compared to the waxy-lipped women cadging drinks and sneaking bills off the bar top she looked like paradise in three-inch pumps.

She was next-door cute, sultry with smoky amused eyes. Her black hair was out of style, cut into a modified shoulder-length shag. I liked it. So did the rest of them. We were sentimental for days gone by. It told us that she went her own way. When you got down to it, that's what we all wanted to get our hands on. A woman who stood apart, especially since we couldn't stand apart from each other.

She was a little younger than the rest of the ladies, maybe ten years older than me. All the curves were still in the right places, her chin just starting to soften a bit. Full heart-shaped lips, a bobbed nose, dimples that only appeared when she gave a slight smirk, which she did from time to time at nobody and nothing in particular. Like the rest of us, she had her own inner monologue going. Hers made her happy. Maybe she was laughing at us.

She signaled the bartender and bought her own drink. A gin and tonic. This wasn't the kind of place for a gin and tonic but somehow she made it so. She wore a nicely fitted black dress, bare-armed despite the chill weather. Was she showing off or had she been dumped here like some of the other ladies? A trucker boyfriend passing through, a husband who'd walked out in the middle of an argument, a pissed-off boyfriend making a point?

I fought to keep from gawking. When the bartender got to me I ordered a Jack and Coke and tried to keep my eyes aimed at the front of the bar. No one had followed me in. I had parked directly outside the front window and nobody had messed with my car. I checked the lot and didn't see the Mustang idling anywhere. I was growing more sure that I'd shaken the crew. I didn't feel so close to my dead bad-dog brother anymore.

"You're not like the rest," she said.

It's what we all want to hear. It's what we all want to believe despite the truth. I took a breath. Then I took a sip, determined not to be lured into this kind of a trap. I gave it a good five count of resistance, then buckled. I was lonely. My heart contained hairline fractures.

"What makes you think so?" I asked.

"You walk with a light step. You square your shoulders when you sit. The rest . . . well, just take a look." She told me to look so I looked. "Every one of them is slumped over. Glowering at nothing, chewing their lips."

"These are rough times."

"Even in good times they do it," she said. "That's who they are. They plod. They're going to plod out to their cars to get their knobs polished. They're going to plod home, throw up in their toilets, and make their wives clean up the bathroom floor."

It was true but it wasn't the greater truth. "Is this the part where you say, 'Just like my father'?"

"No, it's not that part." She grinned again. It seemed an odd time to smile. "I never knew the man. But, sure, most likely he's a plodder too, why not?"

"You intimidate them," I told her. "They're not this forlorn and full of self-loathing when someone as beautiful as you isn't in the room."

"I bring it out in them?"

"It seeps out on its own because of you. Plus, they think you're a prostitute."

"How do you know I'm not?"

"Your eyes."

"Did you just say my eyes?"

"I just said your eyes," I admitted.

"I'm not sure if that's sweet or ludicrous."

"Let's keep things friendly and call it sweet."

She finished her gin and tonic. She didn't smile. I'd stuck an ice pick through the spleen of the conversation. You have to be careful when you call a woman beautiful and your motives aren't clear.

"You're here for a reason," she said, "but it's not to get drunk or laid."

"What makes you so sure?"

"You're too . . . *alert* for that."

I smiled at her. It wasn't a charming smile. It was a convict's smile. I'd never been in prison but I lived the same life, on the same edge. It was my brother's smile.

"Christ," she said. "What is it? Your eyes practically went black. You tightened up like you stuck your tongue in an outlet."

"Now you're flirting with me."

She held her right arm out for me to see. "It was electrical. Look, the hair on my arm is standing up."

She was telling the truth. I finished my drink and ordered another. She swiveled the stool toward me and I turned to meet her. She openly appraised me, her gaze roving my face, down the length of my body and back up again. She tilted her head when she checked out my white patch. She pursed her lips, dipped her chin. "I like it. The premature gray adds something to you."

"Yeah. Age."

"More than that. And not 'character,' exactly, that's just a tired term they use to express something, they're not even sure what. Not character, no. *Resolve.*"

"Who are you, lady?" I asked.

"My name's Darla," she said.

I smiled again, this time with less sharpness. "Come on. Nobody's name is Darla. And nobody uses it as a, ah, stage name either."

"How would you know?"

"I know something about using a fake name."

The corners of her mouth hitched. "And why's that?"

"I spent five years using one."

"And what was it?" she asked. "Your assumed name. Nick Steel? Mickey 'the Torpedo' Morelli? Johann Kremholtz?"

I told her the truth. "I have trouble remembering."

"Well, if you had been named Darla, you wouldn't. And if you knew anything about stage names you'd know it was a damn good one." She leaned in again as if to kiss me, and then drew away as if fearing I might take her up on it. "How about your real name?"

"Terrier Rand."

"Terrier? Because of your tenacity?"

"Because everyone in my family is named after dogs."

She raised her eyebrows. "You people sound like a fun group."

"Not so much anymore."

I reached for my drink and stared at her over the rim of the glass. She stared back at me. She was right about one thing, there was something electrical happening.

"You want to split?" she asked.

Darla hadn't mentioned cash yet. Even in the Elbow Room a working girl would try to get paid up front first. Darla just kept watching me with her amused gaze. It fired me up and gave me the chills at the same time. I wondered if I'd been wrong about her. I was cynical as hell and had maybe jumped to the wrong conclusion. A provocative woman could make you a moron.

She read me easily and let out a smooth, honest laugh. "I don't charge everyone, you know. I am allowed to give away some free samples in order to build up clientele."

"The Elbow Room isn't your kind of corner."

"I don't have a corner yet. I'm not sure I want one. I'm still sorting out my potential opportunities. The current economy cost me a home and a marriage, which was falling apart anyway because my husband was an alcoholic and a meth addict. I'm thirty-five years old with an above-average sex drive and a retail job that pays a buck over minimum wage. I'm being murdered by credit debt and bank loans. So I thought I'd look into making a bit of filthy lucre on the side."

I checked the window again and spotted nothing. "So you're just liberated and progressive?"

"My mother would have called it something else, but sure, why not?"

"I'd say with your sex appeal you'll be rolling in dough in no time."

"That's generous."

Maybe it was, under the circumstances. Everything was relative. Darla glanced toward the front window. She was polite enough not to ask what I was looking for.

She leaned in again and I caught a deep breath of her heady, feminine aroma. She wore no perfume.

She said, "I thought I'd start here. My husband used to stop by this place a lot, usually on weekends, where he'd drink himself sick, and spend his paycheck on crank and other women."

"Why?" I asked. "Considering he had you waiting at home."

Her smile saddened. "Because I intimidated him in bed. I'm not certain why. He was handsome and rugged and very, very good. And I loved him and wanted to make him happy. I would have done anything for him. He knew that. We were terrific together in the beginning. But he felt some kind of pressure, and he became resentful, and eventually he drifted. Got into meth for a while. He'd rather pay a stranger for what I was giving him for free. He couldn't handle the intimacy, I suppose. We were a week shy of our second anniversary when he got into rehab. While he was getting clean we lost the house, so when he was released there was nothing waiting for him except me. That's when we called it quits."

Once you had no home, giving up everything else had to be easy.

"Of course he always denied that he was indulging himself," Darla continued. "Even when I followed him here and caught him in the parking lot with a woman in his lap, the two of them hitting the pipe, he told me it wasn't what it looked like."

"Men caught with their pants down and illicit drugs in their system make rotten liars."

"This I've learned, Terrier." Talking about her husband had put a glimmer of pain in her dark eyes. "Do they call you Terry?"

"Yes."

"Do you mind if I do?"

"No, it's what they call me."

She finished her drink and I ordered her another. "In any case," she said, "I'm not sure this new endeavor is going to work out. Nobody's approached me all night. Not even you."

"You're too attractive for this place. You unnerve the average mook. You'd fit better at the bar in an upscale hotel, if you're really going to pursue that line. Traveling businessmen have an expense account. Their wives aren't around the corner, they're all back in Wisconsin."

"Thanks for the advice. You know your lowlifes. Are you a pimp?"

"No, I'm a thief."

It didn't surprise her. Maybe she understood what having a light step really meant. "Are you a good thief?"

"Just having you ask has wounded my pride."

The giggle floated from her. "I retract the question. Your secret is safe with me."

"It's no secret. Everyone knows we Rands are thieves."

"The whole family?"

"Yes."

"Doesn't being a famous thief interfere with the need to be a sly-boots?"

Some words were naturally funny. *Slyboots* was one of them. I chuckled. "It has on occasion."

I was hungry for her. Her warm sexuality stirred me. I shifted in my seat.

"Now you have time to pursue all your other dreams," I said.

"All I ever dreamed about was having a happy home." She let out a breath that she'd held inside for months, years. "I suppose that sounds silly."

"Not to me it doesn't. Didn't you have any aspirations before him?"

"My aspiration was him. Or someone like him."

"Come on. Modeling and acting?"

She smiled a genuine smile. "Am I so predictable?"

"You're a beautiful lady. Beautiful people get paid a lot of money to show off their beauty on stages all over the world."

We sat quietly for a while. The mooks muttered and sighed and drank and walked in and walked out. Every time the door opened I glanced up.

"You look like you want to make a break for it," she said. "I just can't tell if you want to rush off with me or run away from me."

I could see my expression reflected in her eyes. A little angry, spooked, a touch worried and a lot horny, hopeful but in need of action.

Darla pressed three fingers to my wrist. "Hey, it's all right. I'm in no rush. I'm enjoying just sitting here with you."

She opened her purse and handed me a business card.

"You've had cards made up?" I asked. "This might be a little aggressive. If you advertise, it's tough to argue in court you weren't soliciting."

"Read it first, wiseass."

I read it. *A Great Yarn. For all your knitting and literary needs.*

There was an address in Port Jackson. I knew the street but couldn't picture the shop.

"A yarn shop *and* bookstore?"

"You'd be surprised at how much crossover there is."

I shrugged. "I suppose I would be. I didn't realize there was any crossover between knitting and reading."

"And I live in the apartment above. Stop in if you're ever looking for a book. Or if you take up crocheting. Or—"

She left it like that. She wasn't a bad girl, not as bad as me, but bad enough. I liked the idea of finally finding someone as out on the rim as I was. She'd lost her only love too, maybe because it was her fault, maybe not. She actually had better judgment and discretion than I did. She could be anyone, and so could I. I thought I should take her up on the offer now, but she did the dance of foreplay, and I had to dance along. There was time. I backed a step away and left the bartender a good but not excessive tip and kept watching her, the connection strong between us, the current still running. The rest of the mooks looked on in their average jealousy and mediocre bitterness. I made the door and got in my car and drove in circles for a while searching the rearview for the crew, and when I was certain nobody was behind me I whipped it home.

The next whisper in the dark.

Terry, I'm bleeding.

We were in her parents' bedroom. Her dad was at work and her mother was out shopping with her aunt, and we stole a couple of hours in the king-size to screw around and put the goose down pillows to good use. She was four months pregnant. We had stepped up our plans to get married. I'd talked to the folks at the Montauk Lighthouse and gotten a fix on the cost of having the ceremony there. I hadn't told anyone about the pregnancy yet. There hadn't seemed to be a right time to mention it. Mal was a bruiser but sensitive as hell. He knew I was holding something back. He vibed that it might be good news. He cornered me and tried to wheedle it out of me. I didn't let out my secret.

You choose as much of your life as you can. The rest chooses you.

The memory unfurled as I writhed. I heard myself ask a question and fought to find the proper response.

Terry, I'm—

Kimmy was sitting on the edge of the bed with her back to me, hands in her lap. She slowly turned. Before I saw her face I saw the pad of her left hand, smeared with blood. She held the hand out to show me. Her palm was puddled. I thought she had cut her hand. The blood tipped out across her fingers. I wondered how she had hurt herself. I leaped off the bed to hunt for bandages. The hand gripped my wrist painfully.

"Terry, I'm bleeding."

I finally saw what was happening. I ran to her parents' bathroom and tore a set of towels off the rack and rushed to her. I went to my knees before her. Her legs were slightly spread. The blood boiled out of her. It terrified me. I used the towels as best I could. She lay back but wasn't comfortable on the bed. She wanted to lie on the floor. I helped her down. I propped pillows beneath her. She remained calm through it all. She told me what to do.

"Call 911. Get an ambulance."

"I can drive you to the hospital faster."

"No. Call 911. Paramedics will know what to do."

I called 911. I felt perverse telling them the address, knowing I didn't belong there. I stood above Kimmy curled on the floor and had the sudden urge to throw myself down next to her.

"Don't worry," I said.

"I'm not worried."

"It's going to be all right."

"I know it is."

"I won't let anything happen to you."

"I know you won't."

"Or the baby."

She didn't respond. She smiled, her faith set firmly within me.

My ghosts provoked and prodded me. Some of them were still alive. Some of them had never been born. My dreams were red. My hands were red.

Terry, I'm—

Whether or not I saved Chub was almost moot. I had to save my girls.

My eyes flashed open. They stung from sweat. The room was full of figures, including the old lady Collie had beaten to death. Her lips crawled with criticism or confession. There was no blood on her face. She hadn't had time to bleed. My brother had broken her neck with two blows. The pink tint of her hair flared briefly as the first hint of dawn fell across my bed. The room emptied.

JFK lay across my legs panting and looking worried. I must've been talking in my sleep again. He put his nose down between his front paws and tried to get back to sleep. I slid my feet free from him and checked the clock. It glowed 5:15. No matter when I hit the sack I couldn't sleep for more than three or four hours at a clip.

I took a shower, dressed, and walked the house. I checked on the family, room by room.

My mother slept soundly in the center of the bed, one arm flung out reaching for my father, except he wasn't there. I sometimes woke to find her seated on the edge of my mattress, staring at me. It was a weird habit that I'd picked up from her.

I crouched and put a hand in her auburn hair. My mother remained a beautiful woman even at an age when beautiful women were called handsome. Her lips and chin had softened a bit more but she was still lovely, with a natural smile that always made me feel better. I had a strong urge to talk to her, but there were so many things I couldn't say out loud that it was safer not to try.

It was the fourth time this week my father had crept out. The car was still in the driveway. Either he was prowling on foot or he had a drop vehicle stowed nearby. I'd looked for one but hadn't been able to find it.

Last night I'd waited out on the darkened front veranda to talk with him but he must've spotted me and slipped around back. In the morning he feigned normalcy so well that I couldn't bring myself to brace him about where he'd been.

He was a quiet man who'd only fallen into being a thief because it was the legacy handed down to him. Generations of larceny were in his blood. He could no more fight against it than I could.

My father had never been comfortable as a criminal. He was a good burglar but wasn't capable of pulling off a polished grift. He couldn't steal from someone who was looking him in the eye. He only stole to bring home cash to the family, and so far as I knew he never spent a dime on himself except for the stupid figurines he collected. He didn't live large, had no flash, preferred to be the humble and reposed man that he was by nature.

When I was twelve my father sent me up the drainpipe to a house that was supposed to be empty. It wasn't. While I was hanging halfway out a third-floor window a seventy-five-year-old lady picked up a lamp and swatted me into free fall. A rib snapped and pierced through my side. My old man pulled the bone shard through by hand. My thirty-foot fall was pretty much the end of my father's career as a crook. Having my blood on his hands forced him out of the game.

I wondered if he was back on the streets, sneaking through old ladies' apartments and snatching up Toby mugs, piano babies, and ceramic monks eating bowls of rice.

Old Shep slept the sleep of a baby. He cooed and sighed. He made tiny fists and sometimes bawled. His beard and hair had been recently trimmed. His face was clean and pink. He smelled of baby powder. His colostomy bag was empty. Gramp hadn't strung together more than a five-word sentence in the past two months, but I knew he was still in there somewhere.

I heard my sister cry out.

Dale was having another nightmare. I eased inside her room. Her breath came in quick rasps and she groaned as if trying desperately to speak. If I didn't know what was happening I would've thought she was having a seizure.

She spoke a word that might've been a curse or a threat. With her brow furrowed, a spatter of sweat on her lip caught the sunlight.

I said her name and then said it a little louder.

"Airedale."

She sat up and let out a sob. Her eyes were wide and focused through me. Her wet hair hung across her face in stringy, jagged clumps. I knew what she was seeing. I knew what she was doing.

"It's all right, Dale, I'm here. Everything's okay."

I murmured more gentle sounds. They didn't help. She swung her legs over the far side of the mattress and sat there, facing away from me, more than half asleep, waiting. I waited too. After a while she started to lie down again, dangling awkwardly half in and out of bed. I got her squared away and pulled the blankets up to her chin. I rocked her for a few minutes and she let out another sob. Finally her breathing slowed and deepened.

"Get the fuck away from me, Terry."

I almost listened. I almost left her. But I didn't want to. And I always did what I wanted.

I'd been watching her closely. Sometimes she was sleepy or giggly or on the verge of hyper. I suspected some kind of herbal or chemical fortification. She had thrown herself into her high school theater arts, taking on more roles in plays and even starring in a couple of TV commercials for local businesses. I could see her slipping in and out of identities. Ma called her *My little Bette Davis*.

Dale spent an incredible amount of time texting and locking herself in her room to toy with her computer. Her laptop was encrypted. I knew how to break into a lot of places, but not that.

I snatched her phone and went through it name by name. There were a dozen entries only by initials. She'd been making calls to somebody named ROG. I figured it was a kid named Roger. I tried the number and it went straight to an automated voice mail. I asked my parents about Roger and got blank looks.

I searched her bathroom. I went through her medicine cabinet. Then I caught a glance at my face in the mirror. I looked heavy, rounded with jowls, like I'd gained twenty-five pounds. I checked the glass and found it was bowed out from the top. I gripped the edges of the cabinet and hefted. It came loose in my hands.

Behind it, sitting in a small niche in the wall, was a bottle of tiny white pills. No Rx label. I shook the bottle twice. Maybe antianxiety meds, antidepressants, or sedatives. Or maybe something harder. Whatever they were, they weren't helping her much.

I started to leave and Dale threw the covers off and called from her bed.

"You're always here," she said with a note of accusation.

"I was looking in on you."

"The way Ma does." She sat up. "I hate that. I hate it."

"You were crying in your sleep. I just wanted to make sure you were okay."

"I'm okay. I'm always okay."

"Except when you're not."

"Can I bum a cigarette?"

I shook a butt halfway out of the pack and held it out to her. She propped it between her lips and I lit it for her. She pulled an empty Coke can from under her bed and tapped ash into it. She was sixteen and had probably been smoking for years, but it still felt a little wrong. Smoke curled toward me.

I cracked the window an inch and sat beside her. She tapped ash into the can. "I have a play this weekend."

"Am I going?"

"You and Mom have to. I need you there."

"Okay, then. What's the play?"

"You've never heard of it."

"I might've heard of it."

"You've never heard of it, Terry. It's French."

"It's in French?"

"No, it's French. It was written by a French guy."

There was no point in arguing that I knew what a fucking French guy was.

We were quiet. I listened to her sucking at the filter, taking a deep breath, easing it out again, the hot smoke hanging harshly off her chin for a second before dissipating.

"What pills are you taking, Dale?"

She turned and glared at me. "You've been creeping my room?"

"Does that really surprise you?"

She took a last drag and stuffed the butt into the can, then threw the can at me. I caught it in my left hand. She let out an exasperated grunt. "It shouldn't. I always knew there can never be any privacy in this family, but yes, it still does. Of course it does. I didn't expect my brother to pull my medicine cabinet off the wall."

"I'm trying to protect you."

"That's not your job. Besides, you can't anyway. You worry about yourself, and I'll take care of myself."

"Dale–"

"I've got rehearsal this afternoon. I need to get a little more sleep." She gave me a half smile that was so fake I actually drew away. I got to my feet. Her teeth looked sharp. "Thanks for being here. I'm glad I can always count on you."

She resettled herself under the covers. In a few seconds, maybe with the help of the pills, she was out cold, or pretending to be.

I closed her bedroom door and walked the rest of the house. I looked in on my mother again and my old man was there, snoring beside her.

The Rands weren't heisters. We'd never bulled over a jewelry shop or hit a bank. There was never any reason to put together a crew or look for a getaway driver. I knew a lot of people in the bent life, but for the most part they all belonged to a certain strata. Burglars, swindlers, grifters, pickpockets, card cheats, midnight tiptoers. I was going to need a little help tracking down Chub's new friends.

Wes Zek owned a nice house right off the Great South Bay. A canal ran behind his patio deck and a twenty-eight-foot sailboat was berthed at a private dock. The last time I'd been here the boat had been in shit shape with frayed loose lines, splintered rails, and a worn deck. But he'd put some muscle into it recently, or hired somebody local to fix it up, and it looked well maintained. I could see life preservers stacked on the deck. He'd been taking it out.

Wes had upgraded his security system but still didn't have it tied in with the local police. Looked like it went to a security firm, though, one probably owned by Danny Thompson, the local syndicate boss Wes worked for.

Danny was another former friend of mine. When his father, Big Dan, hadn't turned over the keys to the kingdom as quick as Danny had been hoping, he became a hateful, piddling prick. After Big Dan died Danny started running the mob into the ground. We'd butted heads a couple times since then.

I'd heard that Danny had begun taxing crews, which was a bad move for everyone. It meant he wanted an ear on every major job. Too many people in the know just made for a stronger RICO case later on down the line. It was the kind of thing Big Dan would never have become involved in, but Danny was hurting for loose cash and making a double-handed grab for whatever he could. He wasn't only desperate for respect and status, he was greedy, and he wasn't even smart with his moneygrubbing. He didn't realize yet how much trouble he could bring down on himself.

I knocked on Wes's front door and rang the bell. I gave it a twenty count and tried again. For a sneak thief, I was showing an incredible amount of self-control. Then I walked around to the back door, pulled out my tools, circumvented the system, and crept Wes's place. Like most wiseguys who used a bar, restaurant, gambling joint, or strip club as cover, Wes's business hours were at night and he tended to sleep during the day.

I stepped into his bedroom and found him snoring beside a luscious slip of a girl who couldn't have been any older than twenty. She was naked and awake, sitting up smoking a joint and watching me through tangled hair. A vapid little smile tilted Wes's lips in his sleep. The strain of working for Danny Thompson had been taking its toll on him. He had ulcers. He had anxiety issues. But for now he had the unlined face of a baby in a crib who had just guzzled the perfect amount of mother's milk.

The girl eyed me. She had a sweet heart-shaped face and high cheekbones. Her trim body was headline stripper material. I couldn't stop staring. She was holding smoke in her lungs and finally let it out in a thin stream that broke over her breasts and moved like a cumulus cloud across her flat, tanned belly. She kept watching me. I expected some shouting and screaming and waving of hands about the face, but she just tugged the sheet up over her breasts and kept staring. I got the feeling that if I backtracked out of there she might never mention it to Wes at all.

"Are you a hitter?" she asked.

Her voice was at a normal speaking level but it sounded painfully loud in the room despite Wes's snores. He didn't wake. She'd put him in a coma. She'd been around long enough to know that when he was out, he was out. It told me the relationship was pretty stable, which made me pleased for him.

She pinched out the end of the J. "Are you?"

The question caught me wrong. You didn't usually ask a guy who'd broken in and was standing there right in the bedroom if he was a hit man. If he was, he would probably lie about it or just shoot you in the head. Maybe the weed was especially strong.

"No," I admitted. "Is that something Wes has to worry about now? Hitters popping up?"

"According to him. But I think he's a little paranoid."

"Probably a good thing to be, in his line of work. Unless it's because of the pot."

She drew a wild blond flip of hair out of her eyes.

"I'm Em," she said.

"'M'?"

"Em. Short for Emily. And you must be Terrier Rand."

It made me perk up a little. I didn't like strangers knowing my name.

"Maybe I'm just a hitter who lies."

It got a modest grin. "You're a wiseass. That means you're Terry Rand. He talks about you."

"He does?"

I was a little paranoid too. I didn't like Wes talking about me with his girlfriends, no matter how friendly they were when I broke into his house. If I wanted to chat with a gorgeous woman with a higher-than-usual sex drive and admit I was a thief, that was one thing. Having Wes chatter about me to his sweethearts, that was something else.

"What's he say?"

"He's impressed with you."

"In what way?"

"He likes how you don't take shit off Danny Thompson. I think he's working up the nerve to quit."

"You don't quit that line of work."

Her lips were firmly set, her eyes empty. "It's nice to think it's possible."

"It's stupid and dangerous too." I worried that she might be pushing him in that direction, which would lead to a face-off with Danny. "I need to talk with him."

"Go wait in the kitchen and we'll be with you in a few minutes."

I did as I was told. I felt a little chastised. To prove I was still macho and the master of my own fate, I poured myself a glass of milk though she hadn't specifically said I could. I sipped it with an air of defiance.

I looked around. The four-bedroom house was full of expensive, practical furniture. Chandeliers, marble tiling, a fireplace without an ounce of ash in it. A dining room that sat twelve. A living room with lush leather L-shaped couches, thick white carpeting, a huge HD television and entertainment system. Coaster trays on every end table. The kind of room where you hosted large parties serving martinis and canapes.

There were photos on the shelves and the walls were now covered with classy paintings. They'd been chosen with genuine care. Wes had either hired a personal decorator or Em had moved in or was on the verge of doing so. He'd finally started to turn the place into a home.

I retreated back to the kitchen and sat in the sunniest corner. After a few minutes, Wes stepped in wearing a fancy silk kimono. His hundred-and-fifty-dollar haircut looked good even after sex and sleep. He carried a black sports jacket carefully folded over one arm. It was supposed to hide the fact that he was gripping a .44 that he'd tugged from a specially made leather shoulder holster.

He wasn't smiling now. He turned and called down the hall to Em. "You were right." He slipped the gun back into the holster, laid his jacket on the counter, and faced me. "If I didn't know better, I'd think you actually like catching me off guard, breaking into my house all the time."

"I knocked and rang the bell."

"That's true," Em said, appearing behind him, wearing a matching kimono. I was a little sad to see her covered up. "I wasn't sure if I should answer."

"You shouldn't," Wes said. "Never."

"Okay, I won't." She pecked him on the chin. "I'll get lost now and let you two talk."

"No, you can stay."

He was asserting himself. I understood why but it was bad business. Wes was one of the most even-balanced people I knew in the life, but I'd embarrassed him in front of his woman and that was the kind of thing that might force a display of bad attitude. I had to make it right, and fast, but I wasn't sure how. I sipped more of my milk.

Emily did me a favor. She smiled, gave Wes another quick kiss, and left the room anyway.

He watched her go. I'd ruined their morning. He opened the fridge and banged some shit around in there.

"I'm sorry, Wes."

"For what?" he asked. "For sneaking around my place and sniffing my dirty sheets and checking out my girl in the flesh?" He glared at me. "She sleeps in the raw so you saw her, right? You checked her out?"

"In my defense, man," I said, holding up my palms. "I mean, *come on,* who wouldn't? She's gorgeous."

"You–"

"I'm sorry. Really. Sincerely. Honestly." I was running out of adverbs. "Genuinely."

But he wasn't mad. He was proud of Em's body and glad that I'd gotten to see what a hottie he'd landed.

"Forget it. What are you here for? What do you need?"

"Next time I'll bring cinnamon buns. Promise."

"Terrific. What do you need, Terry?"

I told him about staking out Chub's place and the four-man team I'd seen. Wes found a piece of cherry cheesecake and a half-full bottle of white wine at the back of the fridge. He poured himself a glass and sat opposite me drinking and sticking forkfuls of the cake in his mouth. I started to doubt that his ulcers were all from tension on the job.

"They're slick and professional."

"Most pro crews are four-man," he said between bites. "Any less and the big jobs are out of reach. Any more and the string is so long that they're not as tight and well oiled. They get sloppy and there's a bigger chance someone will talk."

"These guys also pack a lot of hardware."

"You expect something different?"

He finished the wine and pulled a pained face. I got up, drew a glass from the cupboard, and poured him some milk. He took a gulp and groaned. I found a bottle of antacids on the counter and handed him a couple of tablets. He threw them back.

"Why are we talking about this?" he asked.

"I'm worried."

"Worried? You took a five-year hiatus, Terry, but Chub's been working this angle the whole time. He knows what he's doing. And why are you watching him anyway?" Wes paused, waiting for an answer. Then he brushed his hand through the air, erasing the question. "No, forget I asked. I already know the reason, don't I?"

"You do," I said.

When he finished his glass he thumbed away a milk moustache. "Kimmy's not coming back to you, Terry," he said firmly. "You need to forget her and leave them alone."

I sucked a shallow breath in. Nobody liked having their infatuations tossed back in their faces. It's why only close friends could hate each other as much as they sometimes did.

I thought, Maybe this is it. Maybe we're done for good here. I pushed too hard and he went for the sweet spot. This next minute here, it could be very bad.

"I know," I said. "But I can't yet."

He nodded. "There's things that none of us can let go, even when we should."

"You mean women."

"I mean a history that's already passed us by."

My guts let out a cry like a cat caught in a carburetor. I was hungry as hell. I had acid burning. I popped two of his pills. I drank more milk. He got up and started making a sandwich. "We've got ham and provolone. That all right?"

"Great. Thanks."

He pulled out the wrapped meat and cheese, squirted brown mustard on a slice of bread, made some sandwiches, put one on a plate, and slid it across the table to me. "When you bring the cinnamon rolls, make sure they're from Tataglia's bakery, right? None of this King Kullen's bullshit."

"Right," I said. I talked with my mouth full. "Now about this crew . . . can you ask around? Maybe some of Danny's muscle have heard about them."

Wes let out a little grunt of irritation. "You might want to go elsewhere for your information. If Mr. Thompson finds out you're interested, if it gets back to him somehow, it'll just stir him up again. Last time you ran into him, with you playing gunslinger, he nearly put a hit out."

I sat there chewing my ham sandwich. "What stopped him?"

"It wasn't for old times' sake, I can tell you. You Rands just had too much attention focused on you. All the journalists and news channels camped outside your house because of Collie. The protesters at the prison. The girl hanged in the park. His wife saying there was a serial killer loose. All that shit. Jesus, you might as well have been on your own reality show."

The question was nearly on his lips. He wanted to ask if I knew anything about who'd killed Mal, who'd killed the girl in the park. But you couldn't wonder too much about who snuffed somebody else's family or friends, because it might just be the guy you were talking to.

Wes watched me chewing, and I put all my capacity to lie into my face. I was cuddly. I was cute. I tried to make like Bambi. I was an innocent in the cruel woods of life. I didn't know anything. I didn't do anything.

"So . . . can you ask around about this crew?"

He pulled a face. "You aren't listening to me."

"I am."

"You're not. You never do."

"*I am.*"

"You aren't. You think I chat with guys who work the pro strings? You're the only career criminal I know who isn't mobbed up." He paused for emphasis. He stared at me but I wouldn't lift my eyes from my plate. I knew what he was about to say.

He said it. "Why don't you just ask Chub?"

"I can't. We're not exactly on speaking terms anymore."

"Good for him."

I took a final bite, carried the plate to the sink, rinsed it off. I looked through the kitchen window at the bay, the water convulsing, sharp as sheet metal, the wind rising. Dark clouds rolled in from the west. "Doesn't Danny skim most of the crews who work his territory?"

"Not so much anymore, and it pisses him off," Wes said. "They don't pay tribute the way they used to in the old days when Big Dan ran the show. Mr. Thompson's been trying to throw some muscle in that direction, pressuring any pros he hears about. It keeps his soldiers busy and the money flowing in. And he thinks he's earning back some of the old rep."

"Who else would know some heist men?"

He shrugged. "Ask your uncle Grey. He's a smooth old-timer who's got connections everywhere. He could get answers."

"He's working a grift out of state," I said.

"How far out of state?"

"Not far, but he's staying on the move."

Wes grinned. He always grinned when he talked about my uncles. He admired the classic grifters. "I wondered why he hadn't come into the Fifth lately to hit up any of the big games. I thought maybe your fracas with Danny had him worried."

"It doesn't."

"No, he isn't the kind to let that sort of thing slow him down. So talk to him when he gets back."

"I will. But in the meantime, can you think of anybody besides Grey?"

"You never listen to me."

"*I do.*"

"You don't. I've been telling you for ten minutes I don't know anybody who's tight with that kind of action. But really, you don't need to talk to them. You just keep asking around and word will get back. Then they'll find *you*."

He pulled a lightweight .32 from out of his oversize kimono pocket. It had draped so deeply that I hadn't spotted the piece at all. He tugged out the clip, checked it, and replaced it, then checked the safety. He shoved the pistol toward me. "Here."

"You know I don't carry."

"You keep chasing a four-man crew, you'd better start."

I stared at the white-capped waves, waiting for the storm to drive in and hit.

Turning onto Old Autauk Highway, heading past Shalebrook Lake and the college, I caught a glimpse of a piece-of-shit brown Chevy Malibu in the rearview. I looked again and it had faded back a couple of car lengths and switched lanes. Nothing seemed to stand out about it, which caught my attention.

My cell rang. It was my mother. "Are you anywhere near Schlagel's, Terry?"

"That depends. What's Schlagel's? And where is it?"

"The pharmacy. It's on the corner of Shore Road and Elm. Tucked away back there."

"I'm close enough. What do you need, Ma?"

I could tell she didn't want to impose. She fed us, watched over us, and handled all our common, everyday matters alone, and she still always had trouble asking for the slightest bit of help. "Your grandfather's prescriptions. There's three of them. Pick them up and I'll pay you back when you get home. Don't steal them. I still want to be able to shop there."

"I won't steal them and you don't need to pay me back, Ma."

"And your sister left me a list. It's a short list but it's a list."

"Is it in French?"

"What?"

"Nothing. Read it. I can handle lists."

I could hear her slipping on her reading glasses. She didn't like them and always made a small sound of irritation when she put them on. They hung around her neck on a little chain and the chain chimed faintly. "She numbers these things. So, number one is Cool Sea Breeze Vita-activated defrizz shampoo and conditioner."

"Cool Breeze–"

"Cool Sea Breeze," she corrected.

"Cool Sea Breeze Vita-whatever shampoo. And conditioner. They'll have this at the pharmacy?"

"Of course. Next, she needs mascara. Number two. Great Lashes Waterproof Fantasy. It's what she wears when she's onstage. In case she sweats under the lights, it won't run."

"Right. Great Lashes. Waterproof."

"Waterproof Fantasy."

"Jesus, all right, Waterproof Fantasy."

I numbered my own list. One. Your mother, in the backyard, strolling past her flower garden, stepping into the woods, finds a deep grave that will never be deep enough. What expression is on her face? Two. What expression is on Grey's face, two months dead? Three. What is the expression on the face of Bubba John Jankowski on your first night in the cell you'll share with him for the next twenty-five years?

"Terrier?"

"I'm here. What did you say?"

I heard her refolding the piece of notepaper. "There's more but that's all you need to get."

"Read the rest of the list."

"I'll go out later."

"You don't have to go out later. Just tell me the rest."

"Number three. Last item. She's got a star here and it's underlined. She does that because although it's third on the list she wants us to know it's just as important as the other two items. Number three. Intimate Clinical Strength Antiperspirant and Deodorant Advanced Lady Solid Speed Stick, Light and Fresh pH-Balanced."

Holy fuck, I thought. "Okay. Repeat that. Slowly." She did. "All right, don't panic, no problem."

"When will you be home?" she asked. "Gramp needs to take one of those meds with his dinner tonight."

"Just a little while."

"You heard what I said."

"I heard what you said. I'll be home by dinner."

I parked at the curb and stepped inside Schlagel's. I didn't recognize the name because the last time I'd been here the place had been a hardware store. I'd bought a ten-pound titanium jimmy bar here. Collie thought it was hilarious that I'd pay for a crowbar I was going to use to break into houses.

It took me a couple of minutes to navigate the aisles filled with dollar toys, magazines, greeting cards, baby food, toiletries, wigs, candy, and foot powders before I found shampoo. It took until the tenth power of infinity to find the bottles of Cool Sea Breeze among all the other thousands of brand names. When I got to the makeup aisle I let out a groan. It took even longer to find Great Lashes Waterproof Fantasy among all the similar-sounding products. Beautiful lashes. Fantastic Fantasy lashes. Gorgeous Waterproof lashes. I could feel my gray streak growing wider.

Oddly enough I snagged the deodorant the second I turned the corner into the aisle. I glanced left and there it was. I took the four items and hit the pharmacy counter, asked for the prescriptions for Rand. I gave our home address and phone number. The pharmacist handed me four bottles.

Three were for Shepherd Rand. The last was for Pinscher Rand. I checked the label.

Donepezil.

I didn't have to ask the pharmacist what it was. Each bottle came with its own paperwork. But I didn't need that either. Gramp was taking the same medication.

My father was being treated for Alzheimer's.

"You can pay for that here," the pharmacist said.

I stared at him.

"You can pay here at our register. Your medications and your other purchases. Instead of going to the front of the store."

I handed him the cash. He stuffed Gramp's meds into one small paper bag, my father's in another, and then he stapled them together along with the paperwork. He placed the other items into a blue plastic bag with the store's name on it in bold letters and shoved it all toward me with a smile. I scooped it up and hit the door.

The piece-of-shit brown Chevy Malibu was parked in a handicapped spot directly in front of me. I finally figured out what was wrong with it. The car hunkered down much lower than it should have. Its carriage had been reinforced to take a serious beating in case of a high-speed chase. A lot of extra welding had gone into the chassis. It carried more weight but the engine would have been souped to handle it. Chub always made sure the getaway cars he worked on could cope with going over a median or a high curb at eighty without bottoming out.

All of this came to me at once as the four-man crew wearing their look-alike black clothing and wool hats moved in on me. There was no time to make a break for it. Fighting would be useless, but sometimes you had to bare your fangs just to let them know they couldn't walk over you. There were no guns in sight but I knew they'd be carrying. I controlled my panic. I let my muscles tighten. I steeled myself.

I muttered, "Fuck."

I managed to tuck the two small paper bags of meds into my pocket. It felt very important not to drop the prescriptions even if I wound up with two from a .32 in my temple. I placed the bag of Dale's things gently on the walkway beside me just as the driver reached to get a grip on my arm. I'd made a big deal out of my mother reading off the entire list and I wanted to prove that I had managed to find the four items. I had confirmed my usefulness, resilience, and self-worth. You think weird shit when a slick four-man crew with guns gets the drop on you.

"Hey, gents," I said.

I snapped my arm back, spun left, and drove my elbow hard into the driver's collarbone. The move knocked his little hat off. He had short blond hair with a deep scar crease over his ear from an old bullet wound. Someone someplace would recognize him from that. He groaned heavily, took a step back, and reacted the way I thought he would.

He jumped me. It was enough to throw the others off. The driver threw a wild swing. A surge of satisfaction filled me. That excessively calm pro exterior was pretty infuriating. I was glad I could get beneath it. Whatever happened now we'd all be nice and clear on the parking lot cameras.

Two of them grabbed me by the upper arms while a third frisked me quickly and carefully. Number three said, "That wasn't smart."

"Only play for me to make."

The driver put his wool cap back on. The guy who'd wandered around Chub's parking lot looking for trouble walked along behind us and kept a lookout. Then number three put a hand between my shoulder blades and shoved. I resisted out of pure mulishness. This might be my last stand.

A few people stepped in and out of the store. A rushed lady dragged a small boy along so quickly his feet hardly touched the ground. The kid went "Ahh," every time he made contact with concrete. Nobody noticed us much.

I'd never shaken them at all. They'd been on me since I'd trailed them from the garage out to Wantagh Parkway where they'd lost me with ease. Despite my efforts to shake a tail they'd followed me to the

Elbow Room and kept watch while I sat around drinking with Darla. They'd been right there on top of me ever since.

The crew got more insistent, dragging and pressing me along. I thought they might try to yank me into the Malibu, but instead they led me around the blind side of Schlagel's to the back alley.

My uncle Mal always said if you couldn't win a fight you might as well get the first lick in. They shoved me into the alley and I took two quick steps like I might be trying to sprint away, then turned and fought dirty as hell. I kicked, bit, and scratched, threw tight hooks at their chins and cruel body shots. I did pretty well for about twenty seconds. Then they just crowded me and I was all done.

In silence they worked me over for a while. They were pros at that as well. Nobody got too vicious and nobody tried hard to break anything on me, except the driver, who was still miffed about the cheap shot.

I pulled my chin in, tightened my arms across my chest, and tried to stay on my feet. I managed it well enough until someone got a lucky punch to my kidneys.

I fell down, curled up, rode it out, kicked and lashed out some, and then it was over. They let me catch my breath for a couple minutes. I'd done some damage their way too. Good. You never want to be the only guy hurt in a fight.

The bright red at the edges of my vision began to fade. Two of them grabbed me by the arms and got me up again and number three, who seemed to be running the crew, said, "Considering you're in our line of work, you should know better than to get so close."

I spit blood. "You're right."

"So, you planning to deal yourself in?"

"No."

"You followed us the other night. You weren't cutting in? You didn't try to tag us?"

"Not really."

He didn't like the answer. I didn't blame him. He let loose with a flurry of rapid-fire hooks to my belly that went on for maybe ten seconds and felt like forty days in the desert. I fell down again and then they picked me up again and he asked me the question once more. "You weren't cutting yourself in?"

"No," I said.

I didn't understand why they were bothering with this. When you're a thief you expect other thieves to steal from you. There's not much point in asking them why. You already know why because you're a thief too.

"So why were you chasing us?" the driver asked.

"It wasn't exactly a chase."

"No, it wasn't. You're not a very competent tail."

I wiped my mouth and said, "My first time."

"Could be your last too, little doggy."

I let that slide. I didn't have much choice but to let it slide. "I'm not here to juke your play."

"Juke our play?" He frowned and slid his hat a little farther back on his head. A few blond hairs of a widow's peak appeared. "What the hell are you talking about?"

"Ruin your score."

He lit a cigarette and sucked on it slowly, studying me. He was thinking about kicking the shit out of me again but decided it wouldn't work any better than before. The next step was to blow out one of my knees. He leaned back against the brick building, finished his cigarette, and flicked the dying butt over my head.

"Your face is known," he said. "You've been on television. You look just like your brother."

It pissed me off, hearing that. "Not so much."

"You a maniac like him?"

"Not quite."

"So what's it all about?"

A twinge of pain went through me and I almost dropped. I groaned and caught myself in time. "If you know who I am then you know Chub and I used to be friends."

"I hear that was a long time ago."

"It was."

"So then what?"

"So I want Chub out of the life. I don't care about your heist. Or who you are or what you do. I care about Chub. He's got a wife and daughter and if he keeps playing around with strings like you he's going to get sent up. I can't allow that."

Now the driver laughed. It was a brisk short chuckle without any humor to it at all. "You want. You care. You can't allow. Take it up with him. Stay away from us. There's no cool way to say this, but we know where you live. We watched the house. We know everything about your mother, father, sister, your dog, your granddad, everybody. Back off."

"Why the firepower?" I asked. "You're a wheelman. Drivers don't carry. You sit at the curb and wait for the others, and then you get everyone the hell out. Drivers put two hands on the wheel. They don't carry. So why the hardware?"

I saw his teeth this time, but he wasn't smiling. "You might not be a maniac but you are a moron. I'm trying to give some professional courtesy here and you're spoiling it. Are you a suicide case? Do you want us to ace you?"

I felt the barrel of a gun against the back of my head. I didn't know much about guns, but it was big and ice-cold and I had no doubt that the bullet would turn everything above my neck into custard. I thought about my mother standing at my closed casket.

"No," I said.

"You caused us a setback. We can't trust our escape route anymore. Maybe we can't trust your friend Chub anymore either. That might not be so good for him. I ought to kill you for the trouble."

"He doesn't know anything about this."

"It doesn't matter. Don't bother us again."

The barrel of the gun withdrew. I expected at least a chop behind the ear, but it didn't happen. They walked down the alley single file. I stood there wavering and watching them ease away. They moved in perfect sync. They turned the corner and were gone.

I took a step and fell over. I crawled back to my feet. At least one rib had been cracked. A couple of teeth were loose. The blood ran down the back of my throat and made my belly tumble. I went into a long coughing fit that shook everything that hurt.

It took ten minutes to make it to the mouth of the alley. I walked back to where I'd dropped the bag full of my sister's stuff and was surprised to see it was still there. I bent over to pick it up and vomited. I almost tipped over again. I managed to grab the bag and make it back to my car. By the time I got behind the wheel I was seeing double. I wasn't going to be able to make it home.

I drew my wallet, found the card, and pulled out my phone. I misdialed twice. I wiped sweat from my eyes.

A lovely voice answered. I tried to respond but the blood kept running and filled my mouth. I rolled down the window and spit streams onto the asphalt.

"Hello?" she said. "Hello?"

"This is Terrier," I said. "The guy who's not like the rest. That's true, you know. I'm worse. I'm much worse. But I really need your help."

"Where are you?" she asked. I told her. The pain reminded me of my father pulling my broken rib through my side. I was just crazy enough to think about popping some of the meds. I would need them someday. My father was going to die in a wheelchair watching cartoons, lost inside himself. So was I.

"I'll be right there," she said. I heaved bile and blood on myself. I started smiling because I liked the edge of concern in her voice. The worry, the care. Promises to be kept in the dark.

"Hold on," Kimmy said and I slid to the ground and thought, She's never stopped loving me. Chub, you can die. I might even murder you myself. Number four. What expression is on Chub's face when he's in the bin, doing nine to fifteen, and sees his daughter on the other side of the glass sitting on my lap calling me Daddy?

She helped me out of my car and into hers, straining under my weight while my blood smeared her hands. She laid me in the backseat and put a folded sweater under my head. I stretched out gagging in pain, holding the plastic Schlagel's bag full of beauty products tight to my belly. I wondered where the baby seat was.

I passed out and came to on my feet, taking stairs slowly. She had an arm around me, tight on the broken rib. I went, "Nghh." She let me go and I clung to a freshly stained handrail.

She said, "Are you okay to keep going?"

I said, "Nghh." I might have been trying to say *I love you*. I might have been trying to say *I hate you*. I might have been trying to say *I give up on you. I want to give up on you, but I can't.* Call that what you like. Call me what you like.

Her fingers grazed the side of my face. We stumbled up the cramped staircase to the second floor. She unlocked a door and shoved it open. The smell of moldy, acidifying paper sneaked in under the stink of my own blood.

"Here, take these. Drink this."

She stuck a couple pills on my tongue and pressed a tall glass of water against my teeth. The pain flared again and I sputtered and gagged. I heard both pills go bouncing over the tile across the room. She placed two more in my mouth.

"Try again."

I managed to get some water down this time. I knew the Donepezil wouldn't save me or my old man. Nothing had helped Gramp retain his personality, nothing had kept Grey from going crazy. No sane thought had entered my brother's head to stay his hand from killing old ladies and children during his spree. Meds, what the hell was the point. They wouldn't help you hold on to your memories. You had to run them over in your head again and again, dig them in deep, hide them in the layers and folds of every aspect of your life. I had to live in the moment and live in the past.

I had to remember.

I couldn't allow myself to ever forget.

I thought, Intimate Clinical Strength Antiperspirant and Deodorant Advanced Lady Solid Speed Stick, Light and Fresh pH-Balanced.

I turned and hip-checked a three-foot tower of poorly stacked hardbacks. I muttered "Sorry," and stooped to pick everything up. My skull rang four times like some bastard leaning on a doorbell, and then a spray of colors leaped across my eyes.

It wasn't until she had me in the shower lathered up that I realized it wasn't Kimmy at all. Darla was under the nozzle, kissing me softly, saying my name, and I was saying Kimmy's.

Between my feet heavily pink water circled the drain. I wasn't sure if I was awake or even alive anymore. Most of the pain was gone and I was high on something. Felt like Percocet. That's what she'd fed me.

On the rim of the bathtub was the open bottle of my sister's Cool Sea Breeze. Darla pushed forward and pressed me against the shower wall. She said, "You're back, aren't you?"

"I think so. Mostly."

I stared at her gorgeous body and became aroused. She let out a throaty giggle and used her hands on me. I felt an intense shame for some reason I couldn't explain and looked away.

"It's all right," she said, nuzzling me. "It's okay." She pecked at my bottom lip. With her makeup washed away she looked much younger than before, innocent, even chaste.

"What happened?" I asked. "What have I been doing? What have I been saying?"

"You called me, remember?"

I shook my head and it hurt like hell.

"You got beaten up pretty bad. You passed out in your car. You've got a couple of bruised ribs, I think. They might be fractured but you said no hospital. You were in agony and starting to go out of your head so I gave you a couple of Percocet for the pain."

"Why'd you use that shampoo?"

The question made her tilt her chin. The dripping shag fell across her face in a way that made me want her more and also made me want to run. "You seemed obsessed with it. You were holding on to that bag with a death grip. I thought it might relax you."

She angled the shower head and rinsed us off. I said, "You might want to get out. I need it cold. If my eyes close up I'll be useless."

"It's okay, I won't throw myself at you again. If you don't want it, that's fine, just say so."

She stepped out and I shut off the hot water, then stood there beneath the freezing needles trying to center myself again.

Number five. The expression on the face of the beautiful lady who saved you as you spurned her adoring advances.

I climbed out. She was still drying off. She held the towel open for me the way a mother waits to dry her kid off at the beach. She patted me down carefully, avoiding the worst bruises. She opened the medicine cabinet and got out a roll of tape. The pain meds kept me from bellowing while she tightly bound the ribs on the right side.

I checked the damage in the mirror. "Holy Christ."

"It's not that bad. Here." She taped up my nose, my ear, and my right eyebrow. My eyes were already going black. The cold water had helped a little but not enough. I looked monstrous and couldn't believe she'd touched me in any kind of an erotic manner. She appraised her work. "I don't think you need stitches but you should keep the tape on for a couple of days at least."

"You've been to nursing school too?"

"Close enough. The husband I told you about, who liked to drink? He had small, fast hands."

I knew I should apologize for calling her. I'd taken advantage of her. I'd possibly gotten her involved in some real trouble. The crew might still be on my ass and parked right outside. There was no point in checking, I still wouldn't be able to spot them.

I tied a towel around my waist. She wrapped one around her hair and slid into a robe. I tried to read her eyes but my vision was hazy from the beating and the pills made me loose without relaxing me.

She led me to the bedroom, which was stacked with books in every free inch except where there were overstuffed bags and bins of yarn. My clothes were in a pile on the floor.

"Which sells better?" I asked. "The yarn or the books?"

She let out a short sigh that smelled faintly of mint. "Why are you asking me that question now?"

"I have no idea."

"You're stoned on the Percs, aren't you."

"I think I'm a little stoned on the Percs, yes."

Getting stoned only seemed to drive up my curiosity. I still didn't understand the store, or why she was interested in playing the role of a semiprostitute, and whether she was looking to become a real working girl or if it was all a sex game, and whether I was going to have to pay before the day was out or not. I stared at her and her beauty worked its magic on me, and I was full of need and want again, and the loneliness burned through me like diesel. I had a head full of bad wiring. She sat on the bed and looked up at me expectantly. I had sixty bucks in my wallet. The crew hadn't mugged me. I hoped she wouldn't cost more than that, but then again, if I was going to spend time with a call girl, I'd want her to be a high-priced call girl. It was only reasonable. You had to have standards. I could always rob her next-door neighbors. The Percs and the pain were making me goofy.

She said, "Are you sure you didn't mean to ask if I wanted to go to bed with you?"

"Maybe that was it. I think that was it, Darla."

She stretched out across the mattress and her robe slid open at the knee exposing her leg and thigh. I'd just been in the shower with her naked but somehow the curve of her knee did something to me now and my pulse started going haywire. My side throbbed like hell but only distantly, like a drum beating on some faraway ridge.

With one quick motion she drew the towel off her head and tossed it away. She shook out her hair and stared provocatively at me through the disheveled clumps.

It reminded me of that night at the Elbow Room. She sat there just out of arm's reach, the same way as she had at the bar, drawing all attention. The smoky amused eyes were full of expectation. She'd saved me. I knew I'd have to pay her back. She wasn't a woman who did things for free or for righteous reasons. She was as bad as me in her own way, and I wondered how much she was going to hurt me in the end.

Darla held her hand out to me. I took it and she drew me forward. I dropped on the mattress beside her and caught a glimpse of the clock on the nightstand. It was noon. I was still very aware that Gramp needed his meds by dinnertime. My father too, probably. My heart sank thinking of my old man losing himself in our house, unable to remember my voice or my mother's face. I imagined JFK lurching out from beneath the kitchen table, and my old man talking gibberish to him. *Hi doggie.*

Darla said, "Stay with me. Concentrate."

"I'm trying."

"Try harder."

We kissed and my torn lips hurt but not much, and the kiss turned into something more, and she moaned beneath me. I nuzzled the area beneath her ear because it's the spot that Kimmy liked me to nestle in. Darla shirked out of her robe and said, "Terrier." Her heavy breasts swayed as she turned over, urging me, and I moved to her and Kimmy's name was loud in my head, thinking of her.

Terrier, I'm pregnant.

Darla and I made a fast, angry love, full of loss and necessity, and with a cruel understanding that we weren't helping each other much, but just enough for now. It was the sort of brutal sex that hurt, and not necessarily in a good way. We were both driven to prove something to ourselves and each other, and in the end all we demonstrated was how selfish and forsaken we were. I wondered if she could actually be a new love. I wondered if she would, somehow, manage to slip the blade between my ribs and at last destroy me.

I lay there panting with her arm thrown over my belly, her face against my throat. She was smiling. I wasn't. The pain was pushing through. She said, "That was nice." It wasn't. I told her, "Thank you, I needed that." I did. I knew that when my Alzheimer's hit this interlude would be one of the first memories to go.

Darla put her robe back on, left for a few minutes, and returned with tea, some finger foods, and another Percocet. I ate and slurped down the tea without tasting any of it. I popped the pill. She sat beside me, leaving a few inches between us that felt as deep and wide as the valleys of the moon.

"I don't want you to think I was taking advantage of you," she said.

Strange, but there it was. "You didn't. You were very giving. Thank you for helping me."

She nodded at that. "So you want to be with me. You're not just here because you misdialed."

"No."

"Was it because you simply needed somebody? Anybody?"

It was an honest question, and I didn't have an honest answer. Apologizing wouldn't help. Fucking her again wouldn't help. I didn't know why I'd phoned her. Calling my father would have made more sense. Or Wes.

"I was battered," I said.

"Yes, you were."

The pill started to take effect. My head got lighter. I started to drift. I held my hand out to her and she took it. "I'm sorry if you feel like I used you."

"I don't feel that way at all. I was glad I could help you, and let me say that you helped me just as much. We made love and you were sweet and shy and careful. It's been a long time since a man, any man, made me feel so warm and right. I'm just wondering why."

"Why?"

"Why you went to such lengths to show such intimacy. I knew you were different. But you said you were worse. You didn't act worse."

"Did you really want me to be?"

"I'm not certain. I think I might have initially. My feelings about such things are . . . complicated. Even more so after my divorce."

I wasn't sure what she was saying. I was pretty certain she didn't know herself. I wanted to be a proper sounding board and come up with insightful discourse. I wanted to assure her I would never hurt her, except I couldn't, and she wouldn't want to hear it anyway.

"That's what I'm investigating," she said, "those impulses, by doing this."

"Oh."

"Don't look so shocked."

"I'm not."

"Then don't look it."

I tried not to look it. I didn't know how not to look it, so I made an effort to wipe all expression from my face. It hurt. The tape tugged.

"There's a lot of bad people out there," I said. "I think you shouldn't go looking for them."

I thought she was too good for the life, if that's what she was in, but I didn't know why. I didn't know anything about her. I thought maybe I wanted to. A hundred questions were backed up inside me, but the Percocet wouldn't let me get to them.

I found myself on my feet and Darla whispered, "Come back to bed."

I did as I was told.

"I'm not sure I like it," she said, glancing down at my chest. She traced the borders of my dog tattoo, which took up the entire left side of my chest. It covered three bad scars including the one from where my father had yanked out my busted rib. "It's garish, but beautiful, in its own way. Speaking from a purely aesthetic viewpoint." She let the pause hang there for a full three count before adding, "Of course."

I wasn't sure what other point of view you could have besides an aesthetic one when discussing a tattoo, but I was sort of out of it.

She let her fingers roam along the bandages, snarling in the runway of hair leading down to my belly button. She pressed her knuckles into the scar tissue, hissing a little as if the wounds were fresh and she was the one feeling the pain. Everywhere else hurt, but not the scars. They were barely visible beneath the deep black ink of a howling dog. Darla stroked me, stroking the dog's head.

Her robe fell open. She rolled closer. I slid against her and tightened my jaws. She said, "You're one of those guys who likes to be in love when you do it."

"I suppose I am."

"Don't fall in love with me."

"I probably won't, but it's a weird thing to tell somebody."

"I know, but you're the type to fall hard and get hurt."

"If you haven't noticed, I get hurt just fine all by myself."

I expected a titter at least, but she didn't even crack a smile. "Aren't you going to tell me not to fall in love with you?"

"I might if there was any chance of that."

"There's always a chance."

The pain had grown muted. The Percs did their job. Darla's touch became more insistent. She moaned and said my name again. For the first time I liked the way she said it. We clasped and grappled. I squawked when I twisted the wrong way. Or maybe it was the right way.

She kept murmuring beneath her breath, "It's all right," trying to comfort me or simply commenting on my performance. I wondered if she'd picked up any of the beaten-down bastards at the Elbow Room after I'd skipped. As I nipped her shoulder I couldn't help looking past her, searching out signs of male spoor. I was somehow remorseful and jealous at the same time.

Darla whimpered, "Yes."

Our second tussle was brief and full of a sort of blunt affection that wore away into sharpness.

Afterward, her breathing steadied and deepened and soon she was asleep. I checked the clock and the numbers melted together. When they came back into focus two hours had passed. Darla was still sleeping.

A small alcove turned out to be a stand-up kitchen. I found ice in the fridge and dumped it in the bathroom sink and soaked my face. The bruises were turning funky colors already. My nose wasn't broken. The tape job to my side was holding my ribs in nicely.

I watched Darla sleeping. She was even more beautiful in repose. I wanted to join her again. I wanted to run away. I glanced around to see if there was something that might have her real name on it. I crept her place. There was nothing.

I wondered what the proper etiquette was supposed to be. Was I really a client? Was this something more than what it felt like? She'd nursed me when I needed her. She'd eased my agony. I'd helped her investigate her impulses. Maybe we were even or maybe I owed. I found my clothes, stole a nearly full bottle of Percocet, gathered up Dale's products and the prescriptions, and pulled out my wallet. I had three twenties. It wouldn't cover her price, if she even knew what her price was. It was degrading leaving cash behind, but that seemed to be what she needed from assholes like me. I thought of her husband's small, fast hands. I wanted to hurt him. I dropped the sixty bucks. It embarrassed me and I thought that might be her real endgame. A life lesson through humiliation.

I left the way I normally did. Despite the afternoon sun, I cut out like a thief in the night.

I called Chub. He answered with a formal "Wright's Garage," a lilt of laughter hanging there like somebody in the room had just finished a joke.

"It's me."

The second he heard my voice he disconnected. The Percs kept me steady. I tried again and it went straight through to voice mail.

I said, "This is serious. Call me back."

I waited two minutes, then drove over to the garage. I pulled up and parked next to his '64 Shelby Cobra 289 Roadster, another classic muscle car he'd restored himself. I stepped into the first bay and watched the three mechanics he had working for him under the hoods of three different cars. They didn't know anything about Chub's other career. He'd always managed to keep his lives separate. I'd tried that for five years and had still fouled it up.

Chub stood in his office, staring through the front window with a faraway look in his eye. I opened the door and stepped inside.

I could clearly see the outline of a blade in his back pocket. It wasn't much considering how much firepower the crew carried, but it must've given him some sense of safety. It was stupid of him to carry anything except an automatic with a hair trigger on his hip.

If the knife was for me, that was another matter.

He sat down, his feet up on his desk. I said his name and sat across the desk from him. He nodded but didn't divert his gaze. The last time we'd met like this we'd at least shaken hands. I could feel the heavy tidal drag of resentment straining around us.

"Keep it short. What do you want, Terry?"

"To warn you off of the latest crew you've been dealing with."

He shifted in his seat a little but that was it. The vehicle in the nearest bay started up, sputtering and popping badly until the mechanic fixed the timing chain. The car quieted and finally hummed.

"I know all about that already. They stopped over here a couple hours ago and told me they'd been followed from the garage. I knew it was you, you pain in the ass. I had a feeling you'd been watching me. After they shook you, they trailed you home. You nearly shook them a couple of times. The driver was impressed. I can see by your face they told you to go away. So why don't you go away?"

"They know where I live. My family could be in jeopardy."

"And whose fault is that? I told you to quit bracing me, Terrier." He jerked his feet off his desk and leaned forward. "You act like you're trying to protect my wife and daughter, but I know what you're really about. You're hoping I take a header. You want me in the bin. Or dead."

"It's not true," I said.

That got him grinning. Sorrowful and pained, but the old Chub was there, the guy I knew and had once loved. "You can't even find the guts to sound insulted." His expression drifted through different shades of the same things: frustration, pity, disappointment. "You gave that crew a reason to distrust me. For the first time my ass is really on the line."

"It's always been on the line, ever since you decided to plan escape routes and sell getaway cars. What I don't understand is why you're still doing it."

"Ask your father."

"Let's pretend I'm asking you."

"Why was your old man still a cat burglar climbing across rooftops when he had more than enough cash set aside?"

"He was born into the life, same as me. You weren't."

"You have no idea how ridiculous you sound, do you?"

Maybe I did but I ignored the question. "No matter how careful you are you're going to fuck up. Kimmy–"

He leaped up in a blur of motion. He was this close to taking a poke at me but held himself back at the last instant. "Don't. Don't mention her name."

"All right."

"Keep away from her."

"I have."

"I don't believe you."

"Good, you're wising up. You shouldn't believe me, even if I am telling you the truth. I'm a thief and a liar. So is that crew. No pro outfit needs that much hardware on a job. Even the driver was carrying. A driver never carries."

"You scared for me or for yourself?"

"Mostly for your wife and daughter."

He pulled a disgusted face. "Oh, don't give me that shit again. We've already been through this."

I nodded. I tried to find the right words. They weren't there. I licked my lips and almost spoke my brother's name. I didn't know why. He wasn't talking in my head at the moment. "Look," I said, "I'm a jealous, bitter prick, and for the past couple of months I've had a heart full of vipers I wouldn't wish on anybody. What matters right now is that you wise up about these guys. They're righteously bad news."

"Why? Because they beat the shit out of you? You deserved it."

"Probably," I admitted.

"You got what you were after."

"Not quite."

"If they were as wrong as you make them out to be they would've put six in your face instead of letting you walk away. I trust them more than I trust you, Terrier. So back off. I'm not telling you again.

Stay away from me and my family." He glanced aside. He couldn't keep his eyes on me anymore. "Just stay away from us."

There was nothing else to argue about.

Maybe I didn't know Chub that well anymore but I did recognize a man who was full of fear. For all his bluster Chub was worried. The crew had spooked him. Part of it was my fault. They had probably pushed him hard when they found out I'd followed them. I had meant to protect him and I'd put him in danger. They might think he was leaking info. They might think we were planning a rip-off. Only our reputations had saved us so far. But you could never be sure who might overreact, overindulge, overreach.

"Go on, get out of here," he said.

I waited. I had a reason. Chub had a screen saver on his computer showing a recent photo of him, Kimmy, and their daughter, whom I called Scooter. It bounced around and grew larger and smaller. When he'd jumped out of his seat the screen saver had cleared. I waited for it to return.

It took maybe another ten seconds. I let him glower. Finally I saw Scooter's smile.

Chub, Kimmy, and Scooter played in the driveway washing the Roadster. Chub held a garden hose, the water arching in a fine spray toward Kimmy but not reaching her yet. She was trying to dodge, the curve of her jawline shadowed by a tree on the lawn. She had her front teeth champed on her bottom lip, a habit she had whenever she tried to hold back laughter. I could imagine the sound she was making, a kind of choked giggle. He had his head drawn back, a small smile just beginning to break on his lips, a smear of bubbles across his forearm. Scooter had a pile of suds on her head and had her face scrunched in a squeal of joy. All of her teeth had come in. The ache went through me like my father pulling out my busted rib.

I thought, Goodbye, kid.

I hit the door. I got behind the wheel and faded into traffic. There was no point in looking for the crew. If they were still on my ass there wasn't anything I could do about it. For a second I flashed on the idea of visiting Jack "Fingers" Brown, the gun dealer who'd sold Collie the pistol he'd killed with. The fact that I'd thought of him at all was proof that the underneath was still there, waiting to draw me in.

My father stood on the porch with a man who looked so much like my dead brother that all I could do was sit in my car and stare. I was still a little buzzed on the Percs but I didn't think I was so far gone that I'd be hallucinating. Maybe I had a concussion. Maybe I was lying in a coma in an ICU while my parents agonized over pulling the plug. JFK trundled down the steps and crossed the lawn. He rose onto his hind legs, put his front paws on the hood, and stood looking at me expectantly through the windshield.

The guy who looked like Collie was talking animatedly with my old man. He used his hands a lot, waved his arms all around. He bent over violently and guffawed. He flashed teeth. My father showed no emotion and sipped from his beer. He shouldn't be drinking at all. I imagined the arguments my mother had already had with him trying to get him to stop.

He leaned back against the railing like he was relaxed, but I could read tension in his body language. I swung the car door open and climbed out. I stepped up the walk filled with the same dread I'd felt when visiting death row. For my sins I was doomed to repeat myself. I dry-swallowed another pill. JFK stayed close at my side.

My father said, "Here's Terry now."

A chill breeze broke like cold lips on my neck. The guy gazed down at me as I approached. He even had Collie's white streak in his hair, same as me. It seemed like he could barely contain his joy. Number six. The expression on the face of the man who looks just like your brother, who looks just like you.

My father noted my bruises. He cocked his head, a cloud of worry crossing his features. "You all right?"

"Sure."

"This is your cousin John."

"I don't have a cousin John," I said.

"You do," John said. "I'm your mother's nephew. Your uncle Will's son."

There didn't seem to be much of a reason to point out that I didn't have an uncle Will either.

I shouldn't have taken the last pill.

"Hello, John," I said, putting out my hand. "I'm Terry."

We shook. "Oh, I know who you are, Terrier."

"Yeah?"

I didn't like the way he said it, as if he'd been checking up on me. He had a rich deep voice. He had a charmer's grin. He was bad news through and through. I vibed that he wanted to hug me and stepped out of his reach. JFK went and crouched in the corner. He shivered in the presence of a ghost.

My cousin John wasn't drinking beer. Someone had mixed him a drink with a lot of ice. The glass was nearly empty. He took a deep breath and let out a warm laugh that I knew was going to be the precursor to a long story.

"Let me freshen that up for you," I said, and snatched the glass out of his hand. I stepped into the house and made sure to shut the door.

On the stove simmered a pot of stew. My mother sat at the kitchen table, talking quietly on the telephone. We were the last people in the western hemisphere who still had a landline and a phone with a cord. The cord was stretched across the length of the kitchen like a clothesline you could garotte yourself on.

I couldn't read her, which worried me. I threw down the meds and the bag of my sister's beauty products. I was home by dinner. I had done my duty. Liquor and cola and an ice bucket were out on a tray situated in the center of the table. I sniffed at the tumbler. Smelled like Dewar's. I drank it down.

The second she got a look at me my ma said into the receiver, "I have to go now, yes, tomorrow, goodbye." She hung up. She rushed over and checked the tape job and scabbed-over cuts. She gripped my chin and turned my face this way and that, considering it from different angles. She tsked as loudly as a rifle crack.

"You stole the meds," she said.

"I didn't steal the meds."

"And they caught you and they punched you out."

"Ma, listen–"

She ran a hand through her auburn hair. "Now I can't go back to Schlagel's."

"You can go back to Schlagel's."

"We have to find a new pharmacy."

"You don't have to–"

"Do you know what a nightmare it is dealing with the doctor's office and getting them to call in prescriptions to a new place?"

"You can go back to Schlagel's, Ma. Now, forget that, right?" I motioned toward the porch and nothing but a little groan came out and then my voice kicked in again and I said, "This guy? John? He says he's my cousin? What the hell?"

"What are you on?" she asked, staring into my eyes. "What did you take, Terry?"

"Nothing."

"Don't tell me nothing."

"That's not important right now."

"It is important, Terrier. When I ask you a question like this you answer. That's what you do. So, what did you take?"

"Some Percocet."

"I don't like you messing with drugs."

"Ma, I'm not mess–"

She cut me off with a hand slicing through the air. "Don't drink any more liquor, then. Who punched you out?"

"Some of Chub's friends."

"Why did they do that?"

"It was a misunderstanding."

"You need to stay away from him, Terry. You need to stay away from her."

"I am. I will. Ma? This guy? John?"

I dropped heavily into a chair. She grabbed the empty glass from my hand, filled it, and brought it back out to John. His laughter filled the house. I knew he was brimming with schemes and scams and rip-offs that would bring doom on us. I glanced into the living room where Gramp was watching cartoons. He seemed to be grimacing as John's chortle rang through the place.

My mother returned and said, "It's disturbing, isn't it, how much he looks like your brother?"

"I hadn't noticed. What's he doing here?"

"My brother Will phoned earlier this afternoon. My father had a stroke last month. He's dying and wants to see me."

"And you're complaining about the fucking pharmacy?"

She took a breath and shut her eyes and found her resolve. "I'm sorry. It was a defense mechanism. I suppose I'm in denial. It's a lot to take in. I haven't heard from my family in over thirty years. I haven't seen them since I got married. Talking to Will again . . . it brought back a lot of memories."

I'd never met anyone from her side of the family. I knew absolutely nothing about them. After she and my father started becoming serious her parents asked what kind of a boy he was. She told the truth. They ordered her to stop seeing him immediately. She returned one last time to pack her belongings and found the pictures of herself turned to the wall. She never went home again.

"Was that him on the phone just now?"

"Yes."

So, I had a grandmother too. "What was that like? After thirty-plus years?"

"It reminded me how much I missed him. And my parents. And how much I still resent them, for what happened."

My mother was the strongest person I knew, but this family, a family she had married into at the loss of her own, had cost her a normal life. She spent her life in a house devised by crooks, built on fifty metric fuck tons of unfenceable loot stashed away in caches in the walls and ceiling and floors. She'd been braced by the cops a thousand times, had spent all her time holding the Rands together despite our best efforts to destroy ourselves. She'd seen Mal in the yard with his guts hanging, she'd listened to the TV as the crowds outside the prison cheered while my brother died. She watched over Gramp, feeding and cleaning him, engaging him on the off chance that he could still understand enough to deserve human conversation. I suddenly wanted her to leave us and save herself.

"What are you going to do?" I asked. "About your father?"

"I'm not sure yet. I have to think about it."

I wanted another drink. She knew I wanted another drink and moved the tray away from me. I said, "So if you talked with your brother, then why's this one here? This nephew of yours."

"He wanted to come." She peered out the kitchen window at John and my old man freezing their asses off on the porch. My father stayed out there because it was his spot. It was usually the spot where the old dogs rested and kept watch. "I think he's always wanted to come. He seems quite lonesome."

Cousin John wasn't lonesome. He wasn't disaffected. He wasn't eager for newfound blood attachments. The restrained joy I'd seen was all about money and action and some kind of score.

"So even though they threw you out of the house they've kept tabs on you all this time?" I asked.

"Considering the Rand family history, nobody had to exactly

keep tabs. All they needed to do was watch the police blotter. Or the television." She poured herself two fingers of scotch and drained half the glass. I had never seen my mother drink alcohol before.

She reached over and with two fingers plied my gray patch. We were both acutely aware that these white streaks were from her side of the family.

I didn't even know her maiden name. I had always wondered why she hadn't just covered and lied about my father's occupation. I was a liar at heart. If you hit a wall you lied your way around it or over it or through it.

"What do you need me to do?" I asked.

"Right now? Just go out and talk with John."

"Oh Christ, don't ask me to do that."

"Please, it's not his fault that my parents disowned me," she insisted. "He's still family. And I think your father has reached his limit of social interaction. I'm going to give Gramp his medication and then I'll be out too."

"You don't trust him either," I said, noticing the swirl of suspicion in her eyes. "That's why you didn't let him in."

I walked out the door. John was gnawing my father's ears off, talking about movies. My old man hadn't been to a movie theater since 1981, when he'd stolen the receipts for the Mayweather on Fourteenth Street and been chased two miles by a fleet-footed security guard. He stood there up against the porch railing like living stone. No one else would call him antsy, but I could see it. His bubbly dead son was blathering at him.

John turned to me. I got a good deep look at his face. The likeness was spooky as fuck. He didn't bear my brother's scars, those from his youth and the worse ones he'd gained in prison. John wore a soul patch, just a trace of peach fuzz. His eyes were all wrong. He was thinner, softer, and he smiled, apparently pleased to be here. Collie had never been pleased to be here.

"You don't know what it was like for me, growing up in your shadow," John said to me.

"You're at least five years older than me," I said. "How did you grow up in my shadow?"

He chuckled. There was no edge to it. "I was speaking meta-phorically about the Rands. My father, he talked about your mother all the time."

"You knew about us."

"Sure, I knew about you," he said, taking a sip of the Dewar's and Coke. "Doesn't everybody know about you? I mean, I'm not . . . whatever . . . *street,* you know. I'm about as far from that as you can get, I guess. I was coddled. My mom, she was a coddler, a doter. She was a pamperer. I'm pampered. I was her only kid. My mom, to her everything in the world was a mystery. It frightened her. She passed some of that to me. It's just the way she was." He chuckled again, edgeless, a little sadly. "She's been gone almost three years now. Some kind of bone cancer. Took only a month."

"I'm sorry," I said.

"Thanks. Thank you. A nervous woman, but I loved her for it, sort of. I gave her and my dad a rough time when I was in my teens. Spent most of my waking hours doing what I shouldn't have been doing, driving them nuts, making her even more nervous. Granddad, he's hard, he's a hard man is what he is, and he'd give me stern looks, lots of stern appraisals, and stick his finger in my face, and give me orders on how to be a man, what to do to succeed, but it never took. I'd just go back out with my friends and fuck off, do whatever I wanted, had a little maryjane emporium going on the side, ran into some bad dudes, kinda bad dudes . . . well, pretty bad dudes. Had some more trouble. Occasionally heard the Rand name. Profession-ally, you know."

My father wagged his chin in a noncommittal fashion. His beer was empty but he didn't grab another one. He stared at John as if through a microscope, poring over every cell.

John didn't notice. "I probably did all that just because I figured it was something I could get away with, the way you all got away with it. I thought I was sharp. I thought it was in my bones, I suppose. Sorta in my bones. In my blood. Maybe." He shrugged. He had no Rand blood in him but somehow it was my father's shrug. "Then I did some business with some folks who did some business with Big Dan Thompson. I never met him but I heard about him, he had that syndicate style you see in mob films. The mob films that make the mob seem hip. And then, you know, a few years back, that thing with Collie, it was everywhere, you were everywhere, the name, I mean. Your name. I wanted to call, give condolences or whatever, but I wasn't sure if it was the right thing to do. So I kept my mouth shut. My dad, he never stopped talking about Aunt Ellie, she was on his mind a lot."

He ran out sentence after sentence, sort of chuckling as he went, enjoying the gab. John kept his arms moving, his hands flashing, unable to stand still.

"So why didn't he drop her a Christmas card from time to time?" I asked.

"Ah, he got caught up in the fallout too. It wasn't his fault. He was just sixteen at the time. My grandfather, Perry, you'd have to know him. He's . . . rigid. Demanding. Exacting. Not a bad man, just stern, puts his foot down and you know you'll have to fight to the death to change his mind. And who wants to go that far?"

My father kept a cool gaze going. It had to be working on him, knowing that the man who had thrown my mother out of the house was calling her back home again.

"Right, Uncle Pinscher? You've got to remember him."

"I remember him."

"Hard, right? Hard hard man. Steel."

"Yes."

"Don't bother hating him anymore, Uncle Pinscher, he's dying. The strokes took it all out of him. He went from being who he always was to this paralyzed scarecrow with mostly empty eyes. He cries a lot, he's scared like nobody I've ever seen scared before. I never liked him much but I feel sorry for him now. It's why I'm here, really."

My father's face remained placid so I grimaced for him. Uncle Pinscher? My mother came out with another refill for John. My father didn't get another beer. I hung on to my high as well as I could. She smiled and made a little small talk and John yipped and jabbered some more. She asked a few questions. He responded at length. Her face froze in place. She had thirty-five years of indignation under her belt. My mother had never turned her back on anyone in the family for a minute. I swallowed down a surge of hatred for her parents. I wanted to meet these people. Along with that came a vague anger toward my father for falling in love with her and stealing her away.

John snapped his chin up, put his hand on my elbow. His touch made me bristle. "So tell me about yourself, Terry."

I didn't feel like sharing. I looked at him and wondered when the ax would fall. When he'd make his move, when he'd show his true colors, the con man beneath. John waited for me to respond, sipping his drink, my father silent as stone, my mother shivering.

I said, "Sorry, John, I guess I just want to mourn quietly for Grandpa Merle."

"Perry."

"Right."

"He's not dead yet."

"Right."

"It's okay, I understand. Must be rough, having me just drop in on all of you like this from out of the blue. My father said I shouldn't come, but I wanted to. I've been meaning to for a long time, and this just gave me the right chance. I think. I think it was the right chance. What I hope was the right chance." He finished his drink, drew me into one of those nervous, buoyant semihugs, and patted my back with his large strong hands. I couldn't remember ever being hugged by my brother, but if he had, it probably would've made me feel something like this: uncomfortable, disturbed, pleasantly surprised. Against my will, my better judgment, against the tide of time, I hugged him back a little.

"I should be getting home now," he said.

My mother embraced him. Her body language said she didn't trust him any more than I did. My father stuck out his hand. John turned to me. I nodded. He didn't really want to leave. He took a step and remembered JFK.

He said, "See you soon, boy." JFK lumbered to his feet and sat having his broad flat head patted. John made it down the porch stairs before turning again and giving a brief wave. When he got to his car he did the same thing again. After he reversed out of the driveway, he waved again when he hit the street. Collie's presence swelled beside me and pressed against me. My mother and father stood silently. The three of us abided side by side, along with the dog, waiting for the next thing to happen.

My cousin John honked twice and drove off just as Dale pulled up in some new beau's 4x4. The kid had manners and parked at the curb, stepped around the front of the truck, and opened the door for her. He escorted her up the walkway. She introduced him as Tony. He was the second lead in the French play by the French guy. They talked about how narrow-minded the director was. They told cute anecdotes about things that happened during rehearsal. My mother nodded and engaged them, because that was her gift, even while she was thinking of the dying, steely father she hadn't seen in decades calling her back home, even while she shuddered.

I knew she would attend the performance and I would go with

her like Dale had asked. Tony said good night in short order, giving my sister the look, the virtuous pained look of a young man in the opening venture of falling in love, excited about it, scared, a little guilty, wired. He had it bad, and it was inspiring to see. Dale smiled at him, didn't even give the poor kid a peck. He did a little jog as he crossed the lawn back to his truck. He gave a brief wave as he got behind the wheel, exactly as John had done. Dale could no longer hold a straight face as a tortured and puzzled expression crimped her features. A moan broke within her. I knew the sound. The sound was inside me. I got my arms around her just as she burst into tears and wailed, *"Am I going insane or did I just see my mass murdering dead brother driving down the fucking road?"*

We Rands did a poor job of expressing ourselves.
We supported one another, sometimes, but we did it in silence. My
mother tried to ease the burden at the dinner table. She kept up a
steadily lilting monologue. She told us stories out of her childhood
that made her smile without feeling. She mentioned how she and her
brother Will would go swimming in the Bay Shore marina when they
were children, and how later the family rented a house out on Oak
Beach every summer until she was twelve. No, thirteen. No, twelve.
Maybe thirteen. She couldn't remember. It had been a long time ago.
Her tales illustrated almost nothing. I tried to smile through them
but my lips felt like poorly molded clay. She was conflicted about her
dying father and the memories kept beating at her like a squall whip-
ping the coast.

My father put his hand on her elbow and whispered, "It's okay,
baby." For him that was a tremendous show of affection.

The tension kept growing. Old Shep felt it too. As my mother
continued her idle talk and she fed him, he looked up from his plate
of stew and every so often turned his head left or right, watching each
of us in turn. He looked frightened, like he was afraid of being hit.

Afterward Dale went to her room without a word even though I
could see the shouting in the planes of her face, the screaming, the
loss and anger. My parents watched television with Gramp, occasionally whispering to each other or laughing hollowly at the screen.

My bruised ribs were starting to hurt like hell again. I popped
more Percs. The pain dulled. Some of the pain dulled. Some of the
pain, the pain that I couldn't put a name to, sharpened like shivs
working at my kidneys. As the sun set I got into my sweats and went

for a run with JFK down Old Autauk Highway and out around Shale-brook College and the lake. JFK planted himself at the shore near a bench where a couple of college girls sat. He moseyed up to them and stood for a brisk pat-down. I ran the mile and a quarter around the lake, my head growing lighter and lighter. The lamps around the park came up and illuminated the running trails. Each time I looked at the bench there was someone else sitting with JFK, scratching his ears.

John was going to try to hurt us. I had to put a stop to that.

It was stupid to keep running with possibly fractured ribs. My breath stuck in my throat like barbed wire. When I got around again the bench was empty. JFK buried the side of his face against my thigh.

We took it very slow on the way back home. I wondered if the crew was still watching. I didn't mind. I had said what I had to say and the rest was up to Chub.

My phone rang.

Darla said, "How are you feeling?"

"A lot better, thanks."

"You didn't have to leave money, Terrier."

"I wasn't sure of the protocol."

"I'm not certain I have a protocol. At least not yet. But if I did, you're not someone I expected to follow it."

"I owed you for helping me."

"You didn't owe me for that."

"And I stole your bottle of Percocet."

"You're a thief. And you were in pain. I expected you to take it. And the money in my wallet. Instead, you left me cash."

"I'm not that kind of a thief."

"You're the kind who would never steal something important from a friend. That's good to know." A Kia with a squealing fan belt sped by. "What's that noise?"

"Traffic. And my dog panting. I'm out for a run."

"With those ribs?" She let out a grunt of exasperation. "The fact that you're even walking means you must be slamming down those pills. Are you trying to kill yourself?"

"I don't think so."

She let loose with a giggle, warmhearted and a little disparaging. "Well, I'm glad you didn't answer with a definitive yes anyway. That would have ruined the evening completely. I thought you might like to come back over tonight."

I imagined the silent strain still there at home, John's presence remaining behind and conjuring the dead. Dale hiding in her room texting, burning up her laptop, practicing her French, talking on the phone with Tony, talking with ROG, whoever he was. My old man waiting to climb out of bed and take off into the dark. I should keep an eye out. I should follow him tonight.

As I walked along I thought of how Darla's beauty worked its magic on me. I was still full of need and want, and it felt like I always would be no matter what she did to me. The loneliness was on me again, the mad boredom. I saw her stretched out across the mattress with her robe sliding open at the knee, exposing her leg, the taut muscular curve dimpled and shadowed, my pulse full of fire.

I found a bus bench and sat. JFK slumped at my feet, his ears standing up whenever a particularly noisy engine cruised by.

"I'd like to," I told her. "Very much."

"But you won't."

"I can't. My father is disappearing nights and I should watch out for him."

"If he isn't telling you where he's going then he has his reasons. Does he question you on where you've been?"

"No."

"Then maybe you shouldn't corner him."

"You're right, I probably shouldn't."

"But you will."

"Yeah, I probably will."

"There are better things to do with your time, Terrier. I'm one of those things."

"I know that."

"I don't think you do, but maybe you'll learn."

The air grew heavy with the smell of the ocean. That storm was still out there, waiting to roll in. "I thought you didn't want me to fall in love with you."

"I don't."

"I'm the type who falls hard and gets hurt."

"I know," she said with a sexy, throaty hum. "I'd very much like to avoid that."

"Then maybe I shouldn't come by tonight."

"Because it's the kind of night when you might fall in love?"

"Like you said. There's always a chance."

"It's nice to think so, isn't it?" she said and disconnected.

It was nice to think so. I sat there on the bench and watched the headlights burning through the rising mist. It had been a day suffused with hurt, surprise, and kindness. JFK put his head down and began to snore. In a half hour a well-lit bus pulled up to the stop and I locked eyes with the driver and waved him on. He smirked and continued past. There was a long break in the traffic where the dull sweep of the breeze lulled me.

Then JFK raised his head, sniffing the air. We both smelled rain coming. I had stiffened up too much to jog anymore and sort of limp-walked the rest of the way home.

By the time I got back the house was dark. I was hoping my father would be out on the porch again doing his usual thing, enjoying the night or pretending to. I wanted to ask him about his thoughts on John. I wanted to ask him about those long-ago days when he was a kid trying to impress a new girlfriend's tough old man, burdened by a family reputation he didn't want and barely shared in.

I crept the house and checked on everyone. My mother was arranged primly on her back, arms straight at her sides like a long-term coma patient. My father lay there hanging off the edge of the mattress with his eyes shut, breathing slow and steady, but I got the distinct impression that he was faking it, pretending to sleep until I'd gone on my way. He was still a jump ahead of me.

Dale had her door locked. I could pick it in eight seconds but didn't want to push her level of mistrust any deeper into the red zone.

The house swelled heavily with history. The walls were packed with busted scams. The hidden crawl spaces could hide a hundred bodies.

Gramp was still awake. Or at least his eyes were open. I opened the window, sat on the sill, and spilled. It was good to have a confidant who would never betray your confidence. I whispered to him about everything that had gone down over the last couple of days. I went on and on and could barely hear myself. Every so often he intoned some odd phrase.

"We want the goods."

"My bones burned."

"The rest follows quickly."

"Buckets of rain fell beneath a cold moon."

In his own head he was probably confiding in me as much as I was in him. I tried to piece together what he might be remembering, or dreaming, or trying to tell me, but I couldn't make it. His voice ran out on him but his mouth still worked. I stroked his hair. Thick tears slowly ran from his eyes and threaded their way along his wrinkles. I wiped his face and eventually he slept. I shut the window and left.

JFK followed me to my room. I lay back and tried to will myself into the joists and timbers of the house as they creaked. The storm had finally arrived, rain pouring down. I tried to separate the sounds. I waited for my father to hit the front door. JFK lay out beside me, put his chin on my thigh, and began to snore. I put my hand to his powerful heart and felt the thrum of his blood running through him.

I dropped my head back on the pillow expecting to soon hear my old man creep to his car. I prepared myself for the confrontation to come. I imagined a hundred scenarios. I pictured him telling a dozen stories. He was doing second-story work again. He was breaking into pawnshops and flea markets to nab himself more figurines. He had a girlfriend on the side. He was playing high-stakes poker at the Fifth Amendment with Danny Thompson and the other big gun operators. I saw us standing in the front yard nose to nose, drenched. He opened his mouth to say something important, his face full of rage, and whispered the next whisper, *"Terry, I know what you—"*

I woke at dawn to find my mother sitting on the edge of the bed, staring at me with her hand sweeping through my white patch.

She'd been crying. Her bright hazel eyes were a little swollen, shot through with red.

"You don't have to go," I said.

"Yes, I do."

"No, you don't."

My side was on fire. I never should have gone jogging. What a fucking stupid thing to do. All I wanted were the Percs. I was going to need the pills for another week at least. I was going to burn through them.

She kept plying my gray curls. She had the same streak in her own hair and had been dyeing it since junior high. I realized that when she toyed with my hair it wasn't just a signature way to comfort me. Maybe it always made her think of her brother and father. All this time it hadn't been a moment being shared just by the two of us, but also by these outsiders.

Her smile was tinged with turmoil and excitement, the kind that hits you all at once on mornings like this, when you prepare yourself to face someone you thought you hated, and who you knew hated you. "He's my father."

"Does that matter? You haven't seen him in more than thirty years."

"Of course it matters. He's always been my father. He'll always be my father."

"John says he's hard as steel."

"Not anymore," she said, smiling sadly. "Not if he's asking for me."

"Just because he's had a stroke doesn't mean he'll be a sweetheart."

"He'll never be that."

"John is bad news. Don't trust his goofball act. All that hugging and back-patting. All that laughing. I get the feeling we're going to run up against him in a bad way before this is through."

"I think he had a rough start and straightened himself out. It's a rare thing. He doesn't have any siblings or cousins. He's only looking for family."

I sat up against the headboard. Shifting hurt like hell but I didn't let it show. We Rands could do amazing things in order to hide the truth. "And seeing your mother again. And your brother. What's that going to be like?"

She angled her chin away and shadows of beaded rain fell across her face. "They never had anything to do with it. My father was a small tyrant. I was happy to be gone. If he hadn't disowned me over the man I loved he would've disowned me for some other reason. It was inevitable. And I suppose it was inescapable that I'd go back someday."

"I'm going with you, Ma."

"That's not necessary, Terry."

"I want to. I want to see these people."

"They're just strangers. They're not your family. They're not your enemies. He's dying. I don't need you starting up all kinds of dramatics."

"Me?" I asked. "Am I the kind of person who would start up dramatics?"

"You are absolutely the kind of person who would start up dramatics, Terrier."

"I'm still going."

She touched the side of my face, prodded some of the damage.

"Do you want to tell me which of Chub's friends punched you out? And why?"

"Not just at the moment."

"Follow me."

I got out of bed and followed her into my bathroom. She peeled off the pieces of tape and swabbed my cuts and bruises with astringent. She had done this many times before for me and Collie, for my father and uncles. "There's not much swelling, and only a little discoloration. You iced up yesterday, didn't you?"

"Yes."

"Good. You've been favoring your right side."

"A couple of banged-up ribs."

"Take off your T-shirt."

I did as she told me. Her hands went to work on my side gently. She had a well-practiced touch.

"You should have told me yesterday. Don't keep these kinds of things from your mother."

"Sorry," I told her, and I was.

"You didn't tape this up yourself," she stated. "Whoever it was did a good job. You should leave it for another day or two, then I'll change it. Try not to let your side get soaked when you shower. Do you still have any Percocet?"

"Yes."

"Two every four hours, Terrier. Don't pop them the way you were yesterday. Your eyes were practically spinning."

"Okay." I got the bottle and took two dry.

"With a glass of water," she said.

"Right." I got a glass of water from the bathroom tap.

My ma went to my dresser and laid out my clothes for me like I was five years old again. For some reason I found it just as reassuring as annoying. "Are you certain you want to come with me today?" she asked.

"Yes."

"We'll leave after breakfast."

"Okay." It hit me then. "I don't even know your maiden name, Ma."

She moved to the door, took an extra second to answer as if she had trouble remembering, and said, "It's Crowe."

She left and I ran the name around in my head for a while. I hopped in the shower and tried not to let my side get soaked. I washed the dried blood from my hair. I sponged off the remnants of Darla's intimacy. When I got out I wrapped a towel around my waist and walked down the hall to Grey's room.

My uncle was supposed to be on the long grift. I'd packed up some of his clothes in a fancy set of luggage and filled an overnight kit with hair care effects. He'd gone on the gambling circuit before, twice for as long as six months at a clip. I still had a little time before my father would get suspicious.

I'd cut every label out of those shirts, suits, and even his under-wear. Then I'd driven to the Port Authority Bus Terminal and left the baggage sitting in the farthest stall of the men's room. Nothing could disappear without a trace any faster than that.

I splashed my face with Grey's aftershave and used his double wooden brushes to swipe my hair back and forth across my head. I put on some of his threads. They fit well and looked good. Let the shrinks say whatever they wanted. One of the last times I'd spoken with my uncle, while he was still in his right head, he'd told me to raid his closet anytime I liked.

Dale heard me in his room and peeked in while I finished dress-ing.

"You're going to go with her," she said. "Good, I don't think Ma should be alone." She hung back in the doorway and watched me get-ting ready. She tilted her head one way and then the other, appraising me. "You look nice."

"Why don't you come with us?" I asked.

"I have school."

"Ditch for the day."

"I don't do that."

"Of course you do that, you're a teenager."

"I hardly ever do it, and I'm not doing it today. You'll make sure you're back for my show tonight, right?"

"Right."

"Eight o'clock?"

"Absolutely," I said. "Wouldn't miss it."

"I really want you there. It's important to me that you're there. You and Ma. You understand. You know what I'm saying, Terry?"

"I know what you're saying."

"Good."

I caught her eyes in the mirror as I finished buttoning my cuffs. She continued to hover in the doorway. We faced each other across the room, too reserved to hug, too bound by remorse to talk at length. I filled the room with a question. "Dale, who's Roger?"

"Roger? I don't know any Roger." She stared at me curiously. "Who's Roger?"

"Roge."

"Roge?"

"R-O-G. Who's R-O-G, Dale?"

She pulled a face and glared at me. She stepped in. She closed the door behind her. She lowered her voice. "You've checked my phone. You've been creeping me again."

"I wanted to mention it." And I always did what I wanted. "You call the guy a lot."

"How do you know it's a guy?"

"Whoever it is. That's what I'm asking. Who is it?"

"And what business is that of yours?"

"You're my sister. Everything about you is my business."

She let out a weary snicker. "What balls!"

"Dale–"

"You really have no idea how to deal with people, Terry. Even if I wanted to share that with you, do you really believe I would now? After you've been checking my phone? Searching my room? What makes you think that would instill trust in you?"

"Because I'm your brother and you know I'm looking out for you."

"You disappeared for five years without a word." A tight smile slashed its way across her face. "I'm not feeling a tight sibling bond right now, Terry, not at all."

"I just want to make sure you're safe."

"I'm not safe. No one is ever safe. I can't have you even deeper in my life, do you understand? I can't have that." Her voice had a thin core of iron to it.

"Dale–"

"Stop saying my name! All you have to do is remember everything I just told you. You won't forget. You'll do as I ask. That's what you'll do. You'll respect me that much, Terrier. You will. Say you will."

I said, "I will."

"And you'll mean it."

"I mean it," I said.

She was so keyed up she lunged forward and fell into my arms hugging me. She squeezed me so tightly I let out a grunt. I tried to fold my arms around her and hug her back but by then she'd slipped away. She opened the door and shut it behind her, leaving me alone smelling like the man I'd killed.

Part II

FEELING THE DEVIL

So far as I knew, my father hadn't yet said a word about my mother returning to her childhood home. He rarely said a word about anything, but I expected him to expound at least a little about this. I was still waiting for him to share. He sat at the kitchen table looking thoughtful and grim. He was a touch scary when he was grim. Or thoughtful. He caught me watching him and his face cleared. He set his gaze on me. He knew where I'd fall when it came to this topic.

My old man considered my clothes and said, "Snazzy."

"Grey said I could borrow anything in his closet."

"Yeah. You look good. You should dress like that all the time."

"Thanks."

He nodded, mopped up his eggs with toast, drank some juice, drank some herbal tea the color of seaweed. Beside his napkin were three pills of various sizes and colors. "I'm glad you're going with her."

"Sure."

"She shouldn't be alone."

"No, probably not."

"I'd go, but—"

There were only so many things to say when you weren't talking to somebody about something they couldn't talk about. "I understand."

I waited and tried to figure out what I could do to help him. I couldn't come up with anything. JFK sensed my father's mood and nosed into his right hand. My father patted him slowly, heavily on the head.

We finished eating. My old man gulped his pills. A truck horn blew in the street. Dale came down, pecked our mother on the cheek, and said with great intensity, "Good luck. Don't let anyone push you around or make you feel guilty. If anyone tries, walk out. Right?"

"Right," Ma said.

"See you at the play?"

"We wouldn't miss it for anything."

Dale rushed out the door and down the walk and into Tony's 4x4. They kissed deeply for five Mississippis.

My mother took my father's hands in her own. She leaned down and they touched foreheads and she spoke quietly for a moment. I moved out onto the veranda, lit a cigarette, took a drag, and flicked it over the rail. I turned back to check on them and saw her kiss him gently. She peeled away and thumbed tears from beneath her eyes. She shouldered out the screen door, across the porch, and down the stairs. She looked like she needed a second to compose herself so I let her get into my car and reapply her makeup in the passenger-side mirror.

My father came to the door. He waved to her and gave a wholly false smile. He backed up a step so he was out of her view. He glanced at me and his lips dropped into a frown and the frown fell in on itself. He gave me a firm nod. I nodded back. Then he made his way through the house and out the back door to the garage, where he would dust and mull over his figurine collection and think about delicate creations made during terrible times. He would think of what he owned and what he didn't own. What he could get and what he could never have.

I drove my mother back to the family she hadn't seen in more than three decades. It turned out to be less than twenty minutes from our house. I thought of what that must've been like for her, living that close to her family for all these years.

I knew the upscale neighborhood pretty well. As a teenager I'd robbed at least a couple of houses within a half-mile radius. The area had some serious wealth sunk into it.

The Crowe house turned out to be a huge old Victorian restored to perfection. The other side of the family had some cash, and they protected it. The place had a lot of exterior lighting, including four motion-detector spots. Two to illuminate the front yard, and one along each side in case anybody jumped a fence and crossed the back-yard. I could see from here that the windows were wired with glass-breaking alarms. The security system would be tied in to a local company, probably APS, American Protection Services. Their offices were over on Jerusalem Avenue, and they could probably make this address in under four minutes.

The house was surrounded by a seven-foot-high black spear fence tipped with nasty barbed points. It was too tall to be aesthetically pleasing and way too aggressive to be only a matter of privacy. It was meant to be intimidating, imposing as hell. My mother stared with a subtly despondent, angry expression.

I said, "It looks like your old man always expected dad to come here one day and empty the place out."

"It's very different from when I grew up here," she admitted. "My mother used to love gardening. She had beds of flowers all over the yard. There was a white split-rail fence along the sidewalk, not this hideous metal thing with knives at the top."

"Those chevron barbs are meant to hang a burglar up. Guy swings his leg over the top and spikes himself on it, he's trapped." It was such an obvious message it made me snicker. "Did he really think this could stop Dad if he wanted to juke the place?"

"My father had very dim notions of most people."

Set between two looming stone pillars was a gate made of the same metal spears. The gate was open, maybe in an effort to make my mother feel welcome. I'd seen jails less forbidding.

"I'm guessing they don't throw many cocktail parties," I said.

"At one time they did. We always had Christmas parties and Fourth of July cookouts. My parents loved having guests. My father did a lot of business that way."

"I never asked. What's he do?"

"He's a television and movie producer. He used to take me into Manhattan to the studio offices and introduce me to celebrities. I once met . . . I once met–" Her memory faltered and her voice faltered too. "I met a number of celebrities, but I can't remember any of them now." She tried to hold back the wash of emotion, but the tears came again anyway. She flicked her wrists and tried to smear them away.

"It wasn't your fault, Ma."

"No, I don't think it was. But it's sad anyway."

"There's still time to change your mind."

"No, there isn't."

I did a K-turn in the street and backed up the Crowe driveway. I already had a bad feeling and wanted to be able to hop behind the wheel and rip out.

"What's wrong?" she asked.

"Nothing."

"Try to smile."

"I'll do my best." I gave her my smile.

We got out and headed up the extravagant brick walkway. We didn't get a chance to ring the bell before John answered the door with the adorable grin already pressed into place. When it was finally revealed I knew his scam would somehow change my life. He sang out with a loud "Hey-ey!" He grabbed my mother in a bear hug and hefted her heels off the stoop. She allowed him to dance her around for a couple seconds before he led us into the foyer.

Without letting her go he reached aside and stuck his hand out to me. We shook. He said, "You found the place okay? No problems, right?" He said it like he didn't know my mother had lived here until she was twenty. Maybe he didn't. It was make talk that didn't deserve a response, so I didn't give one. He ushered us deeper into the Crowe house.

"Oh," my mother said.

The inside was about as different from the exterior as you could get. It was bright and inviting and looked designed for cocktail parties and charades and celebrity mixers. Lots of homey rooms, some small but most excessively large, all packed with expensive stylish furniture. John asked if he could get us anything, a drink, tea, something harder, an early lunch.

We begged off and he led us into a living room where a man about my father's age stood in the center of the room, arms at his sides like he was on guard duty, just waiting for my mother to walk in.

He dyed out the gray streak the same way she did. He had reddish-brown hair like her as well.

"Ellie," he said.

"Hello, Will."

She moved to him and gave him a brief awkward clench that soon became a genuinely emotional embrace. I was surprised, and a bit jealous, by its intensity.

"You're so beautiful," he said.

"And you look healthy. You're trim, you've lost all your baby fat."

"A long time ago. My wife Stephanie was a nutritionist. She taught Mom how to cook meals without all the fat and heavy carbs. Now we eat plenty of legumes, fruit, and nuts for good blood glycemic numbers and HDL levels."

I had no idea what a blood glycemic number or HDL level was, or if mine were any good, but I tried my best to appear as if they were. My mother opened her hand and motioned to me. "This is my son Terry."

Will raised his chin and went deep into my eyes. He was a man of quick assessments, who judged others instantly on how they presented themselves, how strong their handshake was, how expensive their cologne. I was glad I was wearing Grey's. Will gave my hand one hard squeeze and pump, then didn't let go. "Hello, Terry, it's nice to finally meet you. I'm sorry it's taken so long."

"I suppose I am too."

I tried to say something more but there wasn't anything more. He brought his other hand over and clasped mine in both of his. He smiled and in his smile I saw that he was at as much of a loss as I was. I broke our clutch. He had years to catch up on with his sister and nothing at all to cover with me.

My mother and her brother drew off to one corner of the room and chatted quietly about their father's fading health. He put his arm around her shoulder and brought her in close and gave her a brisk but honest kiss on the cheek, and she fell in close to him. I wondered where my grandmother was. I wondered which bedroom my grandfather was dying in.

John said, "I'll show you my studio."

"Studio?"

"My cutting room. I'm a filmmaker too."

He led me through the house. I got a sense that the place was usually filled with servants or nurses. I could feel the empty spaces where they usually clustered. John stopped off in the kitchen and drew two bottles of imported beer out of the fridge. It wasn't even ten A.M. yet. He handed me one. I waved him off. I had to start worrying about killing brain cells and blood glycemic numbers and brain elasticity. We traveled through a series of corridors that made me think of the Rand house with its hidden panels and fold-up ladders. I imagined the walls snapping open to reveal secret private movie theaters and game rooms.

"You live here?" I asked.

"Yeah."

"You're, what, thirty-five? And you still live at home?"

"I'm thirty-two. You're not all that much younger than I am and you live at home."

"Yeah, but I'm fucked," I said. "Are you?"

"I suppose I am."

His cutting room was an office with nearly every inch filled with something to do with movies. Shelves packed with DVDs, walls covered with one-sheet action movie posters, some signed. Golden age of Hollywood memorabilia. Framed photos of film noir, original film reels. Computer and stereo equipment. Boom mikes in the corner. Horror movie icon models, action figures, first-edition hardcover horror novels. I knew a lot of fences who would go in big for this sort of thing. I could rake in some dough. My instincts kicked in. I looked at the windows and checked what kind of alarm system was in place. It was out-of-date and wouldn't be too difficult.

Except we Rands had a rule that we didn't steal from family. I wondered if it still applied in this case. Were the Crowes my family?

John had an old-fashioned editing machine, the kind that ran actual film and clipped out frames. The floor was covered with sections of film and pieces of tape and piles of dust. The maids never got in here to clean. I imagined that they'd have strict orders to keep out.

"What kind of movies do you shoot?" I asked.

"Wistful ones," he said. "Dreamy meditations on—" He sipped his beer. He let out an angry laugh. "—on who the Christ knows what. Artsy, surrealistic, experimental pieces of shit that pay homage to German expressionism and the French new wave. At least that's what every talentless, pretentious fucker says. And documentaries, like I said. Everyone with a camera thinks he can make a documentary. It's because of reality television. Reality TV lets us all think we can be stars either in front or behind the lens. All you have to do is be self-important, belligerent, promiscuous, or willing to heave yourself off a garage or in front of a car, and you'll be popular. You'll go viral. You watch a lot of TV?"

"No."

"Good, that crap will rot your brain worse than crank." John leaned back against the wall between two posters: *The Hills Have Eyes* and *The Maltese Falcon*. He was bookended by Bogie and a bald mutant cannibal wearing a necklace of bones. John raised his bottle like he was toasting me. "My dad and granddad are both very successful producers."

"Why don't they live in Los Angeles?"

"Granddad was out there for a few years when he was a young man, but he hated it, so he moved back here to New York for the television market. My father has a place out there in the hills, spends a few weeks or a few months at a clip getting studio projects off the ground."

"Must be a nice in for you."

"No. Neither one of them ever helped me much. They mostly hate what I do."

I thought, Here it is. Here's the setup, here's the scam. It's got something to do with his old man. It always has something to do with your old man.

"Sorry," I said.

"Don't be. I've got other interests. I'm into making my documentaries. Don't ask me what subjects. A variety of them. I have a touch of OCD, I think. I've never been diagnosed, clinically I mean, but my obsessions seem to get the best of me. I follow them up. I have a lot of them. But then most people do, I guess, whether they admit to them or not."

I wasn't going to ask him what subjects.

"I've shot some horror films . . . atmospheric ghost stories," John said.

He seemed to be waiting for a response to that. "Okay."

"Some of it was artsy, very Asian, very European. A way to honor the human character, show it in all its flawed beauty. Passionate, erotic, lush, vivid, striking, angry, bitter, vicious, even ugly. But real. Other stuff, not so arty. More primal, you know. Bloody, gory, hot, sweaty, scary."

"I get you."

"You probably don't approve."

"Why would you say that?"

"Because of Collie."

He was right. I didn't approve. I imagined lush, vivid, angry, vicious, ugly, real, bloody, gory, sweaty horror films and thought of my brother's butchery. I'd lived through it, I didn't need to see it on film. I'd already seen it on TV reports, at the time and then again with the upsurge of public interest right before his execution. I wanted to warn John off. I wanted to tell him not to make a documentary about my brother, not to use his story as the basis for some knife-kill flick. I looked at the bald mutant cannibal and the bald mutant cannibal looked back at me.

"I'm thinking of doing a movie on Dale."

That shook me. "What?" A shiver ran through me and my chest tightened and my sternum ground together like my bad ribs. "What did you just say?" The rage was on me in an instant. I covered the ground between us in one bound, gripped his collar, and shoved him hard against the wall while Bogie tilted and smacked him in the head. "Did you just say you wanted to film my sister?"

"Jesus, Terrier, relax!"

I glowered at him.

"Listen, listen, you've got it wrong. Listen. She's very photogenic. When she was being interviewed by reporters about Collie, right before his execution? When all that went down? She never got rattled. The camera loves her, she's comfortable in front of it. She's a sensation. With the show. Everybody loves her."

I let go of him and backed up a few steps. Film crinkled beneath my feet. One match and we were both six-foot piles of ash.

"What do you mean the show?"

"Her show. The show, Terry."

I looked at him. I waited. Bogie eyed me.

"You don't know about it?"

I smiled like I knew about it, like of course I knew about it, let's talk some more. He frowned, worried now.

"I feel bad having mentioned it, then. I figured you knew. Forget I said anything."

I smiled. "As much as I wish I could do that, John, I don't think I'll be able to. So please explain to me what you're talking about, yeah?"

"Maybe you should talk to Dale."

"I think you're right," I said. "Yes, I believe so. I should talk to her. I will talk to her. But she's not here at the moment and you are."

"You're pissed, huh?"

"No, not at all."

"You look pissed, Terry."

"John, tell me what the fuck you were talking about, right?"

He went to his laptop. He punched in a website. I watched my sister appear on the screen and I finally found out what ROG was.

"It's pretty brilliant, isn't it?" John said. "The guy who created it, some guy around my age, his name is Simon Ketch, he's a multimillionaire already. Can you believe it?"

"It's fake," I said.

"That's what Ketch's lawyers are always arguing, to handle any lawsuits, but who knows?"

"I do."

I sat at John's desk staring at his screen with my eyes starting to burn. It turned out that ROG was short for *ROGUES*, a new Web-based *COPS*-like show filmed from the point of view of petty criminals pulling minor acts of theft and vandalism. Most of the kids were boys wearing ski masks or handkerchiefs over their faces. Some street chicks showed up to watch the shenanigans and applaud the illegal efforts. It was all filmed with handheld cameras chasing after the punks while they kicked in doors, busted windows, and ran through houses sticking things like DVD players into sacks and pulling cheap jewelry out of dresser drawers. Third-rate home invasion antics. The kids laughed their asses off the whole time. It wasn't about money, it was all about the mischief.

Except in Dale's case. She was the face of the show. She wore heavy black and red makeup, sexified but almost clownish, with her hair styled in a wild shag almost the same as Darla's. She was skinned into tight leather clothes I'd never seen her wear before. It was a hell of a getup, a real semislick disguise. Most people who knew her wouldn't be able to recognize her, but she couldn't fool me.

She introduced the segments and interviewed the punks under their street names of "Lick 87," "Morgue Baby," and "Godless Kid."

She never said her name but she smiled into the lens, looking beautiful, vivid, and wild, like she was heading out to an underground club.
She ran along with the cameramen like an investigative reporter. She
had a quiet demeanor as if she took all of this very seriously, as if she
had exclusives to breaking news that would soon be on all the net-
work stations.

The B&Es seemed staged to me. I knew the sound of real breaking glass, but when these punks put their gloved fists through the
door or kitchen windows I didn't buy it. I watched Lick 87 especially.
He had the same basic size as Tony, the kid Dale was dating.

"How do they make money on this?" I asked.

"They sell downloads for a couple bucks a pop. The Web show is
popular. Anything that's popular can turn a profit somehow."

I nodded. "And the cops?"

"It's pretty small fry. I doubt the cops or feds are very interested.
There's tons of this kind of shit on the Internet. They can't catch everyone. They can hardly catch anyone. It's all anonymous."

I played some of the segments again. Sometimes these teen Rogues
were inside a house for less than thirty seconds, doing Class-C acts of
vandalism. Sometimes it was worse. They ran in an open back door,
shot paintball guns at folks on a couch, kicked them around some,
ripped off purses and wallets, and continued on out the front door
while people yelled and children screamed. Maybe it was just stupid
enough to be real, but what brand of new outlaw was this? And why
would Dale be involved?

There probably wasn't a Simon Ketch at all. More likely a group
of twentysomethings hiding behind the false persona, selling button-
clicks of idiocy, fronted by a league of lawyers who just wanted to tie
up the courts long enough to make a ton of cash and then split for
some West Indies island that had no extradition with the U.S. It was
a new age of grift that I just didn't understand.

"This kind of street crime and gags have been popular for a long time," John said. "Backyard wrestling tapes, college girls going crazy on spring break. You remember when they'd pay homeless guys to slug it out in back alleys for ten or twenty bucks?"

"Urban legend."

"Nah, you can bet it happened. And teens robbing houses on video has been done before. Ketch just gave it a Web address and some pretty packaging."

That was Dale, the pretty packaging.

"How long has this been going on?" I asked.

"I don't know. I found out about it a couple of weeks ago. It's a pretty popular site and, well, like I said, I'm sort of obsessed with the Rands."

"Growing up in our shadow."

"Right."

"She's sixteen."

He couldn't settle on any single expression. He looked baffled, bemused, embarrassed. He didn't fully get it. Probably not his fault. His eyes were bright and a little brash.

She might be only the host of this moronic show, but it could only lead to worse things. I could spot the escalation in criminal acts just watching the highlights. If it was an act it would turn real soon. If it was real, it might become dangerous soon. People were bound to eventually get hurt. Lots of home owners kept guns around. A warning shot gone wrong might lead to big-time investigations, the feds, RICO.

"How'd you learn about this?" I asked.

"This is what I do. Part of what I do. I surf the Web finding the viral vids. Most of them are kittens playing piano and shit like that, but I find the darker stuff too. The crime stuff, the horror stuff. That's what I'm drawn to."

"John, how did you know this was my sister? Her name is never mentioned. You can hardly see her face. You don't know her at all. Why did you make the connection?"

"That's obvious," he said.

"Not to me."

"Well . . . because of the graveyard, ah . . . "

"Ah?"

"The graveyard . . . desecration."

I stared at him. I kept staring at him. "The what?"

"I didn't want to show you that vid, Terrier. That one, it's not fake."

"Okay," I said. "Show me now."

He held up his hands like I was a cop about to bust him. "Look, I thought you knew about all of this. I don't want to be the one who–"

"It's okay."

I gave the charmer's grin right back to him. I knew I was doing it right because I felt like I was the shill and he was my mark. I was the guy he could trust. I was the buddy. I was the inside man. I could talk him out of five grand or I could have him show me the video of a graveyard defilement.

He clicked through a few Web pages and got to one that made him nervous. "You might not like this."

"Nah, don't worry about it. Hey, John, you think you could go grab me a cup of coffee, man? I'm getting thirsty."

"Sure, no problem."

He left the room and I punched the button.

Teenagers always got a little weird and wired around cemeteries. They made out on top of graves, they played tag among the tombstones. It was a place to get drunk and laid and cause insubstantial trouble without anybody around to complain. They toyed with stupid ceremonial rites of witchcraft. They painted swastikas and pentagrams just for the hell of it. The more famous the corpse, the more midnight visitors showed up to get a look. Adolescents went nuts for local legends.

The summer we turned fifteen Chub and I went looking for the crime scene where a teenage drug dealer from Oyster Bay called the Speed King had tortured and murdered his best friend in front of a group of onlookers. Over some minor infraction having to do with stolen amphetamines, the Speed King beat the kid, stabbed him, cut out his eyes, and eventually tossed gasoline on him and burned him to death. They left the mutilated corpse there and for more than a week the Speed King held tours and invited fellow classmates to come see what he'd done. Eventually word got out to the cops and the Speed King was arrested. Three days later he hanged himself in lockup. We found the spot where the murder occurred and drank a stolen pint of vodka toasting the dead or the living or our own impending adulthood.

The Rogues, all three of them, carried high-powered flashlights through the cemetery. They'd waited for a full moon to shoot this segment of the show. I did the math. They'd been out there either two weeks ago or six. I didn't think Collie's headstone would've been ready six weeks ago, so I decided this is what Dale and her pals had been up to the middle of last month. While I had been watching Chub's garage, my sister had been out doing this. I should've been aware.

The digital audio recorder was extremely sharp. Dale did her bit as a news correspondent. She laid it all out without any feeling at all. Not a hitch in her throat or a throb of anger. The Rogues laughed and talked silly shit beneath their masklike bandannas, making ghost noises, doing the theme music from *Psycho* and other horror flicks. They lit a few candles and placed them ritualistically around Collie's grave.

The stone read only his name and the dates of his birth and death. No "beloved son" or biblical phrases. It was as cold as you could get, which is what he deserved. There was no grass on the icy earth. Maybe there never would be.

John returned with a cup of coffee and handed it to me. I smiled pleasantly and said, "Cream and sugar?"

"I put some milk in. And two teaspoons of sugar."

"I like three," I said.

"Oh, okay."

He left again and I shut the door behind him. Some moments you don't share.

The Rogues kept ramping themselves up. Their laughter got more cruel and vicious. They threw out phrases like "Oh unholy Lucifer" and other idiotic Satanic claptrap.

Dale asked, "Do you feel the devil here?"

The Rogues didn't respond. It went down about the way you'd expect. They spray-painted "kiddie killer" on the tombstone, gave it a couple of kicks, hurled their shoulders against it, wrestled it out of the ground, and then they pissed on it together. They giggled when their streams crossed. I kept my eyes on the kid who was the size and shape of Tony. Lick 87. That fucker had been in my house.

I'd been blind. Dale was in even more agony than I'd suspected, full of much greater rage and self-hatred. She stood there while these little assholes whipped out their wangs and drenched our brother's grave. I knew her contrition. I knew her sense of betrayal. The endless frustration, the unanswered questions, the draw of the underneath tugging her down and down. The earned and the unmerited guilt. But some moments couldn't be shared. Watching a trio of teens jumping around acting like douchebags couldn't have eased her burden any. Something else was going on.

Do you feel the devil here?

I opened the door and John stepped in, holding a sugar bowl with a small spoon in it.

His smile was a little nervous and a little stupid. It was a happy smile. He was happy that I was there. I went deep into his face. I shoved my will into his mind. I was good at reading people but I'd made some bad mistakes in my time. I couldn't afford another one. I looked at the man and I tried to know his heart and intent. I should be sensitive to schemers and killers by now, but in this case, I realized I might have been wrong. I'd wanted to hate him because he reminded me of Collie.

He said, "You okay, Terry?"

"Do me a favor and don't mention this to my parents," I told him.

"Okay," he said, "sure. No problem at all."

"And for Christ's sake forget about filming anything with Dale."

"But—"

"Just forget it, John."

He tried to hand me the sugar bowl but I didn't take it. He set it on the cutting table beside the untouched cup of coffee and started flipping switches on some of his machinery. The faces of film noir villains glared at me from all angles. John plugged a mike into his computer and held it out to me, then sat back like a talk show host. "You wouldn't mind answering a few questions, though, would you?"

He might've been running a game down on me, but I didn't know what the rules were. I smiled again. "Perhaps another time, cousin John."

"Oh, right, Terry, yeah, that would be great." He grinned. He had printed out sheets of notes all over his desk. I saw my sister's face several times. The wild makeup made her appear even more like a harlequin. I looked into his dim, happy eyes and wondered again if he was trying to grift me. He seemed eager to help me. He wanted to be my family.

"It's almost time for lunch," he said. "Gram's been cooking all morning."

"Terrific." I winked at him. I don't think I'd ever winked at another person in my entire life.

"Typical of grandmothers, right? Tries to buy love with money or food."

"Yeah?"

"Granddad is still feeling a little low. You can see him afterward."

"Looking forward to it."

"He takes a little getting used to."

"Don't we all."

I followed him back through the house. An elderly woman who didn't look much like my mother stood at the stove with lots of pans and pots simmering. She moved the ladle around like her life depended on it.

He said, "Gram? Gramma? This is Terry."

Without turning to face me, she said, "Hello, Terry."

"Hello," I said.

My mother and Will were at a large round kitchen table. I could picture them in those same places thirty-five years ago. It happened in every family. You got your spot at the kitchen table and you never moved from it for the rest of your life. You never sat in your sister's seat. You never sat anywhere except in your own, even if you were alone at the table.

Grandma Crowe was practically invisible. I don't know if she started out that way or if she'd been drained of all color and sound until this was all that remained. She could barely raise her voice above a whisper. There was still some handsomeness to her face but no character, no strength or personality. She looked like my mother and looked nothing like my mother. She wheeled and put plates on the table and then spun back to the stove again. I mostly saw her from the back.

My mother tried to engage her in conversation but the old broad refused to respond much beyond a yes or no or "try it with relish." Gramma occasionally stole glances and looked at me as if I were the paperboy or the mailman. She kept herself busy and continued putting dishes down. There was already enough to feed half the homeless shelters in the Bowery, and I knew it wasn't going to stop anytime soon because she just couldn't handle talking to her own daughter after all these years. The food kept coming. She fed her family. She had that much in common with my ma.

I didn't recognize most of the dishes. It looked ethnic and a bit exotic, but since I still didn't know what nationality they were, or that I half was, I couldn't even take a guess. I followed John's lead. I buttered some things and put colorful sauces on others. I wrapped some meats in tiny pieces of sourdough bread and sprinkled lots of pepper and salt around. I swallowed it down but tasted little.

My ma stared after her own mother with her chin pointed and her eyes full of hope, but the old lady beat her at the game. She ignored her even while talking to her. They held an empty conversation about cooking, and my mother brought up the gardens and Grandma Crowe talked a bit about flowers.

John kept up a steady stream of chatter and his father embarked on the same. I couldn't follow anything they were saying. They laughed at private jokes and two or three times even my mother let out a chuckle. I tried to imagine my father and me bullshitting about nothing like that, and I failed.

Then lunch was over abruptly. Grandma Crowe cleared the table one dish at a time and washed each plate separately in the sink, killing each minute like she was smothering it in its crib.

She said, "I think you should go see your father now, Ellie. He's waiting."

My mother stood. So did I. So did Will. He put a hand on my shoulder. He had some muscle to him. He gripped me firmly, doing that massage thing that was supposed to show he was just having his emotions stirred. He held me in place while my mother walked through the doorway.

It was all about assertion and knowing your place. My mother was to go alone. I got that from the top. Will was being emphatic about it but not exactly rude. He had a couple of cigars in metal tubes he kept in his shirt pocket. He handed one to me.

"Let's go sit and talk in the den," he said.

"Sure."

We left John there at the kitchen table looking a little hurt. I followed Will to a room with dark cherry paneling. A huge maple desk dominated the room. Framed photos on the walls showed him with celebrity actors and bigshot politicians. At Cannes, film premieres, and fancy Manhattan and L.A. restaurants. Some of the photos were mounted on wood and metal with cursive engravings: *Will Crowe & Edmund Contino, The Dining Car, 2002*. Contino had headlined the biggest summer blockbusters for the last couple years running.

Other photos showed an icy-eyed, iron-haired, broad-shouldered coot in his late sixties/early seventies with a lot of the same people. *Perry Crowe & Amos Custer, Madrid, March 23, 2004*. Custer was a director who made low-budget sleeper hits that took home an Oscar every once in a while.

One entire wall featured built-in shelves that provided the space to show off seven Emmys and a number of other awards I didn't recognize.

Two leather chairs faced each other at a slight angle, a small antique table between them. A large portable bar covered in top-shelf liquor bottles and decanters was within easy reach. The room tried hard to give off the milieu that million-dollar deals happened here over drinks all the time. For all I knew, they did.

Will clipped the end of his cigar with a cutter and then stared at me expectantly. I slid the cigar out of the tube and handed it back to him. He cut off the end, returned it, then motioned for me to sit.

I did. The chair smelled like thirty years of liquid leather polish and felt like it had never been sat in before. He lit his cigar with a wooden match, then held the burning match out toward me. I put my cigar between my lips and slowly rolled it around as he set the match to it. I took a few puffs and tried not to turn verdant. I wondered what he wanted to say to me that he didn't want John to hear.

"I don't know whether to offer you my condolences or not," my brand-spanking-new uncle Will said.

"If you're not certain," I said, "then I suppose you shouldn't."

"I mean, about your brother. You loved him, so I gather I should extend my sympathies over his death."

"Why?" I asked.

It made Will look at me sadly. I could tell he was a man who looked at almost everybody sadly, for any reason or no reason at all. He rolled the cigar around in his mouth, drew on it, and huffed smoke. "We followed the . . . the case quite closely here. For your mother's sake we were hoping for a reprieve."

"For her sake, and for everyone else's, I'm glad he didn't get one."

"You didn't like him much."

"He killed seven people. There wasn't much to like."

"I thought it was eight."

"No," I said, without explanation.

He cocked his head and his eyes unfocused into a thousand-yard stare and he gazed through the wall and through the fence surrounding the house and went someplace else for a minute. He returned and nodded at me like he agreed with every sentiment I'd ever had about anything.

"Did your mother ever say anything about us?" he asked.

I placed my cigar on the edge of the ashtray. "No."

"Never told you how close we were as kids?"

"No."

"I introduced her to your father."

That caught my attention. My chin lifted.

"Pinscher and his brothers used to race a 1969 Chevelle 396, up and down Ocean Parkway, out on the abandoned airport roads. In movies they always race for pink slips, but we just ran for peanuts. Gas money. Forty, maybe fifty dollars a run." Will smiled thinking about the good old days. "I had a '76 Bumblebee Camaro. There was real muscle to the car, and I had good reflexes. I won my share. Pinscher and the other one, the huge brute–"

"Mal."

He took a long draw on the cigar, let the smoke out with a chuckle. "Yes, that's right. Mal. Malamute. Mal, he weighed too much to be a driver, he was much too big behind the wheel, even in that big-block Chevy. So he always hung back and worked on the engines. Pinscher and the slick one–" Snapping his fingers, one, two, three.

"Grey."

"Greyhound, yes. Grey always had the girls clinging to him without having to earn any sort of prestige by winning races. It all came naturally to him. But your father, he worked for it. One day Ellie showed up at a race. She'd never been to one before, but she turned up with a few of her girlfriends. They stopped in on the way home from a day at the beach. This small group of pretty girls all in bikinis, sunburned, covered in dried sand and salt, their hair flying in the wind, half of them wearing high heels so they could turn heads. Pinscher took me for forty bucks and said we'd be square if I introduced him to my sister. He was pretty slick too, when he wanted to be. And he could drive."

My father was a driver.

I tried to picture him racing down Ocean Parkway out by the closed tollbooths near Jones Beach. It shouldn't seem so weird. All Long Island teenagers looking for a little action or gamble eventually wound up racing down one strip or another. I did it. Of course my dad did it. I had a flash of him as a young man, in his glory, winning a race, and my mother rushing over to him and falling into his arms, the tailpipe hissing. My head was full of movies. Girls in a bikini and high heels. I just couldn't see my mother in a bikini and high heels.

"Your father," Will continued, "he was quiet. Shy really, and very reserved despite the family reputation, which I knew, of course. So I didn't want Ellie anywhere near the Rands. I told him no. I was scared doing it, actually. You didn't talk that way to a Rand."

He kept smoking.

"My fear presented itself as anger. I got in his face. I shouted. I shoved him. I was showing off a little in front of the beach chicks standing around. My father was successful. We had money. I wasn't going to be intimidated by a guy who didn't come up to my shoulder, except that I was. I reacted badly. I was too nervous and stupid to even appreciate the fact that I might have to fight all three brothers."

"They'd never team up on you," I said. "Unless you were playing cards."

"Yes, Grey and Mal only laughed at my little display. The ugly one working under the hood on that three-niner-six. The handsome one with a girl on each arm."

It still wasn't noon yet. Will hadn't offered me a drink, but I reached over and got myself a glass and poured two fingers of rye. I slugged it down and let the heat burn out the image of Grey as a youth surrounded by petite brunettes, the kind of woman whom decades later he'd be driven to kill.

Will lifted his cigar and drew on it. I poured another glassful and tried to sip it and couldn't. I threw it back.

"So Pinscher, he just patted me on the shoulder, smiled, and said,

'All right, friend.' Then he walked away. I was stunned by that. All right? All right, *friend*? Who speaks like that? Who backs down from the kind of jerk I was being? It threw me off completely. It was more embarrassing to have that happen in front of the girls than if he'd punched me or threatened me. Then I would have been the victim. Then I would have gotten sympathy. I called him back. I asked, 'Don't you want the money? I still owe you the forty bucks.' He didn't answer, he just kept walking."

"He'd snatched your wallet," I said.

"So you have heard this story before."

"No. But the pat on the shoulder was to distract you while he went through your pocket. His mind was set. All he needed was her name and an address."

Will chuckled, showing warmth in his eyes, but there was something else in that laughter. An old admiration refined by the sharp-edged years, and a little burr of anger at having been one-upped.

"He stole a photo of Ellie with her name written on the back. And he had my driver's license. He stepped over and introduced himself to her. She was smitten from the first. He took her out to a pizza joint that night, she and her friends, and paid the bill with my money. I had over a grand in my wallet. I was foolish carrying that much but I thought I'd get a chance to show off, wave some cash around. All I had going for me was my father's success and wealth." The cigar smoke boomed from his mouth. "Sharp, your dad. Very sharp. When he wanted to be."

My old man, who could give me the slip night after night, in and out of the house even when I was watching for him, listening for any sound, my will wired to the darkness, and him graceful and silent, sharp.

I vibed that Will's piece was full of fudging or embellishment. For one thing, even in his story he hadn't actually introduced my parents at all. For another, I couldn't picture him going up against my father no matter how much he wanted to protect his sister's virtue or show off for the chippies. Especially not while Mal was around. Nobody would go up against Mal, no matter how angry or stupid they might be. And considering Will came from cash, I didn't quite understand why he didn't just pay the forty bucks and be done with it. Guys must've hit on his sister all the time.

But whatever the truth was, I liked that he was trying to impress me with a part of my own history.

Will reached for the liquor cart, poured himself a short scotch, and refilled my glass with rye. We sat there drinking quietly, him puffing on occasion, me glancing at the door and wondering how it was going for my mother.

"Terry," Will said. "I have something to tell you, and I'm having difficulty broaching the subject."

He waited for me to invite him on or offer reassurance. I kept a cool gaze. Whatever was coming, whatever he had in store around the next corner, it was the real reason why he'd sat me down.

"My father . . . is not a well man."

"I know that," I said. "It's why we're here."

He sucked at his cigar and stared at me for about five seconds too long. I didn't much like his eyes during those five seconds.

Finally he let out a long stream of smoke, and his grin returned. "I don't mean that. He's dying and he knows it, and he wanted to make amends with Ellie, as late in coming as it is. I'm glad for that at least. You don't know how much I've missed her, how good it is to see her again."

Courtesy forbade me from mentioning that he could've lifted a phone at any time.

Will continued. "But when I say he's not well I mean that he's begun to degrade . . . mentally. He may say some crazy things. He may ask for rather absurd favors."

My mother walked into the room with her eyes fierce and her face crumbling. Whatever the old fucker had said it had hurt her deeply, and not in the I'll Miss You Daddy kind of way. He'd gotten a few savage digs in.

But there was some resolution in her expression, even if it was only that she'd never have to see him again. Two fat tears started to dribble from her eyes and my mother did that thing again where she brushed them aside with her thumbs to keep her makeup from smearing.

"He wants to see you, Terry," she told me. "You don't have to go upstairs."

Of course I did. I wanted to see this guy who'd thrown my mother out of the house, once been hard as steel, the starmaker with such dim notions of people. I wanted to hear the absurd favor that had Will on edge. I wanted to give a dying man a slap. He had made my ma cry.

Perry Crowe sat up in bed wearing black silk pajamas, a stack of pillows behind him. The bedspread was folded down to about mid-thigh. His hands hung loosely in his lap. They were big and covered with thick navy blue veins. They looked strong.

There was no indent beside him on the mattress. My mother hadn't sat.

I was surprised there wasn't a couple million bucks' worth of machinery crowded into the room. I expected tubes, heart-rate monitors, oxygen tanks, defibrillator paddles, all of that. But it was just him. No nurses, no panic button near his hand to alert his wife or son or doctor, no bottles of medication on the nightstand. Only a little silver bell for him to ring.

I could almost hear the tinkling sound of it. I imagined hearing it ten times a day for weeks, months. It was things like that tinkling bell that drove people to murder or suicide.

There was a slight tilt to his mouth, the only lingering aftereffect of a stroke that I could see. He had icy eyes. They regarded me intently but dispassionately, the way you watch a movie you're not enjoying that is only slightly less boring than everything else there is to watch.

His shoulders remained broad. I got the feeling he was very proud of them, and that he only sat up so straight to affect an assertive position. He looked good for his age, and healthy too. I vibed another scam at work. He wasn't dying. He'd set the grift up just to get me here so he could dupe me, explain his scheme, embroil me in his plot, turn me into a part of his string. Maybe he'd promise me big money. Maybe he'd pledge to write me into his will. Maybe he'd fork over red carpet tickets to Grauman's or let me dance with a movie star. I thought of Darla on the red carpet.

John had said that the strokes had taken it all out of old man Crowe. That he'd become a paralyzed scarecrow with mostly empty eyes. That he cried a lot, and was scared like no one he'd ever seen before.

John had either been lying or had misinterpreted his grandfather's condition. Maybe he saw fear only because he wanted old Crowe to reach out in need. Maybe Perry had faked him out.

I did my thing. I memorized the layout and likely hiding spots for cash, jewelry, and other valuables. Dresser drawers, armoire, back of the closet, under the mattress. Which paintings might cover a safe, the thickness of the carpet so I'd know how heavily I could tread without making a sound.

Then he started to cough. It was a rough ugly sound that shook him violently, rippled up into his chest, and just kept going for his throat. Every muscle and tendon in his body knotted. His face turned red as a stoplight and the cords and veins in his neck stood out as thick and well defined as sculpted marble. I thought he might be having another stroke and started to break for the door to get help.

Crowe reached for a box of tissues on the nightstand but couldn't make it. I moved and handed him a bunch. He covered his entire face as the cough continued to wrack him. He spit black into the tissues, balled them, and threw them into the wastebasket.

His face showed strain and weakness now as he lay back against the pillows, sucking air heavily. Sweat covered his prominent forehead. His eyes rolled for a second before he was able to refocus through a massive assertion of will.

Considering his current state and that of Old Shep, I didn't exactly have a positive feeling about my impending old age.

"You," he said. "Come nearer. Let me look at you."

I stepped closer.

"Gray already. You get that from me."

"I get it from my mother."

"She got it from me."

It was a small distinction but an important one, I thought. He was a presumptuous prick, ordering people around, crafty and cranky on his deathbed. I owed him nothing. He had treated my ma badly.

"Which one are you?" Crowe asked.

"Which one am I?"

"Your breed. You're all named after dogs, aren't you?"

I could see him trying to hike his bloodless lips into a smirk. A thin sneer managed to crease his face. It tickled him to think I'd be embarrassed by my own name.

"You like making people feel like shit, don't you, old man?" I said. "Puts you in the power position, in control of the situation. But you can't humiliate me with my name. I'm Terrier Rand."

I was lying. I'd pretty much always been embarrassed by my name. I'd once crept a death row guard's bedroom while he and his wife slept because he'd made me say my name aloud.

"Tell me something about yourself, Terrier," he said. "Have you ever been in jail?"

"No."

"How did you avoid it?"

"The answer is no, I'm not going to tell you anything about myself."

Crowe's ashen face firmed up. He scowled. "You're a real hard case, kid."

"Why did you want to see my mother?"

"That's between her and me."

"You'll explain it to me anyway."

His eyes shifted left and right, as if he was searching for a witness, like he needed to confirm that this conversation was happening.

"What is this?" he asked. "What do you think you're doing?"

"You'll tell me. Because if you hurt my mother in any way I'll—"

"You'll what? Kill me?"

That wasn't much of a threat to a guy who would be dead in a couple weeks. "No. But I'm sure I could think of some way to ruin your last days, if you make me prove a point. Somebody like you with money and position must have a lot of secrets. I'm a thief. I can find them. I crack the vaults where your dirty shame is kept. I can hand them over to Will or John or Granny in there. Or just my mom. Or the media."

His face tightened again and a hint of fear gleamed in his eyes. I let him do the work of scaring himself.

But after a moment I realized it wasn't fear at all. It was pride.

"I'm glad she brought you," he said.

"Why?"

"I was hoping she'd bring one of you."

"There's only one of me."

He showed his teeth. They were white and perfect and fake as Washington's. "I meant one of her sons."

"There's only one left."

"I wasn't sure."

"You didn't care enough to find out."

He had something else to say but couldn't get it out fast enough before the cough hit him again. It was like the aftershock of an earthquake. Not quite as bad as earlier but it rumbled on even longer. I handed him tissues and he spit up and tossed them in the trash. When the spasm finally ended he lay back, more drained than before, pale as hell with powdery traces of salt on his cheeks.

With that weird look of arrogance and conceit still in his eyes he watched me. His smile was a little more honest this time. I felt that neediness rise again. I glanced away from him.

"What if my father had shown up instead?" I asked.

"I knew that wasn't going to happen. Ellie wouldn't have allowed it. She loves him too much to subject him to me again after all these years. She wants to protect him. But you. You can handle yourself, Terry. You're trouble. And you like being trouble."

I noticed he'd called me by my common name. So he'd known it all along. "What makes you say that?"

"I can read it in your face."

"I look like my mother. I look like my cousin John. I look like you."

"That's how I know you're trouble."

He was a feisty old fart. The strokes hadn't done much to lessen the steel in him. I didn't know why he'd wanted to see my mother again but it wasn't because he wanted to make amends. Not the fearful kind of amends that other dying men might make. There wasn't an ounce of fear in him that I could see.

"Have you ever seen any of my movies or TV shows?"

"No."

"You're lying. Everyone's seen at least one of my hits."

"Not me."

He liked that. He'd spent a lot of time in the company of men who kissed his ass because they wanted in on his empire.

He gestured toward my face with his right hand. "You've been fighting. You're a fighter. That's good. Have you been in jail?"

"Why do you keep asking? Why would you want to know that?"

"Because I do. Have you?"

His questions had taken on the air of an interview. I had braced myself not to give the man an inch, but already I could feel myself compelled to do exactly that. "Overnight once or twice."

"But not prison. Not hard time."

"No."

"Because you're too smart to get caught."

There was nothing to say in response to that. My father may have never boosted anything from this guy but I knew my old man. He'd slipped in and stood at the foot of this bed at some point in the last thirty years, and just stared at his enemy in the dark.

"What did you say to my mother to make her cry?" I asked.

"I apologized to her for throwing her out of the house. I said I was sorry for all the wasted years."

"No you didn't. She was hurt."

"Of course she was. Have you ever told anyone who's been angry with you for a long time that you were sorry? Do you think it changes anything? Because it doesn't."

I put my hand on the headboard and leaned in close.

"What is it you really want, old Crowe?" I asked.

"I want you to rob a place for me," he said. "Maybe kill a man. Possibly two. You can handle that, can't you?"

"No," I said.

"You can't handle it?"

"No, I won't do that. I don't do that."

All the talking was definitely causing him some strain. His gaze was unfocusing more and more. The cough shook through him almost continuously now. "You're a Rand," he hacked out. "You're a born criminal. That's what you do. That's all you do. That's all you'll ever do."

He gasped for breath and I handed him more tissues and he spit red. I wondered if my mother achieved some kind of closure. I hoped it had been worth it, for her sake.

"You have something better to do?" he asked me.

I thought about what else I needed to do. I needed to help Chub get out of the bent scene so that he could lie in the arms of the woman I loved and live a life I coveted. I needed to fight with my sister and try to turn her away from a mogul who made a fortune on the stupidity of kids. I had to drink beer with my father while we stood together staring off into the night wondering what to do next with our lives. I had to find out where my dad went at night. I had to think about Darla some more.

I thought about the thrill of creeping. I thought of snatching loot, any kind of loot at all, plunder that might bring in a little cash or none at all. It didn't really matter. I had one talent.

"There'd be significant money in it for you," my grandfather said. "I'll pay you twenty thousand."

"Is that significant money to you?"

"All money is significant. And we're not talking about me."

"Yes, we are."

There was a knock at the door. Crowe glowered a few more seconds. He called, "Come in." Gramma entered. She was either extremely polite or they had separate bedrooms. I couldn't imagine knocking on the door of the room in which you slept. Maybe that's what happened after fifty years of marriage.

She said nothing. She didn't turn her head a half inch to look at me. She carried a glass of water and two pink pills in an open palm. She presented the meds to him and he examined them before plucking them from her hand and swallowing them. He took the proffered glass and managed to sip from it without choking. He gave it back without saying thank you. She left without a word but at the door hesitated a moment. I read potential love in that instant. I thought she wanted to offer me advice or warn me away. Or ask for my help.

Then the instant passed and she closed the door behind her.

No wonder he didn't need the pill bottles stacked right next to him. She carried them with her and handed them out one by one. She was the one who always had to watch the clock and give him his next dosage. I felt sorry for the lady even if there wasn't enough of her left to sympathize with.

"Who do you want me to rob, old Crowe?"

"A movie studio."

"What?"

"Co-owned by Will and myself."

"Co-owned with whom?"

"With each other."

I thought about Norman Rockwell, Ozzie and Harriet, and *Father Knows Best*. "You want me to rob your own son?"

"One of our ancillary companies is All Hallows' Eve Films, a production company dedicated to independent horror films. Slasher fare, mostly. Half-naked teenagers being butchered by mad killers."

My breath hooked deep inside me and wouldn't come loose. I

shut my eyes and thought of Collie killing kids. I heard their voices and I heard his. I opened my eyes. I stared at my grandfather and understood that he knew all about me and all about my brother.

"Classy," I said.

"Don't be petulant. It's unbecoming."

"You've got odd notions of what's becoming."

"It's a profitable business."

"Sure. And John's shot some movies there."

Crowe frowned. The wrinkles in his brow looked like they'd been carved in with a nail file. "He fancies himself an auteur. He wants to be hailed as the new Godard, another Bergman, as if the world hasn't long passed those dreary surreal depressives by long ago. But he's compulsive and driven. And to some extent he has style. Will indulges him in these whims despite the fact that he knows the truth. That John is a fool."

"I'm getting the feeling you didn't take him to the circus a lot when he was a kid. Never spoiled him with ponies and puppet shows."

Crowe's strong hand came up and waved away what I said. "But it keeps him out of greater troubles, I suppose. At least he has something he cares about, and his work is mildly popular so it gives him some professional satisfaction."

"And you make money off him."

"It turns a small profit."

Crowe had another hacking fit. I reached over and patted him on the back. When I touched him he drew away like I was knifing him.

I retreated, crossed my arms, and waited.

"The company is currently managed by Erik Blake," Crowe continued when he could breathe again. "He's an affiliate partner who's overstepping his bounds. Blake's a former low-level studio manager who got in trouble with methamphetamines and lost everything in L.A. He was a poor choice to be put in charge but Will doesn't always think these things through. Blake was readily available, talented, and supposedly living a life of sobriety. And perhaps he is. But he's also cooking the books and skimming off the top and the bottom. He's assigned distribution rights he doesn't fully own."

"Sounds like something the accountants and lawyers could settle."

"I prefer a more discreet and hands-on approach."

"Easy to say when they're not your hands."

He laughed at that. It wasn't a feel-good laugh. It grated.

"Why do you even care about any of this?" I asked. "It hardly sounds like your bread and butter."

"A good deal of my money is already tied up in other ventures, investments, and business opportunities."

I could vibe what he was really saying. His normal channels had dried up on him and he relied more heavily on the good old red-blood Americana B and C movies than he wanted to. I wondered what all his New York and L.A. cronies with him in the photos on the wall might think of that fact.

"And what would I be stealing exactly?"

"Whatever you can find of value. Cash, contracts, master tapes."

"Are those kinds of movies still shot on video?"

"No. I'm speaking of the digital masters. The flash drives."

"You can't steal computer files. You can copy them but you can't vanish them. Not unless you want to blow the place up."

"There's a half-dozen films that haven't been released yet. It's been his way of leveraging me. Find them. Get me the copies. As you say, once the copies are out he loses his control of the situation."

"Why? If it's really yours and Will's, why not go in and just take it? Why this dirty business?"

"Blake is . . . unpredictable. He may be dangerous."

"But not for a fighter like me? Not for someone smart enough to stay out of prison?"

"Take care of the problem and you'll be paid well."

I moved around the room. I wanted a new angle. I wanted to see him in a different light. I stepped to the footboard.

He still looked hard as steel. He still looked like he wanted to scrape me off his boot heel.

"Why do you care?" I asked.

"Pardon?"

"Why do you care about an ancillary C movie business when you've been a major name in Hollywood and television for decades?"

He pulled a face. He didn't have much practice in explaining himself. He just said to do something and usually got people to jump. His top lip curled and uncurled. I waited. So did he. I figured I had more time than he did. I was right.

"Times have changed, Terrier. I do very little business on the West Coast now, and Will's track record has been spurious at best in recent years. His last two films were significant losses. As were mine. In this business you're only as good as your last hit. And even that is forgotten very quickly. My last show won an Emmy for writing and it was still canceled by mid-season. It remains a commercial loss that continues to taint me. We need steady income. AHE turns a profit without a substantial investment on our part."

"Doesn't it cost you credibility?"

"No. A success is a success. Credibility and awards count for little. Perhaps even nothing."

"So the ancillary business has become the primary source of income?"

"It's an important revenue stream for the time being, and it's ours. Besides, I don't allow anyone to steal from me."

I moved in closer and hovered over him like the angel of death. "Shouldn't you be busy making amends and begging forgiveness from the Lord and all that?"

His eyes got darker and he showed true anger for the first time. I'd finally gotten under his skin. Sometimes it took a while but I always swung it in the end.

"Is that what your brother did?" Crowe asked. "You were with him at the end. How did he handle his death? Did he supplicate himself?"

He hadn't, not even to me.

"How much cash will be on hand?" I asked.

"We've only recently ascertained that Blake's been liquidating assets for months. Perhaps as much as a quarter million."

I scoffed. I rarely scoffed and it felt good doing it. "No one keeps that kind of cash around. Unless it's drug money. Is that really what you're into, old Crowe?"

"Stop calling me that."

So his name could get to him too. "That's your species isn't it? Crow? Your feathered, winged, egg-laying type of vertebrate?"

His lips were deep red with his blood, his face mottled by irritation.

"Or would you prefer I call you Pop-Pop?" I asked.

"No." He drew the back of his hand across his mouth. A smear of pink was left on his knuckles.

"So why the hell did you mention killing people?"

"He has a bodyguard called Nox. He's usually armed."

I waited for more but Crowe wasn't giving anything else up. He was run-down and worn-out. We were getting into his secret territory now, his most savage strata. Nox must be a really big bastard if Crowe thought the only way into his own studio was to kill the guy.

"I'll give you twenty thousand," my grandfather told me.

"I'm the thief," I said. "You're the shill. The inside man just unlocks the door, and you're not even doing that. The shill gets ten percent, not the other way around."

"You want ninety percent! Are you out of your mind, boy?" It got him rearing. "You don't dictate to me, Terrier Rand. No, boy. No. No." And firmly, once again. "No."

"Then maybe I'll keep it all."

He knew he'd made a mistake with me. I wasn't as easily manipulated as he'd been hoping. He'd juked his play. He was a thief but not a very good one, at least not in this fashion. He almost said that he wanted to forget it. I could see it in his ferocious eyes. He wanted to take it all back and do it over a different way. I knew the feeling.

"Goodbye, Grandfather," I said. "Nice meeting you."

I walked out of Crowe's bedroom. My mother was waiting for me in the kitchen, smoking a cigarette. I'd never seen her smoke before. It spooked me a little. I wondered who had given it to her. Gramma was at the sink still hand-washing dishes. She was keeping up a steady stream of prattle. None of it had any real meaning. My mother was listening and putting in the odd comment here and there. Gramma didn't turn when I entered. I was suddenly very glad that I hadn't been raised with these people in my life. They were a pretty fucked bunch and we hadn't even gotten to the marrow yet, the real blood and bone. My mother ground out the butt in a fancy glass ashtray, rose, and kissed the old lady on the cheek. Gramma didn't say a word after that.

John and Will were nowhere to be seen. I wondered why. Ma and I made it out the front door and my mother snapped at me to give her another cigarette. I did. I lit it for her. She took a drag and coughed. The sky remained heavy with the assembling storm that was also growing inside me, ready to break, ready to pour. We walked down the driveway and climbed into the car.

I sped out through those lethal spear-tipped gates and hit the road.

She said, "Jesus Christ," and I said, *"Jesus Christ."*

On the ride home my mother watched the side of my face as I jockeyed aggressively through traffic. It looked like it had been raining off and on all morning long, but I hadn't noticed inside that house.

She had something to say. I had a lot of questions of my own. I wondered if I should tell her anything about Dale and the Rogues. I was going to find the pricks who'd pissed on my brother's grave and kick fucking hell out of them.

I finally turned and met her eyes.

"He asked you to steal something, didn't he?" she asked. "Pull some kind of grift?"

"Yes."

"My father brushes on being a criminal."

"All rich men do."

"He's embezzled and taken kickbacks and been investigated a few times. More than a few times."

"And always cleared himself, I'm guessing."

She let out a deep, small sound of exasperation. She shook her head slightly. She was having an intense argument with herself and both sides were losing. I knew the heart of it. She would be thinking how foolish she'd been to say, *Of course it matters. He's always been my father. He'll always be my father.*

The car was full of barometric pressure, as if a hurricane were about to wash us off the highway. We are all meant to tell our mothers the truth. Being in old Crowe's presence had brought out the evil little boy in me.

The pressure built. The defroster was on high but couldn't keep up with our hot breath. She looked sidelong at me, then glanced away, then looked back. She fumbled for my cigarettes but was too annoyed to light one. She threw it into the foot well with a groan of disgust. "Did you agree?"

She was breaking a cardinal family rule. We didn't talk about our larcenies, petty or otherwise. The Rands didn't discuss plans with each other, unless we needed help pulling off the filch.

"Not exactly."

"What are you going to do?"

"I don't know yet."

I could almost feel that other guy in the car with me. The one I'd been when I'd worked on the ranch for five years, trying to escape my family. That time was a blur but at least it had been straight. My mother had never wanted me to come home.

"Don't do it, Terry," she said. "I know it's your nature. The nature we gave you. But don't do it."

"Ma—"

"They're not your family. They're not even my family anymore. I was very foolish to go back."

She began to cry so hard that I had to take the next exit, park on the edge of the service road, and hold her for a while. She hadn't had any idea what to expect from those people but it hadn't been this.

"What did he say to you, Ma?"

"It doesn't matter."

The wipers thumped in sync with my pulse. My ribs were starting to hurt again. I could feel a fever rising with the pain. The windshield began to fog over. "Tell me anyway."

"He said he loved me. But he doesn't. He doesn't love anything anymore. My mother used to be a vivacious woman. She used to have so many talents and hobbies and such capacity in so many ways. But you saw her today."

"I saw her."

"She's a ghost of herself. She couldn't even look at me. She said nothing. Nothing. That's my worth to her. To them." The sobbing overtook her words and she shuddered in my arms. I tightened my grip around her.

"It's okay."

"There were times," my mother said, hiccuping for air, "over the years, not many of them, no . . . but a few, when I questioned the choices I'd made. Or at least . . . hoped . . . that one day . . . we could settle this, put it behind us, and they would call or visit." She laughed bitterly. It was a kind of laughter I had heard many times in my life, but never from her. "It's embarrassing. They humiliated me in front of my son."

"Ma, you've got nothing to be embarrassed for."

"I should have broken his jaw. I should have forced my mother to see me."

"She saw you. She was the one who was humiliated."

She drew away from me, found a packet of tissues in her purse, and wiped her eyes and face. She blew her nose. I put on the defogger, threw the car into gear again, and gunned it back up onto the on-ramp.

"Terry," she said, and there was a thrum in her voice that shook me. "Despite the fears, and the doubts, and the worries. Despite having to deal with the police from time to time. Despite what happened with–"

I tightened my hold on the steering wheel. I slid over into traffic and the mist bathed the front end.

"–with everything over the years, and taking care of Gramp, despite it all, you see, I've lived my own life. It couldn't have happened that way in my father's house. Don't mistake my tears for dissatisfaction. I love your father. I love you and Airedale and the life we have. Do you understand?"

"Of course," I said.

"Do you?"

"Yes, Ma."

Old coot Crowe wouldn't have gotten as hard and mean if he hadn't put up that spear fence to keep my dad out. My mother could've been an actress starring in her father's films and TV shows. She could've been a movie star, living on the beach in Malibu, with a husband who was a Hollywood executive, with a blond, empty-eyed hunk of a pool boy lover, and a gaggle of rich children whose worst crimes were getting wasted at the Viper Room and flashing crotch shots at the paparazzi.

She didn't know it, or wouldn't believe it, and I loved her for not saying it, but she'd made the wrong choice.

We pulled up at home and I went in first while she fixed her face in the rearview mirror. In the kitchen I popped more Percs. We still had hours to go before Dale's play. It was her big night, a chance to show off a talent that hadn't been bred in the bone.

My father watched television with Gramp, crumbling crackers into tomato soup. He ate a spoonful and then fed one to Old Shepherd. He saw the look on my face and gave an understanding grin.

He said, "Can you believe that bastard thought a second-rate security system would ever keep me out if I actually wanted in?"

It was a very rare showing of ego in my dad, but I thought he had plenty of reason. It hit me right and I let out a laugh that made JFK roll over and look at me.

"Why didn't you ever boost him?" I asked.

"No point," he admitted. "The damage was already done."

"But you walked around his den at three A.M. a few times."

"Sure."

"And why didn't you ever tell me you were a racer?"

He thought about how to answer the question. Twice his lips began forming words but he stopped himself both times.

He finally let out a half chuckle. "It was a long time ago."

Sometimes my father's reticence annoyed the shit out of me. He went on feeding his old man, a sign of things to come. I wondered if the Donepezil was helping at all or if it was just a daily reminder of his oncoming illness. I'd sworn I would never let it happen to me. I'd promised myself that I'd take the easy way out, but I wasn't sure if I had the guts. Jumping off a ledge was one thing. Jumping off because you thought you might lose yourself five or ten years from now was another. And if you waited too long, you'd probably forget you were on the ledge at all.

I thought we could sit on the porch and I'd give him the entire rundown on what happened at the Crowes' Nest. And he could tell me about the good old days of dragging down Ocean Parkway with his brothers.

But when my mother appeared he took one look at her face, put the bowl down, and followed her into their bedroom.

I thought, Wherever he goes at night, he's not cheating on her.

I finished feeding Gramp and sat there staring through the window at the sky starting to show some blue. When he finished the bowl I wiped his beard and flipped the station back to cartoons. Gramp sat up a little straighter. I was eager to move. The Percs were doing their thing. My ribs didn't hurt. I was a touch high. I kept wavering on whether I should pull a big rip-off and fuck over Crowe good.

I went up to my room and lay on the bed. JFK came with me. He got up on the mattress and put his front paws on my chest. The tape job was holding. The Percs put me all over the place. I thought I should pay Simon Ketch a visit. I thought I should juke Erik Blake and his sidekick Nox before they finished cleaning the studio out and burned the place to the ground. Could there really be a quarter mil on the premises of All Hallows' Eve Films? If I brought that much money home what would I ever do with it?

JFK's tongue lolled. He kept ratcheting his head at me. I must've been talking out loud again.

I phoned Darla and got her voice mail. I said something about getting together for dinner. I had difficulty expressing myself because I kept thinking she was with another man. Or selling books or yarn. I imagined her shag haircut wet with sweat. I grimaced. I wanted her. I thought I wanted her. I wanted to hear her voice. I felt a short sharp stab of guilt and thought of Kimmy. I mooned. I twisted in the breeze. It was stupid but it was human.

I had to either get a job, go to college, head back out west, or commit entirely to being a second-story man. Instead of pulling Chub out of the life maybe I could throw in with him.

My mother appeared in the doorway. "You've been up here for hours. Do you want to talk?"

"I don't think so. Not right now."

"All right. You know I'll always listen."

"I know."

"Don't forget we have Dale's show tonight."

"I haven't forgotten."

"Dinner will be ready in a few minutes."

"I'll be down."

I didn't go down. I fell asleep and dreamed awful dreams and woke up in the dark panting and sweating. I felt certain I'd just had a premonition but couldn't remember what it was. The great mystery of life wasn't what to do with it but that you were lost and needed to find a way out of the black room and off the edge.

I took another shower. I let the hot water clear my head and get my blood moving again. My face was looking better. I removed most of the tape and butterfly Band-Aids. I wanted to look good and show support for my sister. I wanted to warn her off the Rogues and get her out of New York. Maybe she'd be safer in L.A. waitressing and going on auditions and following a dream that might break her heart eventually but wouldn't land her in the bin fifteen to life.

My father found me in my room. My old man said, "Your mother wants to stay home tonight."

I didn't ask why. She needed time alone, and staying with Gramp was about as alone as you could get. "I'm on my own?"

"No, I'm coming with you."

To anyone else this was a trivial moment but to us it was big. My father rarely left the house to go out in public. He never left it with only me. We didn't take in ball games. We didn't go sailing. We didn't catch movies.

"That all right?" he asked.

"Sure."

"I want to leave a little early, maybe get a chance to see Dale beforehand and wish her luck."

"You mean 'break a leg,'" I explained. "Wishing an actor good luck before a performance is actually bad luck."

"I can't tell my daughter to break a leg. I know too many guys who've had their legs broken."

He wore a black sweater and dark slacks that would've looked nice on anybody else, but on him it made him look like he was getting ready to go creep an apartment complex. I wondered if he might be planning on paying a visit to old Crowe tonight.

"You want to ride with me?" he asked, handing me a cardboard ticket that read ADMIT ONE.

"I'll follow you," I said. "I have something to do after the show."

My mother had a dish of salmon and greens waiting for me in the kitchen. I was hungry and dug in. Above that, I was painfully aware that I had to start being more concerned about the health of my brain, even if four-man pro crews were going to keep kicking the shit out of me.

My mother said, "You don't mind?"

"Going to the show with dad? No. But he can stay home with you. Dale won't care."

"I think she might. Just tell her I wasn't feeling well."

"She'll be fine. Will you?"

"Yes."

"You know you can always talk to me too," I said.

"I know."

She gazed lovingly on me with red-rimmed eyes and I knew my course was set.

We got to the cars and I let my old man pull out first. I followed him to the high school and was surprised to find the auditorium packed. My father and I found our seats. We were in the fifth row center. I made sure I sat up straight so that if Dale peeked out from behind the curtain she could see how invested I was in the show.

Ten minutes later a matronly teacher I didn't know stepped out to a smattering of applause and asked that everyone turn off their cell phones. She introduced the play, discussed the playwright for a moment, and then asked us to enjoy the show. I clapped like my hands were on fire.

There was a dramatic flare of music: violins, cellos, bombastic bass drums, and a lot of brass. The curtain went up. The set was dressed like a European parlor room. Actors came out wearing Renaissance clothing. There were kings and queens and fops and courtly gentlemen in white wigs and ladies-in-waiting. They said their dialogue with a lot of bite and while coyly looking at the audience. The kids snapped off a lot of double entendres, some of which I figured out on my own. People laughed and yawped. Maybe it was funny and I wasn't in the right mood. Maybe it was a case of the emperor's new clothes. I didn't want to be a bitter prick but it felt like that was all there was. Maybe I just needed to turn myself in to the cops. Aside from the Cell-Block-C ass-raping, it couldn't be much worse than living the rest of my life like this.

Dale played a married woman whose husband was apparently having an affair with a countess, but not really, so she attempted to seduce the duke's son. They ran around a bedroom chasing each other and then hiding in the armoire when other couples broke in and chased each other around and hid under the bed and behind the curtains. At one point there were four couples concealed in the room from each other. The audience roared. My father chuckled through-out, which for him was laughing like a maniac.

Dale was good. She owned the stage when she was on. She had a bright, confident energy and she put real feeling into the words, even when she didn't have to. She paused in ways that amplified the power of what she was saying. She offered up body language that gave insight into the character. She struck poses, she stared and smiled. She wasn't just a vessel for someone else's ideas. She made the work her own and gave herself over to another identity. The comedy had a real grounding thanks to the contrapuntal way she emoted. Dale under-scored the action. She gave it honesty, significance, and purpose.

When the curtain came down the audience exploded. The cast took their bows and the applause throbbed louder and louder. When Dale came out I got to my feet, clapping and whistling.

After the final group bow together the lights came up and folks started to split.

"I watch her reading lines with your mother," my dad said. "And I've seen her in other shows, but I never really picked up on just how talented she is. She's amazing. She's the real thing."

"Yes, she is," I agreed.

"I'm proud of her."

"So am I."

"I just wish I could figure out what the hell the whole play was about. All those people running around hiding. Kids in the curtains? It was very . . . very . . ."

"French," I offered.

"Yeah. Exactly."

Along with the other relatives of the performers we crowded around the foot of the stage waiting for the kids to come out. Soon they appeared to gasps and hoots from their parents. The mother of the lead actress had a dozen long-stemmed red roses to present to her daughter. When Dale emerged in her street clothes my father swept her up in a ferocious hug. He found the words to tell her how wonderful she was. Dale looked shocked but happy. She thanked him and called him "Daddy," something I hadn't heard her do since she was ten.

He stood there unsure of what else to say so he repeated himself, telling her again how talented he thought she was. He swept his hand through her hair. Then he mentioned that Ma wasn't feeling well and was sorry she couldn't make it. She let him off easy and said she had some last minute things to do backstage and she'd see him at home. He said he understood, nodded to me, and walked lithely toward the exit with the rest of the crowd. I hung back with the stragglers, Dale beside me. She took a breath and looked at me like she wasn't sure she expected a kind word or an ax in the neck.

"You were fantastic," I said.

She gave me a guarded grin. I caught a whiff of her Cool Sea Breeze Vita shampoo. Her mascara hadn't run. She had great waterproof fantasy lashes. "You really think so?"

"I do."

"Did you understand the play?"

"Not in the slightest."

I saw a flash of her real smile. "I told you."

"It was French. It seemed very French."

"It was."

"But I didn't need to understand all the ins and outs of the story to see that you're a terrific actress, Dale. I mean it. You were centered. You put a tremendous authenticity into the performance."

"That's very generous of you to say."

"The characterization . . . swallowed you. The others were playing to the assembly, but you were up there for yourself."

I didn't know if it sounded like a compliment. I wasn't expressing myself as well as I wanted. I fought for clarification but couldn't explain myself any better.

"Thank you," she said.

"You could've gotten the lead. You were better than the girl who took it."

"You think so?"

"I do. And I think you let her grab it. I just wonder why."

"The lead wasn't the most interesting or important role."

"So you outfoxed her."

"I did."

"There's my sis." I put my arm around her shoulder and pressed my lips to her temple. She tightened up and I released her. "I'll drive you home."

Her face closed like a fist. "I'm going out with some friends."

"Can you give me a few minutes first? I think we should talk."

She backed up a step and held her hands up to ward me off. She spoke with a hushed edge. There were still a lot of people around, split off into groups, neighbors and friends who hadn't spoken for a while, loud and laughing, talking about local theater, talking about the PTA, talking about church. "Oh God, no, please don't say things like that, Terry. I never want to talk to you when you say things like that. No, don't you know that yet? Never."

"I don't exactly want to do it either. But we need to discuss *ROGUES*."

She seemed to consider it. "No," she said. "I don't think so. I don't think I'll talk to you about that, Terry."

"Dale—"

"Cool it, Terry. Just go home. Thank you for coming. But go home now."

"*They*—"

In my head Collie said, *You know what to do.* I had no idea what to do. I took her by the shoulder and led her away from the receding crowd and noise. I got her up against the emergency exit, leaned in close, and put my mouth to her ear. *"They pissed on our brother's grave."*

"Is that what bothers you?"

I scowled and pulled away from her. I champed my teeth on my tongue and tasted blood and let my mouth fill. Somehow it settled me. The underneath called, or maybe I called to it. I breathed deeply.

"*Yes,*" I said. "No. It does, but–" The words still weren't there. Maybe they never would be. I fought for them. I couldn't find them. I was getting to be more like my old man, more like Gramp. I had to eat more salmon, more brain food. Collie tried to talk for me. I faded back another step.

My eyes cleared. "Look, that whole Web show is going to go down. Those punks are headed for jail. You can't get hooked up with–"

"I'm not hooked up with anybody. It's good money, it's viral video webisodes, and it's part of my portfolio."

"You're sixteen. What the hell do you need a portfolio for?"

"I'm leaving soon, Terry."

"Leaving?"

"I'm going to L.A.," she said. "It's already in the works."

"In the works?" A few minutes ago I thought maybe she should head to the West Coast, but now I was filled with a deep dread at the notion. "What are you talking about?"

"I can't stay here forever. I need to go. You booked out of here five years ago. I need to leave now too."

"I was wrong."

"You weren't right or wrong. You just did what you had to do. I'm doing the same. I've got some friends out there already."

"No, Dale, I was wrong," I admitted. "I left for foolish reasons. I ran out on my girl. She had to suffer through the worst days of her life alone because I couldn't face that kind of pain. I'd give anything to be able to unmake that mistake."

"It was your mistake, not mine. I'm not running out on anybody, Terry. I'm just leaving. As soon as I can."

"Tell me about Simon Ketch," I said. "Is he for real?"

"I'm not talking to you anymore, Terry. Maybe never again."

She turned away and headed back for the dressing rooms. I moved through the crowd, pulling wallets and putting them back, just for the hell of it, just to keep my fingers nimble, my mind on the grind. Then I left to go rob my grandfather's movie studio.

All Hallows' Eve turned out to be the largest building in an industrial park in Islip. The security system was older than I was. I tricked out the wiring in under a minute and eased inside with my satchel and tools.

The studio was pretty much what you'd expect from guys who churned out low-budget slasher films. It looked like an assembly line for fast action and quick pack-ups and reshoots. The place was split into four separate sets designed to look like cabins in the woods and sorority houses where young women could run away from killers holding machetes and chain saws. There were catwalks twenty feet in the air and a lot of stage lighting. The walls were all white to catch bright splashes of faux blood. The place smelled faintly of air freshener, disinfectant, and the unmistakable odor of freshly smoked meth.

At the back of the building was a large office with triple locks. The door and frame were solid, unlike the walls and doors of the sets. I got out my tools again and within a minute I was inside. I was still a little rusty.

Framed poster art decorated the walls of the office. I thought I saw cousin John's room design flourishes. Sexy, seductive women gazed down at me as faceless figures in cloaks and capes rose behind them hungrily. Various awards stood out on shelves choked with DVDs bearing the AHE logo. Best Murder Scene. Best On-screen Death. Best Shotgun-to-the-Head FX. Six expensive-looking cameras covered with thick cloths had been stacked side by side. There were five laptops at five desks. The biggest desk had a fancy nameplate that read Erik Blake.

I went through the drawers of each desk and pulled out all the discs and flash drives I could find. Together they didn't add up to more than a couple pounds. I tucked them all into the satchel. Physical media was dying out. Everything was downloads and streaming now.

In the bottom drawer of Blake's desk was a .38 S&W. I pocketed it.

It took me thirty-five seconds to find the safe. It was beneath a mismatched piece of carpeting under the empty watercooler. I moved the cooler aside, opened the cache, and saw the faceplate to a forty-year-old safe. I wasn't the world's best jugger. It would take time to crack it. Unless Blake and Nox did what most lazy pricks did, which was leave the dial a couple numbers off so the latch would open immediately. I tried it. It didn't work.

If Crowe was right about the quantities of money then I expected drugs to be inside. I guessed that Blake and Co. probably wouldn't trust their memories when it came to a safe combo. The number had to be around here somewhere.

I found it taped to the underside of Blake's keyboard. I gave him points for at least making a modest effort to throw off a burglar. I tried the combo and it didn't work. I reversed the numbers and was met with a satisfying click. I popped the latch.

Inside was a ten-pound bag of meth and maybe a hundred grand in cash. There was also a set of cooked books. I went through them carefully. In a half hour I could see how Blake had been making additional films on the same sets with the same casts, distributing them under the table, and selling them outright to another company called Fireshot Pictures, all on Crowe's dime. Blake took the extra cash he made and invested it into his meth business, conveniently cutting Crowe out. He paid his kick-up to the Thompson crew but only about a quarter of what he really owed. That would work in my favor.

I took the money and the cooked books. I left the drugs.

I toyed around on Blake's computer. He had pictures of himself with the casts of girls in various states of undress as a slideshow. He was short, lean, and a little fish-eyed with an ingratiating smile. He wore his hair tight to the scalp with overly moussed ringlets spread out across his forehead.

Different killers popped up in horrific poses: Bear-Face, Driller Killer, Mudd the Maniac, No-Heart, and others. The makeup FX were pretty good. The poster art worked about as effectively as anything I'd seen in the theaters. No bald mutant cannibals, but you couldn't have everything.

Blake not only managed the office and directed some movies but he starred in them as well. He played a supernatural murderer called the Blade and even billed himself as Erik "the Blade" Blake.

I found a file of his work schedule. He was due in at seven A.M. to start prepping for a flick called *No Boundaries*.

The last couple of days caught up with me. I felt a cool, deep exhaustion rippling through me. The pain in my ribs had become a sharp, short shiv. I threw back another Perc. I knew I should stretch out. There was a nice leather couch up against the far wall. I lay out, put my feet up, and let myself drift and nod. It was dangerous to be here. I liked the feeling. After a couple of hours napping I felt better and phoned Darla.

The first time it rang through to voice mail so I tried again. This time she picked up. "Hello, Terrier."

She knew how to say my name in a way that made me actually proud of it. "Hi," I said. "Sorry for waking you."

"It's okay," she said sleepily. "What time is it?"

"Nearly three in the morning."

"Do you want to come over?"

I did, actually. "I can't, I'm in the middle of a score."

"A score? You mean you're stealing something right now?"

"More or less. More more than less."

"And you stopped to call me?" A husky purr entered her voice. "I'm touched. That's very sweet. A girl likes to feel important."

"Listen . . . I know your douchebag husband was your aspiration, but have you thought of acting as a creative venture in recent years?"

The question didn't throw her. She took it with ease. "In what regard? I've never had any training."

"Well, how about B movies? Horror fare. Being chased around with a guy with a butcher knife. Topless, probably."

"Those kinds of movies usually star teenagers with perky tits."

"You can show them all up. I have an in with a producer of slasher pictures. I don't know. Figured I'd ask, in case you wanted to pursue it. It's not yarn or books, but it might be fun."

She took a deep, erotic, semisleepy breath and let it out slowly. It fired my pulse. "You do continue to surprise me, my friend. What's your in with him? Is this the person you're stealing from?"

"The less you know the less you'll have to deny later on, if you're ever asked."

"I see."

"So what do you think?"

"You sound excited by this."

"I wouldn't say that," I explained. "But I have some stuff going on in my life that's got me on my toes." I glanced through the hundred grand again. "You can try it out for a while and see if you like what it offers, if you want. All Hallows' Eve Films." I read some titles off the posters. "*Killing Vault. My Bloody Grandma. Nun Will Survive,* and nun is spelled N-U-N. *Stake Through Your Heart.*"

"And this is all right with the powers that be."

"Part of being a criminal is sort of stealing the power from the powers that be."

"I always heard the mob ran Hollywood."

"The mobs run everything."

"When can I see you again?"

"I'll be in touch."

"Thank you for thinking of me."

"I do it a lot."

I disconnected and went through the DVDs on the shelf until I found a couple that were directed by cousin John. I loaded one called *Hello, Baby, Goodbye* into Blake's laptop.

There was an actual storyline, which surprised me. Narrative arcs in horror flicks seemed to go out with the grindhouse movie theaters on Forty-second Street in the late eighties. The plot wasn't much but it was there. Boy meets girl, they fall in love, they try to have a kid and can't, girl is artificially inseminated, baby turns out to be maniacal, boy looks for sperm donor who turns out to be a serial killer. Violence, bloodletting, revenge, potential redemption, love conquers all ensues.

John had a moody style about him, lots of shadows and high angles, intentional lens flares, distant tracking shots. Dramatic close-ups. There was emotional tension, some complex characterizations, a lot of unspoken dialogue written in the actors' expressions, and the blood was only used to accent story, mystery, atmosphere.

The film ended with the young lovers renewing their wedding vows on the lawn of the Montauk Lighthouse. I recognized the spot immediately and my back went rigid. It was where Kimmy and I had planned on getting married.

The grand vistas of the cliffs and the ocean, with the lighthouse in the background, and watching the guests all raise their glasses of champagne got to me. John had laid out some big money to rent the area for the afternoon. I rewound and replayed that final scene a couple of times. I heard myself laughing angrily. I popped the disc out and made as if to hurl it across the room. I caught myself and froze. I replaced the DVD in its case.

Blake came in early. At five to five I heard a car pull up outside. I peered through the blinds and saw Blake and a big guy I assumed was Nox park and climb out of a cherry red Taurus, each holding a large Styrofoam cup of coffee. Nox looked like every thug I'd ever seen. Tall, massive, with a dull expression, no neck, and a face that had lost ten thousand bar fights.

I shut the door to the office and reengaged all three locks. I heard the men come in and futz with the alarm system keypad. Blake's voice was thin and high-pitched. He discussed his shot list. He talked about actresses he wanted to fire for being late constantly. Nox said nothing in return.

I took up post behind the door. The locks turned and clicked. In they walked.

When they got three steps inside I gently swung the door closed behind them.

"Hello, Blade," I said.

I held his own gun pointed loosely in his direction.

Fear and shame passed over Nox's face. I knew what it meant. He wasn't armed. He hadn't been expecting trouble at the office at five in the morning. He was exactly as stupid as I'd anticipated.

Blake didn't rattle. He eyed the methamphetamines on the desk, sipped his coffee, and said, "So who are you? Wait, let me guess. I know your face. You're Johnny Crowe's little brother."

"Close."

"I can tell you belong to that family. You all look alike."

"We do. But we're not all the same."

He frowned, blowing trails of steam. "Whatever that means. You want to direct too? Or maybe star in a couple of features? Meet some of the girls? No trouble at all. You want your girlfriend to star? We have a shoot going on today. I can always use a new face."

"No, thanks," I said. "I've already got a job. I'm a cat burglar."

Nox thought about rushing me. He thought about tossing the hot coffee in my eyes. He thought about getting those huge hands around my throat and choking me into submission. I pointed the .38 at his belly. I hated guns but they came in handy on occasion to help keep certain situations from derailing.

I cocked the hammer, released it, and cocked it again to make sure I had his attention. His shoulders slumped.

"You and Perry have been at odds lately, Blake."

"He's a prick."

"True. But it's his and Will's company."

He sneered. "I made it what it is, not them. They'd never even seen a horror film before I got involved. Neither one of them."

I tabled that for the time being. "You've also been cheating the Thompson syndicate out of about ninety large a year the last three years."

"Wait. You work for Danny Thompson?"

"Everybody works for him, Blake. Even you."

It sounded properly threatening and profound. Nox couldn't keep himself from nodding his huge head along.

"I won't tell them anything," I said. "I'm here to deal."

"What kind of deal do you want to work out?" he asked.

"It's already worked out. The drugs are yours. Take them. Sell them. But not around here. Make your nut and your kick. The cash? That's mine."

"That's a hundred fucking g's, you bastard!"

I reached into my satchel and pulled out master copies of a couple of the unreleased films he'd been planning to sell to Fireshot.

"Here, you can have these two movies as well." I tossed them next to his crank. "Perry and Will won't ever know about them. Sell them to Fireshot. Make some more cash. It's severance pay. You've got a week to get things in order here at All Hallows' Eve. You can stay on as an actor, a director, as upper management, if you want. But you don't rip off the Crowes anymore."

It annoyed him so much he dropped his coffee. He took a step toward me. I gave him a hard look.

"I'm Erik the Blade, man!"

"Whatever. You can still show up and get paid. On the books. All legal. I admire your work ethic, coming in before five in the morning on a Saturday. Stick to your schedule on *No Boundaries* this week. Keep things moving smoothly."

"How much do you know about your people?" he asked. "You have any idea what you're getting into? I get the feeling you're out of your element."

"I think I'll get the hang of it. So, is it a deal?"

"Just so we're clear . . . if I refuse you give a call to the Thompson family, right?"

"Right," I admitted. "But that's up to you. I'd rather you stayed on."

It pretty much hit me at that instant. Old Crowe owed. He owed my mother and father. And he owed me. I aimed to collect.

I don't allow anyone to steal from me.

"I'm stealing it," I said.

"You're stealing it? Stealing what?"

"Everything. All Hallows' Eve."

At six-thirty I crept the Crowe house. My grandmother's bedroom would be next door to Perry's, I guessed. Just close enough so that if old Crowe needed to shout for a pill she'd hear him and come running.

I slipped inside. It was still dark out. There was a night-light bathing the room in a soft bone-white glow. I watched her sleep. She was a handsome woman now that I got a chance to actually see her face clearly. I saw a hint of my mother there.

On her nightstand were easily thirty bottles of meds and a couple of different boxes with the days of the week on them for dispensing pills. I didn't recognize a lot of the medication, but those I did fell into two categories. Heart meds for Crowe and antidepressants for her.

Whatever happened to her had happened slowly, steadily, the way it does for all of us, over a great amount of time. No one's personality is subsumed overnight. It might not be subsumed at all, except here in this place, in the presence of her husband. Maybe that just appeared to be the case. She was bound to have her secrets too. Maybe she screwed the pool boy. Maybe she was as nuts as her husband. Maybe she plotted perfect murders. Maybe she loved horror flicks like cousin John. Her eyes moved beneath the lids. She could still dream.

"Grandmother," I said.

She woke instantly, without a start. Her eyes found me. She wasn't surprised or scared.

"I thought you might come back, Terrier," she said.

"Why?"

"To do something awful to him."

"To him? Or for him?"

"Either. Both. Are you going to kill me?"

There was no emotion in the question, just the barest lilt of curiosity. Like somebody asking how do you get to the highway, make a left or right? She was tough at the core despite the servile attitude and the inability to look my mother in the face. She was full of regret and resentment, but had learned to live with it well. Much better than I had.

"My God," I said, "you people. Why would you think I'd do that?"

"I think it's what he wants. And because you must hate us."

"I never even knew you existed up until a couple days ago."

"All the more reason. Do you want money?"

"Everyone wants money, but no, I don't want your money."

"I have a lot. I'll give it to you."

She reminded me of Gramp. There was something else alive in her someplace deep, but it was buried there under paralysis. She hadn't moved an inch since I'd entered. She watched me steadily. The pills were doing their job. She wasn't depressed. She was feeling no pain. She was feeling nothing at all.

"I'm confused," I said. "Are you offering me money *not to* kill you? Or are you paying me *to* kill you? Or him?"

She blinked at me. Her lids came down and her eyes stayed shut for a three count, and then she opened them again. "To just go away."

"Why wouldn't you talk to my mother?"

An animal moan started to climb from her throat. She covered her mouth with her hand and squeezed her eyes shut until the moment passed. "Because I'm ashamed."

"Everyone's ashamed of something. You had a chance to put some mistakes behind you. Why didn't you take it?"

"You can't put a mistake like abandoning your daughter behind you."

"So how does ignoring her when she's face-to-face with you for the first time in decades make it any better?"

Her small, wrinkled, age-spotted hands balled into fists and she thumped the mattress once, like a child. "It doesn't. Nothing does. I begged him not to call her. But he wouldn't hear of it. He never hears what I say. He wanted to tell her he was sorry. And he was. He truly was. But he wasn't sorry enough. Not nearly. He'll never be sorry enough. Not after what happened. Not after what I allowed to happen."

"You're probably right about that."

I stood. She fumbled for her pills. I watched her carefully. She only took two. It was probably foolish thinking that a septuagenarian might off herself. She was simply too used to the way things were. That's why all this talk of murder and fear. She was just that shaken by what had happened yesterday.

There was nothing left to say.

I went away, like she wanted.

I stepped into old Crowe's room.

He'd hidden a few things the first time around so he wouldn't appear so weak. Two IV bags were pumping him full of fluids. A colostomy bag was now in view hanging off the side of the bed. There was an oxygen tank propped next to the headboard, with a mask placed on the closest bedpost. I opened my satchel and set it beside him on the bed. I picked up the tinkly bell and rang it once.

His eyes opened. He went into a coughing fit for a solid two minutes while I passed him wads of tissues. He was hacking nothing but blood after a while. When he was done there was a nice rosy glow to his cheeks.

"Here's your money," I said. "And the discs and flashes containing about fifteen films that haven't been released yet. Also another dozen that were produced at S&D but were sold under the table to another studio called Fireshot Pictures."

"Fifteen! Those bastards have been busy doing a lot of straight-to-video franchising at my expense."

He huffed heavily. I wondered if he'd go for the oxygen mask in my presence or tempt fate some more. He eyed me and then eyed the tank. I turned it on for him and unslung the mask from the bedpost. He held it to his face and sucked heavily.

"And all right under Will's nose. And John's."

"And yours."

"And mine, yes. Just so."

"Blake had a pretty sophisticated operation going."

"Did you kill him?"

I sighed. "You really think it's that easy, don't you?"

"Maybe not. Maybe it's difficult. But I need to know if you did it."

"No, I didn't. I told you I wouldn't. You shouldn't have asked me. It's insulting and stupid."

"What did you do to him?"

"I made him listen to reason."

My grandfather thought about that for a moment. He seemed to be trying to figure out if I was lying. In the end he decided not to pursue caring.

"Fireshot is Sal Domingo's outfit," he said. "I guess that son of a bitch knew the whole time."

Sal Domingo was another big name in Hollywood who'd won awards once upon a time, had his ups and downs, his hits and misses. More misses than hits recently. It was news that he did a couple of season finales for some hit TV shows. It was news he'd filed for bankruptcy but wasn't going to lose his mansion in Roslyn on Long Island Sound.

"All you hotshots have a plan B to keep the cash rolling in, huh?"

"It's not only practical, it's a necessity."

"You couldn't invest in a coffee shop franchise? Maybe open a health food store?"

"In this economy? Too risky."

I leaned in. "All right, now I want something from you, old Crowe."

He let out a knowing grin that tilted too far to the left. "The twenty thousand?"

"I already took that," I told him. "You're going to get on the horn today and contact some of your friends on the West Coast. My sister Airedale is an actress. She's sixteen and she's good. She's also a real beauty. Get her some auditions. Get her a couple of walk-ons and cameos. Connect her with a good acting teacher, a vocal coach, all of that. I want her set up somewhere nice in Los Angeles so I don't have to worry about her."

His sneer also tilted to the left. "That's impossible."

"You're a dream-maker. So make it happen."

"I tell you it's absurd. Do you think I'd care anything about the indie horror film industry if I still had my connections in Hollywood? If I had any choice at all?"

"You don't know anybody anymore?" I said. "All those guys on your wall? You burned all your bridges?"

"I lit the fire to some of them. Others blew up or fell over on their own. That's how it is."

"That's how it is for a prick like you. You still know the town. You know other old coots just like you. I bet you have a favor or two that's still owed you. You can motivate Will into helping out. He's probably got a few pals left. I'm not asking for Oscar gold or a ten-million-dollar offer. Just a little action getting her started."

He scoffed. He was used to it. He was good at it. "She's sixteen and you want to send her into the business? Do you know how many girls are ruined that way? By drugs? By the casting couch? By the pressures of trying to make it in the industry? By their own drives?"

"Probably as many as get wrecked doing anything. But Dale won't be alone. You're sending John out to go with her."

"That's ridiculous," he hissed.

"John wants to go. And he's not just an auteur, he has real talent. You'd know that if you ever watched his films."

"I have. They're pretentious."

"They're stylish. He could do better things if you backed him."

The old man waved his hand in the air, shook his head, and dismissed it all with a flat final chop. "None of this is worth discussing. Your demands are ludicrous and I refuse."

"Then I'll turn everything over to the cops," I said.

"Turn what over!"

"Blake's cooked books. Your recent movies have been paid for with the profits from a thriving methamphetamine business."

He hacked blood and wiped the froth from his lips with the back of his hand. "I had nothing to do with that and you know it!"

"Your lawyer can explain that to the D.A. while you await trial on Rikers. Personally, I think I could do time pretty easy if not for the ass-raping. How about you?"

His expression shifted from anger to shock to dismay and back again. He looked away and then looked back. There was a nasty curl to his lip. He was going to say something vicious about my mother or father or brother or sister. I didn't want to hear it.

"Just do what I tell you to do, old man," I said.

He settled back. He fought to keep from coughing. He squirmed beneath his blankets and I tried not to like seeing him do it. "And when would you want this miracle of miracles to happen?" he asked.

"Before you croak. So make it soon."

The IV tubes dripped with a quick cruel rhythm. "You're quite an unpleasant person, Terrier."

"Just yesterday you said you liked that I was a fighter."

"I was wrong inviting you into my home."

I felt my bitterest grin beginning to maul my mouth. I felt like I was onstage, performing for a one-man audience, some surreal comedy that would make a profound sense to anyone bright enough. I felt very French.

"You didn't invite me, but I walked in anyway," I said. "I can do it anytime I want. Remember that. You're sorry now, but not enough. You'll never be sorry enough, old Crowe."

The fatigue hit me on the drive home. The ass-kicking, adrenaline high, and three days of overmedication had me crashing, almost literally. I was weaving so badly on the LIE that I exited the first chance I got. I took the back streets to the house. I pulled into the driveway and nearly plowed into my father's car. JFK knew there was something wrong and crawled out from under the porch and followed me inside. I climbed into bed and he lay at the foot of the mattress.

My phone kept ringing. I had it on vibrate which was even more annoying as it danced across my nightstand. I stuck it between the mattress and the box spring. Over the next couple of hours it went off a few more times and I felt the vibrations like the massaging magic fingers of a cheap nooner motel.

Every time the phone went off I was roused from troubled dreams that immediately drew me back down into them. I sweated out the pills. At some point I got up and took another Perc. I listened for Dale's voice. I saw myself at the top of the Montauk Lighthouse, holding hands with Kimmy on the catwalk deck. It was windy. Her wedding veil passed in front of my eyes. I think we jumped or maybe I pushed her.

When I woke up Collie was sitting in a chair beside the bed, holding an uncapped bottle of beer, watching me sleep.

"Hey," John said. "Your dad let me in. He told me to just come up." He proffered the beer. "He really puts them away, doesn't he? It's barely . . . I don't know . . . one in the afternoon, and he had a row of empties along the porch rail. He handed me a couple of bottles. I guess he wanted me to give you one."

I reached for the Percs. I threw another one down dry. I was running out. I had to raid a few more medicine cabinets. The pill got stuck halfway down my throat. I grabbed the beer and took a deep pull. It wasn't until the bottle was a third of the way empty that I realized it was nonalcoholic.

I wondered if giving John the extra beer was my father's way of letting me know he was trying to quit drinking. I wondered if I would question every action of his from here on out.

"Those are Percocet, aren't they? Threw my back out once doing some handheld camera work. You shouldn't be drinking with them."

"It's nonalcoholic, John," I said. I got up and washed my face, dumped the beer down the sink, combed my hair, and threw on fresh clothes. I had the twenty g's in a hidden cache behind the toilet tank. I grabbed half of it and stuck the wedge at the small of my back, nestled in my waistband. When I returned, John was looking at the backyard. He'd opened the window a half inch and an icy autumn breeze blew in. I liked the feel of it.

"Did Perry talk to you?" I asked.

"He did. How did you know that?"

"He mentioned some things to me during our conversation. He's got a lot of faith in you. He seemed sorry he didn't support your career more earlier on."

"I told you, he's changed. He gave me contact information for friends in the industry. He's never done anything like that before. He thinks I can start over again out in L.A. He said he was too rough on my documentaries and other projects." John's eyes grew moist. All any of us really want is our fathers and forefathers to give us a nod now and then. "And he asked me to help Dale too." John reached into his pocket and unfolded a piece of paper. "He listed casting agents, voice coaches, managerial teams."

"He's got a big heart."

"Why didn't you tell me yesterday that Dale wanted to go to the West Coast?"

I rolled with it. "She only mentioned it after I got home. I called—" I had to chew my tongue to massage the word loose. "—Grandpa up and asked him for the names of some scouts and acting teachers."

"She'll be leaving the show. Leaving *ROGUES*."

"Yes."

He roamed my room as if it were his own, touching things, observing, trying to fill in whatever gaps he had about me. The place was pretty barren, and I wondered what that told him.

"Look," he said, "about yesterday, I'm sorry I took off on you the way I did."

"It's all right."

"But my dad, he's sort of an emotional type. Seeing your mom again, talking to you about better days, the good old days, and knowing Grandpa only has a little time left, it all caught up with him and hit him hard. He wanted the two of us to visit my mom's grave together. The cemetery's just a mile down the road from the house, I used to walk there all the time, pick wildflowers, silly, yeah? But she liked wildflowers, so I picked them, would put them on her grave. It's a nice cemetery, looks more like a park, right? Clean, well maintained, grass is trimmed, the trees are beautifully landscaped. It had been a while since we'd been there. We thought you'd still be sitting with Grandma when we got back, but you and your mother were gone. Why didn't you stay longer?"

"We're sort of emotional types too."

"Yeah, yeah, okay. I can see that. I can understand that."

I reached out and put a hand on my cousin's shoulder. "How do you feel about it, John? Are you willing to go back to Los Angeles?"

He brightened. "Of course. It's been my dream to try again. I guess I've been scared to make the effort, a truly serious effort, because I've already had my ass handed to me once, but if my grandfather has some faith in me, if he's learned to put his faith in me, and he's willing to back me, then I don't see why I shouldn't try. I've got some cachet now, believe it or not. My horror flicks are pretty hot, they move well, the fans know me." The planes of his face fell into a frown. "But I don't think I really understand what anybody expects me to do for Dale. I mean, I haven't even met her. She doesn't know me at all. Aren't we getting ahead of ourselves a little? It all feels . . . rushed, you know?"

"That's how you know it's right. When everything comes together to move you forward to a particular place. Fortune favors the bold."

"You're worried about her. You're worried she'll get in deeper with Simon Ketch. You want her off the Web show."

"I do," I admitted. "And you're going to help me do just that." I pulled out the ten grand. "Here. It's just some start-up cash. So you can rent a nice place."

He tried to back away. "You don't have to give me money. I have money."

"Take it anyhow. I expect you to watch over my little sister while she navigates her way through a business that ruins a lot of people. You already know something about it. Take advantage of your name and use it to open doors. Don't let Will's or Perry's failures shove you into a corner. Use their earlier successes as a springboard, John."

"You sound like you want to come with us."

I hadn't thought about it. "Maybe I'll pay you a visit a couple months down the line."

"Right." His voice was full of vigor. He hadn't had a good shot of optimism in a while. "Yes, absolutely. I tried to make it in the biz, but not hard enough. Grandpa . . . my dad . . . they never thought I should go into moviemaking in the first place. They kept saying I didn't have the aptitude. The right attitude."

"Prove them wrong. Even more wrong than they already are."

"I'll try," he said. "I want to do a documentary on Collie too."

"Oh Christ," I said, "no, don't. No."

"People are very interested in him. Right before the execution he was on television a lot. He did dozens of interviews. He wasn't sorry for a damn thing. No regrets at all. Calmest-looking guy I ever saw on death row. People nowadays, they're intrigued by anyone who can keep some sort of cool about them. Your average guy is coming apart, falling to pieces, living in terror. He's losing his mortgage, he's got no health or life insurance, he's neck-deep in credit debt, he's on unemployment and it's running out."

"And you think people are going to admire a sprce killer who wound up strapped to a gurney and was put to death?"

"I wouldn't put it exactly like that," John said.

"I bet you wouldn't." I tensed up and my ribs ground together all wrong. I swallowed down a grunt. "Listen, I watched a couple of your films. I thought they were well made. Chic. Sleek, despite the material. You can always fall back on making more horror movies, if that's what you want, if that's what's hot, if that builds your cachet. You could go work for Sal Domingo's outfit if it comes to that."

"How do you know about him, Terry?"

"Perry told me. Just keep any of the ugliness of the biz from my sister, John. Do you understand? You're not in charge of her, but you are watching over her. I'm trusting you with one of the few people that matter to me in this world."

"Thank you," he said. "For trusting me, I mean. And believing in me."

He was dreadfully naive. Hollywood would grind him up all over again, even with a few connections and his last name. But Dale would learn from his mistakes. She'd watch him in action and understand what not to do. She might wind up turning it around for him.

"When do you think you'll be ready to go?" I asked.

"There's nothing keeping me here. I don't have any work slated. I haven't dated anyone in six months. I can pack up my cameras and film equipment, my editing machine, all that, clothes. Start making some calls to rental agencies in L.A. I don't know. A month or two? When does Dale want to go? Doesn't she still have school?"

"We'll work out all the details over the next few weeks."

He smiled at me. It was Collie's smile. It slid inside me like a shiv. He stuck out his hand and I shook it. He held on for a long while, like we were partners now, our fates entwined. Perhaps they always had been. I felt it too. He was blood of my blood.

"Let's have dinner this week," he said.

"Sure."

I stood at the top of the stairs and watched him walk down. I had a strange sense of déjà vu, but I didn't know why. I had no memory of this, but there was still that powerful sense of repeating the past. I listened to his voice recess in the depths of the house, my mother and father answering him. The high flutter of her false but pleasant laughter.

I waited until I heard the front door open and shut. I waited until the television was on and Gramp's cartoons were doing vicious things to one another with frying pans and shotgun shells.

I moved down the steps and out onto the back porch. I took up post. My gaze strayed to the woods. The oak, maple, and pine flailed in the wind. Leaves whipped around wildly, circling and rising in funnels like dust devils. I heard a car approaching. I slipped around the side of the house and watched Dale's boyfriend pull his 4x4 halfway up the driveway. They kissed almost modestly.

He chucked her under the chin. She got out and gave a brief wave. He hit reverse and she turned, not bothering to watch him go. He hit the road and gunned it hard. He drew attention to himself. If he was Lick 87 of the Rogues I hoped he kept pulling fake shenanigans and didn't step up to the real thing. He'd get busted pretty quick. My sister started for the front door.

"Dale," I called.

She walked around the house like she was headed for the gas chamber. We moved side by side to the back porch. I sat on the glider. She said, "It's too cold out here." I ignored her and waited. She finally sat beside me. Her breath smelled of hot sauce, antacids, cheap booze, and mints. She'd gone out last night to celebrate after the show. Or to diagram her getaway to L.A. Her gaze swiveled around the yard. She checked the back door to make sure our parents weren't nearby.

She got in close to me and I said, "Listen, were you serious about what you said last night? About moving to the West Coast?"

"Yes. It's already in the works."

"What does that mean?"

"I've asked some friends of mine who are out there to help me get a place and a day job. Then I start hitting auditions."

It wasn't in the works at all. It was smoke and empty talk right now. What friends could she have out in L.A.? People she'd met online? But the heat was there in her face. She was going to make it happen soon, even if she had to hitch out there on her own, thirty-seven cents in her pocket. She'd go on the grift, she'd snatch wallets, she'd get away with it for a while, and then she wouldn't.

"I've got ten grand for you," I said.

"What?"

"And the names of some dramatic coaches and professional casting agents who might be able to help you in Los Angeles. Also the names of some studio folks who might help fast-track you into walk-ons, cameos, stuff like that."

She drew away. She was wary as hell. She had every right to be. It sounded like I was grifting her, telling her something that sounded too good to be true. In our family, it was possible.

"How did you do this?" she asked.

"Our cousin John did it. He's made a few small movies. Documentaries. Horror flicks. He lived on the West Coast for a while and now he's moving back. I asked if he'd put you up for a while and show you around the town. You'll be staying with him."

"Our cousin John's a filmmaker?"

"Yes. So's Mom's brother, Will Crowe, and her father, Perry Crowe."

Dale cocked her head. She licked her lips. She looked at me, then she looked away, then she looked at me. "We're related to Will and Perry Crowe? The TV and movie producers?"

"That's right."

"And no one ever told me this?"

"I only just found out about it myself."

"Mom is heir to Hollywood royalty?"

"They're not so fancy."

"And she never said anything? And nobody told me? You didn't tell me?"

"I'm telling you now, Dale. I only learned about it when I went to visit the old fucker. He's stuck making horror flicks now. His company's called All Hallows' Eve."

"They own AHE, the horror movie production company?"

"Yeah."

"I could work for them! Easy!"

"Not so easy," I said. "All the girls have to run around topless and get butchered."

"So what? I'm not bashful!"

"I'm bashful enough for both of us."

For some reason that made her grin. "But what's the money for? I don't need that kind of money."

"Everyone needs money."

"I have money, Terry. *ROGUES* pays very well. I've got lots of money. I get paid in cash, off the books."

"Where do you keep it?"

"In a bank."

"If it's in a bank it's on the books."

"In a bank deposit box."

"Good. Well, you can always use more. I'll wire more if you need it. John's got plenty too. This way you don't have to work three waitress jobs to cover your initial costs. You can focus on acting and school."

"I told you I was quitting school."

"You are not quitting school," I said. "You're going to go to night school or summer school or whatever the hell you need to do to get a diploma and then start college. You're staying away from this Simon Ketch prick and that Internet show. If you do this thing you do it right. All of this is nonnegotiable, Dale."

She let out an exasperated breath. "You're still pushing me around, Terry. Don't you see that?"

"I see it," I admitted. "But I'm right. I'm helping you to get out of here and to follow your calling. You still need a stable foundation of education. A high school diploma, a college degree."

"You never went to college!"

I glared at her. "You want to be me?"

Her nose and cheeks were turning red. Her frosted breath iced up my throat. "What do Mom and Dad have to say about this?"

"I haven't told them a damn thing. That's your job. You clear it with them. You talk it out and you explain yourself. You get their permission. You don't run. You think things through and you do this the smart way. John knows the ropes. He can open a couple of doors with his name. You listen to him as much as you can."

"So he's there to keep an eye on me?" she asked.

"Yes," I said.

"You trust him a lot for someone you just met. And whom I've never met at all."

"I trust you, Dale. He just knows the area and some facets of the business. But he's got his own life to live. You've got yours. Promise me you'll go easy on the booze and do nothing harder than weed. And you stay in touch with Mom and Dad. And me. And if you ever want to come home you don't think about it for any length of time, you just do it. You catch a plane and come home. For whatever reason."

"And if I call bullshit and decide to keep working with the Web show?"

I answered honestly. "Then you're not as smart as I thought. And I suppose I'll have to find out where Ketch lives, creep his place, and get some bad dirt on him. He's already got a ton of lawsuits against him, right? I'll turn up the heat and do my best to take him down. If he's even real. If it's a board of directors, I'll do the same to each of them."

"You have a real mean streak in you, Terrier."

"No," I said. "I don't. I'm just protective of the people I care about. And I'm willing to go to the wall if I have to." I pulled out a pack of cigarettes, drew two, lit them, and handed her one. We sat there smoking for a minute. She started to shiver and I put my arms around her and pulled my little sister against me, remembering when she was a kid and I used to read to her.

"Really," I continued, "think about it, Dale, how many more staged home invasions can you do? Or real ones, before the cops come down anyway?"

She knew I was right. She wanted to resist because that's what we Rands did, even when we were being cut a break. We were contrary people. We did have mean streaks.

"All right," she said.

We smoked our butts down to the filters and then flicked them into the grass.

I stood and a wave of sadness rushed over me. She saw it and said, "Oh . . . don't. Don't do that. Don't cry. Stop. Wait, wait. Shhh." She jumped to her feet, took me in her arms, and pulled my head down to her shoulder and I laid my face there. She held me.

We stood there in the chill, the two of us sharing space and guilt and fear. I squinted against the wind and because I didn't want to have to see the woods.

"Thank you," she said.

I could've told her I loved her. I should've reassured her that everything would be all right. But I was mired by that strange and unmistakable sense that the past had doubled back on me. That time had slowed, had nearly stopped, but was about to pick up to a screaming speed again.

My father stood at the back door. He pushed open the screen and looked at me with an indignant heartache. It wasn't his heartache. He was showing me the face of my own heartache.

He gestured with his chin.

He said, "Come inside. You're going to want to see this."

My mother sat on the couch watching television. A breaking story unfolded. The set was too loud with people talking breathlessly into handheld microphones. The on-the-scene correspondent was impatient with the cameraman. He wanted a wider angle. He said, "As you can see over my shoulder . . . over my left shoulder . . . there . . . that's it, right there—"

His hair became winsomely mussed in the late afternoon breeze. A lot of cops milled in front of a bank in Hauppauge. I inhaled sharply.

Gramp's chin rested on his chest. He didn't turn his head at all. His eyes were open and he caught me in his peripheral vision. I could see him in there trying to fight his way back to life. He mumbled some gibberish as I stepped close.

Dale knew that whatever was going on, it was going to be bad. She'd seen Dad's face too. She held her hand out, caressed me lightly on the wrist, then went to her room. I stood behind Old Shep and propped myself against the back of his wheelchair.

My mother knew I'd been overdoing the pills again and said, "You must be hungry. I made lentil soup. I'll get you some."

"Thanks, Ma."

She brushed past my father and put a hand on his chest, let it stray to his hair for a quick run-through on her way to the kitchen. We were constantly giving one another small reassurances. My father took up his seat in the center of the couch.

I'd been keeping an eye on the papers, waiting for the heist to go down. I guessed at potential targets. I'd been wrong. The crew had bigger aspirations. They'd been pro and sharp and clever, but they never should have gone for a bank. Not with three crew members and a driver. The only ones who ever get away with robbing a bank are the dumbasses who reach over and snatch a handful of bills from the till. It's easy to escape with a thousand bucks. But getting into the vault, trying to pull down millions, getting the feds on your ass, that was either overly ambitious or extremely stupid or both.

Wrecked against a flagpole in the bank's parking lot was the dark green '69 Mustang fastback that Chub had sold the crew. It looked like a stray shot had taken out a tire. The driver had wiped out hard. His body was still wedged behind the wheel, neck turned at an impossible angle. It seemed like a million-to-one accident.

"No matter how much you plan—" my father said.

The on-site correspondent turned his chin, listening to his earbud. "Early accounts state that the robbers may have gotten away with up to eight hundred thousand dollars—"

How'd they get away? They had no wheels. They had to boost a car on the lot. Whose and how'd they get it? Carjacking at the corner light? Were they holding some little old lady hostage in the backseat of her own station wagon?

The only reason my father could've known I'd want to see the news is if he knew that Chub was working with strings. The only way he could've known that was by following me. While I'd been wondering where he was going nights he'd been wondering the same thing about me. Except my father was a better creeper than I was. I'd never sensed him on my tail at all. Even with having to take the Donepezil he was just as good as ever. He'd found me out.

My mother brought me a bowl of soup and a chunk of whole-grain Italian bread. I sat beside my old man and ate it without tasting it. He and I were going to have to have a long talk soon, but not right now. For the next half hour we watched as the story continued unfolding.

They hadn't been after the vault. They'd sat waiting at the back door of the bank for when the armored car brought in cash. I wasn't sure if it was the smarter play. No dealing with customers, no going up against time locks, no fighting with the managers for keys, but quadruple the security. Did they have an inside man riding in the armored car?

It looked like things had gone smoothly through most of the score and then somebody went gun crazy. None of the witnesses seemed certain who'd fired first. Three security guards were dead, all of them retired police officers. One had only recently come on board after serving three decades with the Suffolk County Sheriff's Department.

"It's going to be bad," my father said.

Already the commissioner had issued a hard-nosed statement. The case was being treated as a cop killing. There was a big reward. They were going to beat the bushes and shake the trees. They were going to rattle the world and the underworld. They were going to drag in everyone who'd ever done a job with the crew, everyone who'd ever gotten a piece of any of their pies. The tremors were going to reach far and wide. The earth would crack and a lot of people were going to fall in. The feds were going to do damage to the perps and anyone harboring them. No one would be able to breathe or rest until the crew was found.

They had the corpse of the driver. From there they could get the names of the rest of the crew. They'd been tight so it wouldn't be difficult. Informants would be tripping over themselves to cough up whatever they could. Nobody protects a cop killer–there's too much heat. By-the-book cops develop itchy trigger fingers.

If the other three members of the crew weren't shot on sight they'd go straight to death row unless they had something to barter with. The D.A. would leverage his position until they turned over evidence on every crook they ever worked with. That included the Thompson family.

I could picture how it was all going to go down. Danny was going to turn up the flame and try to have the three others hit before the cops got their hands on them.

Even though the Mustang that Chub had sold the crew was clean and legal, the feds would still come knocking eventually. With Chub's record they'd put him in the hot seat. I wondered if Danny would consider Chub a part of the crew.

If he did, he'd have Chub clipped too.

For good measure, someone might mention my name as well. Things could get rough.

I said, "I have to go."

My old man said, "Be careful."

His voice had real iron to it. He knew what was going to happen too. He didn't want me to get caught up in it, and he didn't want me to drag the family through it either. But it might already be too late where that was concerned.

I grabbed my jacket. I rushed to the front door.

Outside, JFK let out a greeting of happy barks.

Someone was coming up the porch steps.

I opened the door and Kimmy was standing there on the veranda, holding Scooter in her arms.

She said, "Hello, Terry," and her daughter mimicked her with a squeaky voice I'd been hearing in my dreams for years.

"Hallo, Tewwy."

Number seven. The expression on the face of
the woman you once loved who no longer loves you.

I'd only been this close to Kimmy physically one other time in the
past five years. A couple of months ago I'd stood on her front walk,
watching her and Chub and their girl coming out of their house.
Scooter had run a few cantering steps down the walk, not watching
where she was going until she'd almost crashed into my legs. I bent
and hugged her and her face fell in on itself in shock and fear of a
stranger. Kimmy had looked at me in surprise, Chub with a cautious
curiosity. Maybe we could've started down the road of becoming
friends again. If only I had said the right thing, or done the right
thing, or acted in the correct manner. Instead, I'd bolted.

I had to keep reminding myself that Scooter wasn't my daughter.

I had to remember that Kimmy was no longer mine.

I wondered if Darla wanted kids. She had told me not to fall in
love. I wondered why I was going to such extremes to never find love
again. We Rands continued to be driven upon the rocks.

I said, "Come in."

They came in. Scooter looked down at JFK and stuck her tiny
hand against his wide snout. He lapped at her and she squealed. She
cut loose with some kiddie chatter that I didn't understand. JFK got
it though and jumped up on his back legs and gave her a kiss. She
guffawed. Despite it all I couldn't help smiling. I let out a chuckle. My
laugh got a little louder. I wanted to hold her. I could go crazy with
how much I wanted to hold the little girl, and the woman too.

Kimmy was tense as hell. In our kitchen she checked left and
right, looking for lurkers. JFK and the kid kept playing. I tried to

smile. Kimmy's eyes spiraled with anxiety. Some of it was because of me. The rest because Chub had to be on the run already.

"I phoned," she said. "You didn't return my calls."

That meant Chub had given her my number. I hadn't expected that. The toddler reached for me. I caught her chin between my thumb and forefinger.

"I'm sorry," I said. "I haven't listened to my messages today."

She sat at the kitchen table and tugged Scooter onto her lap. I sat across from her in my brother's seat. She looked hard at me, studying my tics and my tells, searching out my lies even before I'd had a chance to say anything.

Scooter started reaching for items on the table. The centerpiece, the place mats, the salt and pepper shakers. All of it stolen, of course, all of it originally belonging to someone else, but ours now, stamped with our history. Scooter wanted to fill her hands. She wasn't my kid but Chub was a thief too. Maybe she was destined to be a grabber. I looked at her and the powerful mantra filled my head. *My girls. My girls.* And neither of them was.

Kimmy said, "Terry—"

JFK did me the favor of drawing focus. He kept putting his paw up on the kid's lap and she'd laugh. He'd turn his head one way and his ears would flop in that direction, and then he'd go the other way. She was a chatterbox. She spoke in a goofy singsong. For every dozen words I thought I might recognize one.

"Tewwy—"

Sometimes there's no starting point, nowhere to jump in that isn't full of breaking waves. So I said nothing. I simply asked the question.

"What can I do?"

Kimmy had to pry the salt shaker out of Scooter's chubby little fist. She slapped it firmly back down on the table and the kid snatched it again immediately.

"Chub called and told me he was in trouble. He was rushed and said it was all a mistake. He told me to get out of the house for a few days and go home to my mother. He didn't sound it but I know he was scared." Her hand moved like a separate small animal looking to bite something. It came for me and latched onto my wrist. "What isn't he telling me, Terry?"

"I don't know."

"He left his cell phone behind. I checked and your number was in there. You've spoken to him recently, haven't you?"

"No," I said.

"You've been outside our house."

"No, I haven't. And I haven't seen him."

"You're lying. You never used to lie."

I used to lie all the time. I made promises I couldn't keep. I deserved whatever I got. So did Chub. But Scooter, the kid, reaching for me now while JFK licked the tips of her shoes, she had to be protected.

"I'm not lying, Kimmy. Give me a chance to look into it."

"It must have something to do with this bank robbery. All of these ex-policemen who've been killed."

"I wouldn't know."

"Is he still helping to plan scores? Is he still selling cars to getaway men?"

I pictured what kind of hitter Danny would throw at him. I imagined that the remaining members of the crew might want Chub done away with just so he couldn't give them up. He was hiding from the cops, the feds, the people he worked with, his wife, me, and the syndicate.

Her grip on my wrist loosened. She withdrew. It was like the tide going back out, taking me with it.

"Do you have his phone with you?"

"Yes."

"Give it to me."

She opened her purse and handed me a cell.

"Go to your parents' place. I'll–"

"My father died two years ago. It's just my mom now." She jounced Scooter on her knee. "I'm sorry, I don't know why I said that. I know it's not important right now."

"I'm glad you told me. I'm sorry about your dad. Go to your mom's. Don't stop back at your place. I'll call you tomorrow."

"So you do believe it's serious?"

"I don't know," I said. "But I think it would be safer for you and Scooter to–"

"Scooter? Why did you call her that?"

Because I didn't know the kid's name. Because I didn't want to know. Because whatever it was it wasn't the name I'd have picked for my daughter. The first time I laid eyes on the baby, from a parked car nestled across the street from their house, Kimmy had been playing with her on the front lawn as the toddler wobbled away. Kimmy had called her "Scooter" then. That's what she'd always be to me.

I didn't answer.

"We need some things," she said. "Diapers, bottles. I can stop and buy them on the way."

"Don't shop in your usual stores."

"Why not?"

"Just don't. And only use cash, no credit cards."

"Oh Jesus–"

"Don't flip out," I told her. "It's just a precaution."

"I don't have much money in my bag, only forty or fifty dollars–"

Chub had a fat stash hidden away. If he decided to skip the country I had no doubt he'd have plenty of money set aside. I wondered if he had three new identities already worked up as well. Passports cost big bucks.

I opened my wallet and handed her some bills. "Here."

She took them. Scooter snatched a couple from her and waved

them around. Kimmy said, "You just gave me over a thousand dollars in hundred-dollar bills, Terry."

"Oh."

"That's what you carry in your wallet? You still have no concept of money. You're still stealing."

"That surprise you?" I asked. "I'm a thief."

My mother walked in. She let out a choked sound of shock, smiled broadly, and shouted, "Kimmy! Oh honey!"

She rushed Kimmy and grabbed her out of the chair and embraced her and the baby hard. The kid liked it. She squealed some more, still clutching a few C-notes. My ma rocked them both, patting Kimmy's back, rubbing it, speaking softly in her ear.

In a minute my mother started whispering, "Shhh, shhh, it's all right, you're fine, everything is going to be fine."

Kimmy was sobbing quietly against my mother's chest. The two of them clung together with Scooter in the middle.

Kimmy shook and the baby giggled and my mother tightened her hold gently. Ma kissed Scooter on the forehead and the baby went, "Aye-haa!"

My mother glowered at me over Kimmy's shoulder.

Finally Kimmy pulled away and said, "I'm sorry," grinning with embarrassment.

"*Sowwy!*"

"Nonsense," my mother said, "just tell me what the trouble is. Let me help."

"You can't, Mrs. Rand. It's not that I don't want to tell you, but I don't know what's happened."

Her voice broke and my ma reached out and massaged her arm. She glanced at the baby and smiled. My mother put her index finger on Scooter's nose and the kid went, "Ding-dong!"

My mother lasered commands into my brain. *You will help this girl. She was going to be your wife. You'll do anything and everything for her.*

I nodded once.

My mother said to Kimmy, "Let me get you something to eat, dear."

"No no, nothing for us. I should be going. I need to get the baby . . . home."

My mother put a hand on Scooter's head and rubbed at the downy strands of blond hair. She said, "Oh, she's so beautiful. Such a treasure."

"Yes, she is," I agreed.

I gave Kimmy a longing look and put my hands out and she hefted the kid into them. I held Scooter and pressed my forehead to hers and tried to bend the world to my will. I made silly noises and Scooter giggled like crazy and flapped around in my arms.

My ma pressed her cheek one last time to Kimmy's. "You're always welcome here. Whenever you like. Whatever you need."

"Thank you."

"You're family," my ma said. "You'll always be family."

Kimmy's bottom lip trembled. My mother hugged her, kissed her loudly on the forehead, turned and left. When the kitchen door swung open I saw my father there on the other side. Our eyes met for an instant and then he was gone.

Scooter threw money around, JFK tried to snag her shoelaces with his remaining teeth. Kimmy and I stood there presented before each other.

"Find him, Terry," she said.

I said, "I'll make it right. I'll find him. I'll make sure nothing happens to him."

"Promise me."

"Kimmy, look–"

"Promise me, Terrier Rand."

I sucked in a deep breath. "I promise."

The words caught in my throat like razors, but she seemed to want to give me the benefit of the doubt, even though there was no doubt.

"He knew you would help us. He wouldn't have kept your number in his phone if he didn't trust you."

"As soon as I find out anything," I said, "I'll call."

She picked up all the money and pocketed it. She knew she'd been ignoring Scooter so she took a minute to rub noses with the kid, make some goo-goo sounds. Kimmy hit me with a haunted but hopeful smile that nearly took out my knees.

The woman who wasn't my woman said, "Goodbye, Terry."

The baby who wasn't my baby said, *"Goo bye-bye, Tewwy."*

Part III

HELLO, BABY, GOODBYE

I stood outside of Chub's garage watching and waiting, the same way I had for months, knowing murder was creeping nearby in the night. I could feel it in my guts. It might be Chub's murder. It could be mine.

Now that I'd found out my old man had been following me I was attuned to other creepers. Somebody was here, and I couldn't shake the feeling that they were already on to me. It didn't matter. I had to get inside and see what I could find out.

I'd retrieved my phone. I did the obvious and clichéd thing of replaying Kimmy's messages. She sounded warm and engaging with only a hint of alarm. She sounded a little sheepish at having to phone me at all. It must've been horrible for her.

I went through Chub's phone too. There were no messages, no names that stood out as being potentially dangerous. If anybody managed to track it they were going to discover me. Maybe that would be good enough.

The four bays in the garage were each filled, one with an SUV, one with a van, two with early-seventies Chevies. I checked for blood. Chub could've been taken down already. It wasn't a thought I wanted to dwell on. I had to creep the area as carefully as possible.

Nothing seemed out of place. It didn't appear that there'd been a fight. Nobody had tossed the joint. It didn't look like anyone had gotten his hands on Chub here.

The feds would be by soon enough. The minutes were burning off one by one.

I was still going with the idea that he'd made a run for it. If he was smart, and he was, he'd have diversified and invested so that Kimmy and Scooter would be set up for life if he ever went in the bin or got clipped. He'd have bought real estate. We used to talk about retiring south to North Carolina or Florida. Neither of us had ever been farther than Jersey at the time, but the discussions helped us to believe, at least for a while, that it was possible to do something else, to be something else. That had seemed important then.

He'd have land, a house. Maybe more than one. Maybe out of state, maybe upstate. Maybe an apartment in Manhattan. A place he could go to ground if he ever needed it.

I hunted through his office cabinets and desk drawers and came up empty. Nothing showed me where he might've gone. I booted up his computer. It wasn't password protected or encrypted. It wouldn't be his real computer. He'd have a laptop somewhere safe.

I watched the screen saver. Chub, Kimmy, and Scooter played in the driveway washing the Roadster. I had pretty much memorized every pixel. My memory, like their images, was frozen in place. It would always be in motion but immobilized. Chub with the garden hose, the water arching toward Kimmy, but not reaching her, never reaching her. Her face turned as she tried to dodge, front teeth champed, holding back her laughter. Scooter with suds on her head, her face scrunched. I tried to force the image to move on. I pushed the film forward. I got them breathing. I heard the noises they were making. Kimmy choking back the giggle, Scooter shaking her head and the soap bubbles trailing off.

There was a safe in the corner of the office, hidden under a set of shelves obscured by racks of oil and transmission fluid. Unlike the one at All Hallows' Eve, Chub's was an old, simple model that I could've cracked inside of ten minutes. It made him seem sloppy, and that was the whole point. The first safe was meant to be found.

There had been a newer and more compact model hidden directly under the first. You had to shift the floorboards in a proper pattern to lift them out. The safe had been filled with maps and plans for various getaways, along with ninety grand in cash. I knew it was only one of his caches full of escape money in case he had to make a run for it. I loosened the boards and pried them up. As I suspected, the safe was gone.

Chub would've moved it after I'd come through the first time. The question was, did he have time to grab his money and weapons and get himself to a safe location or was he being run ragged out there?

I worked the office for another half hour and came up empty. I kept an eye on the doors and windows and still vibed a creeper weaving around me. I held out little hope that Chub would give me a call if he really needed my help. There was a chance he was a step ahead, but he wouldn't be able to keep it up for long. Neither would I.

On a hook in the office I found the keys to the Challenger out front. Another ragtop, red on red, with a wide white hood stripe running down between the scoops. It wasn't exactly going to fade into the background.

I slid in and out of broad shadows. I had already gotten rid of Blake's gun and wished I hadn't. I waited for the other creeper to make his move. I stared at my car parked at the far side of the lot. If anybody was going to ambush me, that's where they'd do it. I kept an eye out, moved to the Challenger, slid in behind the wheel, started her up, and tore ass out of there. Still nothing. I was paranoid but I wasn't wrong.

The driver had been sharp enough to follow without my knowing it, but I doubted any of the three remaining members could do as good a job. If the crew was around, and they planned to tail me, I'd spot them. If Danny Thompson already had a syndicate hitter on the move he'd likely be of the old-school goombah variety and I'd see him.

Maybe it was a highly motivated fed. Maybe a cop in the freezing darkness with just his own loneliness keeping him warm. I gunned my new car out of the lot and roared up the highway. The Challenger was pure power. I wondered if my father was putting along behind me. He'd once broken into Chub's house to take a look at Scooter when she was an infant.

My old man, he'd been losing his family and himself for years now. Maybe in the girl he saw a scant hope of redemption for the Rand name, the same as I did.

By definition a burglar has poor social skills. I didn't like to ring a doorbell and wait for entrance. I felt uncomfortable bringing something into a house rather than snatching something away. I didn't go through many doors in the daylight. I preferred kicking in a window to knocking.

I wanted to talk to Wes before I braced Danny Thompson. I needed to know if anybody on the street had stepped up with any information.

I prowled the neighborhood and kept an eye on the Fifth Amendment. It never closed. There was always something happening at the bar. Either drunken gatherings, business dealings, major poker games, mooks counting their book, drug deals going down, or hookers keeping the wiseguys happy.

The security was for shit, like most security on mob-owned places. They thought muscle and guns would scare off anybody from juking the joint.

I watched who came and went, but I wanted a closer look. I parked around the block, climbed over back fences, hopped up onto the Dumpster, and hit the roof. I perched on an overhang just below the rain gutters, staring through a partially opened window.

Like Perry Crowe, Big Dan Thompson had had a brag wall of himself with sports stars, singers, and Hollywood idols. Then Danny had taken most of his old man's photos down and stuck up a few of himself with B-list coked-out models, actresses, and bureaucrats. He sank a lot of money into political campaigns for the wrong reasons. It wasn't so he could get a handle on the rich and powerful and turn them to his best use. It was because he wanted to be a part of a world he didn't understand and that didn't want him in the first place. He smiled with senators who would never take his call no matter how big a check he cut. I bet Danny didn't mind so much just so long as he could get a nice eight-by-ten to hang in front of the other syndicate guys. He cared more about playing the part than being the real thing.

I'd had my first drink of hard liquor, seen my first thousand-dollar bill, and had my first woman here at the Fifth Amendment, all on the same day. The waitresses and pretty bartenders earned extra cash by taking the chief players back to the private lounge. When I turned fourteen Big Dan invited me in and showed me the delights of that back room, all on his ticket, the same way he'd shown Danny a few weeks earlier on his birthday.

Back then, Danny and I had been buddies, the two of us having come up in our fathers' footsteps. We'd gravitated toward each other because we understood one another. Our families did business together while we watched and waited for our turn at bat.

Big Dan had broad tastes and used to put in requests to my family for particular pieces of jewelry, watches, diamonds, sports collectibles. My old man would show up and Dan would personally go through boosted items, a jeweler's eyepiece always on hand.

The past and present continued to collide. I watched Danny holding court with the usual thugs and mutts and out-of-town mobsters. I didn't recognize anyone. Some of Danny's stooges wandered in and out from the back room, whispering in Danny's ear. Wes stood at Danny's right hand looking strained, but he always looked that way. I wondered if what Em had said could be true, that Wes was really trying to work up the nerve to quit the Thompson family. I didn't even know if it was possible to quit the mob or what would happen if he tried. I imagined it might involve blowtorches.

I sat poised there for over an hour. The temperature continued to drop. I listened to Kimmy's messages again. My ribs started to fuss and I took one of my few remaining Percs. I sank my fists deep into my pockets and tightened my arms to my sides to control the trembling. I kept waiting for something to happen. Wes took call after call, played some poker with the others, and popped antacids when nobody was looking.

Finally it looked like Danny told him he wasn't needed anymore and said he could take off early. It was almost eleven.

Wes got in his car and drove home. I climbed down from the roof, ran through the alley back to the Challenger, and followed Wes. I stopped at a liquor store first and got a good bottle of wine.

Ten minutes later I stood at Wes's front door, listening to the heaving wind blow whitecaps across the bay, hugging the bottle to my chest.

Em answered. She saw the look on my face and it made her smile. "Terrier Rand, waiting patiently on the stoop. I'm guessing that goes a bit against your grain?"

"Not at all," I said, trying to turn up the wattage on my smile. "I voluntarily enter the social contract and accept all its rules."

"Right. You look like an eight-year-old who's had to sit through a two-hour Sunday mass in a suit and tie." She stood straight and aimed her chest at me. "I'll try not to take this as an insult to my tits. I think they're well worth breaking into the house to check out."

"Agreed," I said, holding out the wine.

Wes stepped up behind her. He didn't smile. A hint of doubt clouded his face, but that was all. He took the wine and handed it to her without a word. He gazed behind me at the darkness of his yard.

She said, "I'll go . . . get some glasses," and retreated down the hall.

The keel of his boat rose and dipped and slapped around the canal hard. The dock groaned. It sounded like a dying woman trying to make it to shore.

"Why didn't you just crawl through a window at four in the morning?" he asked.

"Because you've got a girlfriend now."

"That stopped you?"

"That stopped me, yes."

He didn't know what to do with me. Ask me in for a glass of the wine and a plate of cheese or chase me off. He knew what I wanted. I could only bring him more trouble.

I followed him to the living room. I sat heavily on the comfortable couch and practically melted there. The cold cramping began to leave my muscles. Em handed me a glass and served the wine. She sat beside Wes and they both took turns sipping from the same glass. She was hoping that maybe we could have a quaint conversation like normal people. I hated like hell to disappoint her again.

"I can't help you with Chub," Wes said. "That was one of his cars, right?"

"Right."

"I already told you that Mr. Thompson keeps me out of that end of the business now."

"I know. I want to know who Danny has running that part of the show. I couldn't tell from who he had around him tonight."

"You were at the Fifth?"

"Yeah."

"You mean you were casing the Fifth."

"Yeah."

"You never learn, do you? You just don't learn."

"I've learned a few things."

He glanced at Em, a touch abashed. I realized I'd embarrassed him again. Nobody likes to admit that they've been replaced in the company, whether they're selling insurance or aluminum siding or running mob matters. He sipped the wine. I hoped it wouldn't aggravate his ulcer.

She said, "I suppose that's my cue to get lost because the menfolk want to discuss diabolical acts and the business of being wicked."

"You make it sound a lot more fun than it is," Wes said.

"That's my natural gift, honey bear."

Em gave his ear a lick that brought out a glowing flush across his forehead. She gave me a little toodle wave and walked from the room. I hoped one of these days we'd actually be able to talk for more than a minute or two.

Wes ran a hand over his face as if he could wipe some of the red away. He burned brightly. I remembered the time when Kimmy could do that to me. Hit a pose or say a word, make a particular sound that clung to her bottom lip and made me change colors, hop from one foot to the other, break into a sweat. I envied him these early days of love.

"Terry, don't you dare say any—"

"Honey bear?"

He sighed. "A guy named after a dog shouldn't act high-and-mighty."

"I think it's quite sweet, Mr. Bear."

He didn't have many friends to break his balls. "Look, so I bought her this gold locket with a little bear on it. It's got a little pot of honey and—" He checked to see if I was laughing. I wasn't. I wasn't making fun of him at all. He was my friend, maybe the only one I had left in the world. He saw it there in my eyes. The happiness I had for him. He grinned a bit.

"Well," he said. "You know how it goes."

The dock moaned loudly. He'd had new windows put in his house, but they'd been installed improperly. A slight draft played along my neck hairs.

"I need to find Chub," I said.

Wes nodded. He looked grief-stricken but resolved, like a father set to tell his kid that there's no Santa. "You can't do anything for him, Terry. He's either dead by now or he will be the minute anybody spots him. If the cops find out he was helping that crew they'll pop him on principle." He finished his glass, poured himself another. "A bank job. And a bank job pulled when the armored car guards are there, no less. What were they thinking?"

"I don't know," I said. "Does Danny have hitters going after Chub?"

"Of course he does. Chub and the others. And anybody else who might snitch when the feds come kicking ass. He knows that crew will blow the whistle on every job they ever pulled or heard about to keep the death penalty off the table. And if they're professionals they've got info on something Mr. Thompson doesn't want made public. He's got to cover his ass. And you said the guys in the crew were very tight. That means they're going to ace anybody who can finger them. Chub might catch a bullet coming or going, but he's going to catch one. You might too, if you get in the way. You need to stay out of sight."

Wes used a lot of euphemisms instead of saying the word kill. Each one set my teeth further on edge. He took another sip of wine and licked his lips. He looked at me over the rim of the glass.

"Maybe I can talk Danny out of it," I said.

"You never learn."

"I've learned a few things."

"If you try to talk to him you'll wind up with a bullet in your ear. He doesn't like you to begin with. And now you're someone very close to someone with a bull's-eye on his ass. I'm serious, Terry, do not shake things up further."

"I need to know which of Danny's guys is going after Chub and where I can find him."

The wine was lubricating his wheels. He kept pouring it down. He was scared and this new twist in the biz wasn't sitting well with him. He wasn't on firm ground with the wiseguys anymore.

He looked at me coldly for a moment. "Maybe you shouldn't bother, Terry. If Chub does get clipped then–"

"Shut up, Wes."

"–maybe you'll get Kimmy back."

"Shut the fuck up, Wes."

"Isn't that what you want?"

The draft was beginning to annoy the hell out of me. It was like a tongue flicking against my skin. I shifted six inches to the left and rubbed at the back of my neck.

Wes was still waiting for an answer. He wanted a gut-wrench response. I gave it to him. "Yeah. It's what I want. But I'm not going to let him die because I'm a bitter screwed-up asshole."

He nodded, his carved stony chin jutting. "Okay, now I know for sure you mean what you say."

"If I didn't, would I be here?" I asked.

"Maybe. Maybe you'd try to help him out just to keep your conscience clean and prove to yourself that you weren't out to steal his woman and watch him die. And when the time came maybe you'd kill him yourself."

Christ. It was the third time in three days that someone thought I had it in me to snuff out a life like swatting a moth. What in the hell was I putting out there into the world?

"The name of the torpedo?"

"Walton Endicott."

"He's not using goombahs anymore?"

"There aren't that many left around. Most of them have run to Chi or L.A., either mobbed up there or gone legit or retired. He puts his regular boys on the street to find out whatever they can, then Endicott follows up."

"So where can I find Endicott?" I asked.

Wes shrugged his huge shoulders. "I don't know. He doesn't work out of the Fifth. He doesn't like to be seen with Mr. Thompson. He seems to think that working with wiseguys is beneath him. He's the real thing, Terry. The kind they don't make anymore. A professional killer. Pure ice."

"So how'd he wind up on Danny's payroll?"

"He works for whoever will pay him. Times are tough for everybody."

"I guess so."

Wes had more to say but needed to work up to it.

"There's something else, Terry." He craned his neck and checked down the hall to make sure Em was out of earshot. He slid to the edge of his seat, gesturing for me to do the same. I leaned in. "They say he uses a needle."

"What?"

"He kills with a needle." Wes enunciated clearly, striking each syllable like banging flint together.

"A needle? What do you mean? Like a syringe?"

"I don't know."

"Like a knitting needle?"

Wes shrugged again.

"Or like a hat pin that some old ladies still wear? Or like a stiletto maybe."

"Jesus H., I don't know. A needle. That's what they say. That's all I know. He's put the shits into some of the Thompson soldiers that you'd figure would never rattle. I'm telling you, you can't go up against this guy."

"I don't want to go up against him," I said. I reached for my cigarettes and Wes gave me a look like I'd just spit on the floor. He was taking this new home owner's pride a little far. I stuck the pack of smokes back in my pocket. "I just want to talk to him."

"He doesn't talk. Guys like that don't talk. He's racked up a lot of numbers, Terry. We're talking triple digits."

"Oh bullshit."

"I'm serious. You pay him and the job gets done, period. He doesn't make mistakes like the other boys might. He's a very nasty customer. Let it lie. Chub called his tune."

All of it was true. Chub had made his choice. I didn't want to go up against an iceman torpedo. But I'd made Kimmy a promise I never should have made to make up for a promise I didn't keep.

"You never answered me before. What's the name of the new mouthpiece that Danny's listening to? That's how Danny got ahold of someone like Endicott, isn't it? Even Big Dan never used somebody who performs hits with a needle."

Wes didn't want to give me any more information. He hadn't wanted to tell me as much as he already had. He knew he was putting me in harm's way. But I was calling my tune. "Guy's name is Haggert. Eddie Haggert. He's not a ginzo, but he was a trusted confidant of Big Dan back in the old days. Guy's about seventy, a former middle-weight, fought at the Garden a couple times. Drives a big Caddy and talks about it like it's his mistress. He came out of retirement to help the Thompson family, mainly because he was bored and wasting away."

"I didn't see anybody like that at the Fifth tonight."

"He wasn't there. He was coming in late."

"That's why Danny wanted you to leave."

"Yeah. Haggert thinks I'm soft and weak. He scapegoated me and blamed me for the family nearly going belly-up, the prick."

I scanned the framed photos around the room. I looked here and there at Wes and Em smiling like mad, in the usual New York tourist spots. Top of the Empire State Building, in front of Radio City Music Hall. It was quaint and endearing at the same time. I could feel my jealousy wanting to hate him now too. I wondered if anyone in my family ever visited a psychiatrist. I wondered if Collie had just needed a couple months of cheap self-explanatory therapy to avoid his execution.

"The boss can't take the blame," I said. "That's why he's the boss."

"Right again. Anyway, Haggert is teaching Mr. Thompson how to do it hard. Lots of beatings, burning down businesses for extortion cash, breaking kneecaps, clipping rats. Like it was in the rotten old days. But it's working."

"Why aren't the cops coming down on him?"

"He's good at deflecting investigations. And Mr. Thompson is spreading more cash around. Cops who were clean and idealistic a few years ago are worried over their mortgages now. There's a lot more gray area when the national debt is twenty trillion."

"That's why Danny's overreacting like this situation?"

"It's not an overreaction, it's his new business model. Wipe out all enemies and all possible complications. It's his last chance to make any kind of a statement to the other syndicates. If he doesn't do something big to save the family business he knows he'll get squeezed right out. He's poured a lot of cash into Haggert's and Endicott's pockets just so he could impress the guys who are impressed by that sort of thing."

Danny had a lot to prove, especially to his old man. Now that Big Dan was dead, Danny was really going out of his way to dazzle him. "Is it working?"

"Yes. Mr. Thompson's gaining back some ground."

The wine was gone. Wes had pretty much finished the bottle on his own. He looked at his glass like his future was just as empty.

"How bad is it for you now?" I asked.

"When your boss doesn't trust you in this thing you don't get a severance package, you get severed."

"Em seemed to think you were quitting."

"I tell her that to try to keep her happy. But she's not an imbecile."

"You really think Danny would clip you?"

"Me, you, Chub, anybody he feels might be a bump in the road."

"I didn't know it had gotten so bad."

"You should've. Out of all of us I'd still say you're at the top of his list."

"I thought it impressed you, how I didn't take shit off him."

"It does. It also scares me. For Christ's sake, be careful."

He wasn't just talking about my well-being. He was asking me to tread lightly. If I put Danny in another bad mood, Wes might be the one who got two in the back of the head. Or a knitting needle through the eye.

I got back up on the roof of the Fifth Amendment. Danny Thompson was still at his father's station, the corner table where all the real business got done. The hive was buzzing. I watched more and more cars pull in. The thugs, soldiers, and big shots spread out across the bar drinking and flirting with the chick bartenders. Cigar smoke hung heavily in the air now. The men hugged each other and kissed one another on the cheeks. Even the non-goombahs did it. You pretended to love the guy you might someday mow down. It went back to the Garden of Gethsemane.

A few of the high rollers took women upstairs to the private rooms. I listened to their vacuous giggles as they followed the men, carrying drinks and plates of sandwiches and appetizers.

I checked my messages and had a new voice mail from Darla. "I'm still thinking about your offer. Maybe you can come over tonight and persuade me one way or the other. Stop by no matter how late it is, if you'd like."

A half hour later I spotted Eddie Haggert swing around the corner in a vintage '59 Cadillac Fleetwood Sixty Special. Sporting a fake fender scoop, chromed ice cones, three-row bullet rear grille, extraordinary fins, and a molding that wrapped from the front to the back, this was fifties flamboyance at its best. He was old-school all right. The good old bad days.

He slid from the Caddy and moved across the lot with the fluid grace of an ex-pro athlete, much like my father moved. A shout went up when he walked in. Danny got to his feet. Danny didn't get to his feet for anybody.

They did the kissing and hugging thing. Danny waved his boys away. He and Haggert went into a huddle. They were in deep discussion for ten minutes. I could see the sweat on Danny's brow. He usually talked much too loudly when discussing business. His father had never raised his voice, not even when he was furious. You never knew who might be listening.

But Danny had learned to keep it down. He spoke calmly, controlling himself, sipping a large dark beer. I'd seen him for the first time in five years a couple of months ago and he'd put on a lot of weight, shifting uncomfortably in his seat, wearing a suit a couple sizes too small for him at the time.

Now he'd dropped a few pounds and looked healthier, stronger, a little more like his old man. Danny's silky blond hair had receded into a prominent widow's peak, but he no longer appeared to have the nervous tic of constantly brushing his thumb across it. Haggert's company had given him a boost of confidence.

I was pretty sure Haggert was going to make a run to take over the whole show. He'd come out of retirement to jockey his way up to being the number-two man. I didn't see a guy who'd drive a boat like the Fleetwood Sixty Special being happy unless he had all the power. A roughhouse boxer like that didn't get back into the ring unless he wanted to win the title.

Nobody drifted near Danny's table or the back office. It was time for a midnight snack, and the kitchen was busy.

Haggert had the same cool as Big Dan, as most of the old time players. He wore a three-thousand-dollar black suit and still went in for cuff links. He had his white hair sharply parted on the side, something you didn't see much of nowadays. He had a rawboned handsomeness to him, huge powerful-looking hands even as he used a tiny spoon to stir his cappuccino.

His smile seemed genuine and he had a habit of chuckling as he spoke, his shoulders heaving gently. He had dark blue eyes that were, somehow, a little too warm. There was a forced gentleness there that you knew you couldn't trust. I found myself liking him from afar, and realized just how dangerous that sort of thing was, considering I was hanging on to the rim of a roof staring in at a bunch of wiseguys.

I had my tools with me but I didn't even need them to get into the back office. The ventilation was bad in the building so they kept a lot of the windows open a crack, even during frosty autumn evenings. I went around the back of the Fifth, popped one of the window frames of the office, crawled inside, crossed the room, locked the door, and propped a folding chair under the knob.

I searched the small room as quickly and efficiently as I could. I wasn't expecting to find anything of use but it was a better place to start than plan B.

Thirty years of useless paperwork was piled up everywhere I looked. Anything of real importance would've been shredded or locked up. They were sloppy but not quite that sloppy. I started at the computer. It wasn't encrypted. Nobody encrypted anything. There were files of transactions in a code I knew would be easy enough to break if you put a little time in. It wouldn't give the feds much. It wouldn't give me anything.

A second set of books would be hidden away someplace. A third set someplace else. Maybe written out, maybe on other computers. Most of the Thompson dealings were legit, like most underworld action nowadays. There was still a rotary phone on the desk. Like my own family, Danny was a holdout.

I checked for anything that might help me get a line on Walton Endicott. I didn't think his cell number would just be sitting out in the open. But then again, it had to be somewhere. Danny played at mobsters, not spies. Information wasn't going to self-destruct. They had to be able to get in touch with the torpedo. I could see Haggert memorizing such numbers and destroying the evidence, but not Danny.

Big Dan used to keep a small safe in the corner, but it wasn't there now. I figured they might move it around, but they wouldn't get rid of it. I checked the whole place but couldn't find a new stash for it. I went back to the computer and played around some more. I couldn't find anything to give me an edge.

The doorknob rattled.

"Hey," a voice called. "What's this? Somebody in there?"

"Just a sec," I said.

"Just a sec?"

"Just two ticks."

"Two ticks? Who's that?"

"Give me a minute here, Chico."

". . . Chico?"

I kicked back in the chair and thought, Shit, plan B, we're going to have to do this the hard way.

He had the door unlocked but still couldn't get in because of the propped chair. I pulled it away and the door flew open and a huge bruiser stood there with the same body and face and expression as about ten thousand other guys who'd performed the same function for bad guys going back to Capone.

"Who the fuck are you?"

"You wouldn't happen to know Endicott's number, would you?" I asked.

He carried a Sig Sauer compact in a shoulder holster. He must've bought the holster first because the compact fitted loosely in it. He had his hand on the butt of it but hadn't yet drawn the weapon. I smiled and held up my hands. The smile annoyed him enough to make him pull his piece. He held it on me while he patted me down.

He took my burglary tools and said, "You trying to rip us off?"

"In a manner of speaking," I said. "So, you know this Endicott fella? Supposedly kills people with some kind of needle?"

The tough spun me around, gripped me by the neck gruffly, and shoved me forward with the barrel of the Sig Sauer planted in the middle of my back. He pushed me out into the bar. There was a ker-fluffle of activity. Some guys yanked their hardware. The dude who had me shoved me toward Danny.

"Mr. Thompson, we have a–"

Danny didn't let him finish. He looked up from the table and waved me over with two fingers, the way Big Dan used to allow passage to his corner.

He didn't like to be called Danny but I had no idea what the hell else to call him. Mr. Thompson sounded excessively formal.

I said, "Hello, Danny." It might miff him but we were headed in that direction anyway, no matter how it started off.

He didn't lock up the way I expected. He looked practically serene and let his face slip into an easy smile. He reached out and shook my hand. "Terry. You're losing your tan. Sit down."

Haggert drank his cappuccino and wore an amused smile. I didn't know if he knew who I was but it was a good bet. Or maybe that was just my ego talking. As I sat Danny let out a chuckle, cool, controlled, confident. But it was already too late for him, and he didn't even know it.

More top wiseguys came in and walked up the stairs. I smelled shrimp scampi smothered in garlic-butter sauce. The back room door opened for a minute and I saw some bigwig out-of-towners playing cards, women waiting patiently laid out on sofas.

The last time Danny and I had met face-to-face I'd held a Desert Eagle on him. I'd snatched it off one of his soldiers and shot the guy through his leg with his own gun. I was in as dark a place as I'd ever been before. I'd planted the pistol in Danny's ear. I'd drawn stacks of stolen money out of my pocket with my left hand and tossed them, one after the other, onto the table. They bounced and fell into his meal and then into his lap. Eventually I believed him when he said that he hadn't had my uncle snuffed.

I could feel the slow embrace of history forcing me along a particular path as if we had rehearsed this many times before. It was a strange ballet, perfectly executed for ten thousand nights, about to be performed once more. I was a bullet ballerina.

I kept my eyes on Eddie Haggert. Now that I was up close I could see all the scars of his early boxing years pounded into his face. The thick tissue around his eyes, the pulped nose. Both his ears were cauliflowers mostly covered over by his white hair. All the knuckles on both hands had been flattened.

"Get you anything?" Danny asked me.

"Sure. Coffee. Black."

He motioned one of the waitresses over and put in the order. Then he turned to me. "From what I remember you don't like coffee much. You must've been casing the place for a while out there. Getting nippy, is it?"

It was an astute observation. I'd made a mistake. It wasn't much of a mistake but it proved I wasn't as focused as I should be.

"So, Terry," he said. "You juking me now?"

"Not exactly," I explained.

He nodded at that, slowly, with great dramatic emphasis. I felt sorry for him. He had to dwell on every gesture, every word, run each thought through his head five times over. Despite his newfound reserve he just didn't have the natural disposition for the job.

Haggert watched him. I wondered how long Danny might have.

"Not exactly," he repeated. "Care to clarify that a bit?"

"All right. I wasn't stealing from you, I was hunting information."

"What kind of information?"

"We're getting ahead of ourselves," I said.

"You're right, we are. First off, let me introduce you to my new lieutenant, Eddie Haggert. Eddie, this is an old friend of mine, Terrier Rand."

Haggert stuck his hand out. I took it. I could feel the immense power within him even at seventy. At thirty he must've been a total butcher in the ring.

"I know the name," Haggert said. "Family of boosters. Brother went a little berserko and paid for it in the chair."

He was looking at me like he expected a response, so I said, "Almost right. He got a hot shot, not the chair."

Haggert opened his jacket. He withdrew a cigar from his shirt pocket and offered it to Danny, who wagged his chin. It was important to show proper courtesy, even in these circumstances. He then proffered it to me. I waved him off.

"You a nutjob like him? I'd say you had to be at least a little cracked to do what you just did. Trying to rip off your old friends."

"I creep everyone. That's what I do."

"You're overstepping."

"That's what all of us at this table do."

It made him laugh. He pulled a cigar cutter out of his pocket. I wondered if we were going to do the chopping-off-fingers bit. I got ready to swing out of my seat. I eyed the stairs. I could be halfway up them before anyone could get a bead on me. The trouble was what happened after that.

The coffee came. I waited. Haggert clipped off the end of his cigar but didn't light it. He held it in his left hand. He picked up his cappuccino in his right. Danny was working on a JD on the rocks.

You had to play Danny Thompson with a soft touch, but you couldn't go too soft. I could vibe his self-doubt still chewing him up inside. He had a cap on it, but it was there. It seemed that the longer you hung in with somebody the worse you hated him in the end.

"What were you chasing, Terry?" Danny asked. "Or do I really have to guess?"

"You don't."

"You were looking for some kind of line on Chub."

"Yeah."

"And you want me to let this thing with that cop killing crew go."

I shook my head. "Not at all. What you do with the crew is your business. But Chub isn't part of the crew. I want you to leave him out of this."

He drained the rest of his JD, held the empty glass up, and rattled the ice cubes around. A girl brought a fresh glass out to him immediately. He took a deep drink, let out a sigh. "You asked my old man the same thing, if I remember correctly."

I nodded. "You do."

I'd only gone up against Big Dan once. Chub had tuned the getaway car for a string that had taken down a massage parlor owned by the Thompson mob. The heisters blew town with fifty large and Big Dan thought Chub ought to pay him back. I asked Big Dan to let it slide. He didn't like my asking. He ordered four of his men to kick the shit out of me. I didn't fight back. Big Dan had let Chub slide anyway, as a favor. I didn't take any of it personally.

Danny rubbed his thumb over his widow's peak. I'd set him on edge. Tics never really disappeared or died. "And, remind me, what was his response again?"

"He had his boys work me over," I admitted. "But he also let Chub go."

"He was a nice guy, my old man."

I wouldn't go that far, but I smiled complacently anyway.

"How'd you hear about my plans for Chub anyhow?" he asked.

"I know the way the game works, Danny."

"Okay, but tell me this: Why do you even care?"

I finished my coffee. "You know why."

"I'm not sure. Old times' sake? Or because you can't bear to see her hurt? Your ex-girl." Another possibility occurred to him. "Or because she asked you?"

I thought I kept my face as impassive as possible, but he immediately read the truth.

"So," he said, "she asked you. And even though she's his wife now, and you broke her heart once already, you've come around again to beg for a guy who took everything you left behind."

There it was, laid out hard and cold. I wasn't appealing to his better nature. Danny Thompson didn't have a better nature in front of his men, in his father's seat. But there was no reason to lie now.

"To be fair, that wasn't plan A."

"Plan A didn't pan out for you, Terry." Danny laughed. "You're better off letting him get what he's got coming. Maybe there's still time for you to pick up the pieces. They got a kid now, right? A little girl? So tell me. You sit up late at night thinking about all the what-ifs? What if she was your lady? What if the kid called you Daddy? What if you could do it all again? You imagine pink dresses and bows in the hair? You check your rearview and see a baby seat back there behind you?"

Haggert rolled his unlit cigar from one side of his mouth to the other. He was very interested in what might happen next.

"Let Chub go, Danny." There was nothing shameful in asking please, so I did. "Please." Danny was already a dead man. I saw him with a sewing needle in the eye, a syringe in his carotid.

"It can't be done," Haggert said. "And maybe now that we got you, we don't let you go either."

I looked at the old man. His scalp was very red and clean where it showed through his part. "Should I be talking to you?" I asked. "Or him? Far as I know this is still the Thompson syndicate. I've done business with them all my life. You I don't even know."

"I'm his lieutenant," Haggert said, "his right hand, so you can talk to me, if you've got to talk at all. Apparently Daniel respects you because of the common history he shares with your family. But that doesn't count much when it comes to bank jobs that leave three cops dead. When cop killers go down they take everybody with them. We can't let that happen. You're not stupid, kid, you know it's the truth."

Haggert relaxed in his seat, handsome for an old dude, his cuff links burning.

"Chub wasn't part of the crew," I said. "He wasn't on the job. He didn't shoot any ex-cops. He just sells souped cars. And he sells them clean and legal."

"He sells them to the wrong people. That makes him accountable."

I cleared my throat like I was going to make a final impassioned plea, a grand soliloquy, a speech in French. There was a lot between Danny and me. Secrets we could barely remember. Blood and bullshit. I'd called him out. You didn't forget such things, ever. You never forgave them either. I showed him my teeth. I had a couple more buttons to push. I felt sorry it had to be this way. My expression said, You'll always be a disappointment to your old man, even in hell.

He couldn't take it. No one could. He choked back an ugly bleat, swung on me, and caught me flush in the jaw. Even though I knew it was coming it still hurt. I acted startled and leaned into him, got him in a clench, and he put his hands on my chest and shoved me off.

He had the good sense to appear sorry for his strong-arm tactics. He straightened his tie, took a sip, and wiped his mouth carefully with a linen napkin. He cleared his throat. He let an eight count go by.

He said, "You remind me of times I'd rather forget, Terry. I'll see you around. Just not here. Never again. You're not welcome anymore. My men have new orders. You come around again you'll get clipped on sight. You walk in the door or climb in the window and no one will ever see you again. Your mother won't have a grave to visit. Remember that. I'm washing my hands of us once and for all."

"Okay, Danny," I said. "Good luck to you."

He beckoned his thugs. "Boys, show Mr. Rand out."

Four of the Thompson legbreakers surrounded me, putting on a nice show, like we were all friends. Chico waved me out of my seat. They walked me to the back door and into the dark lot. Thank Christ there was no kissing. While my back was still turned Chico threw a jab into my kidneys. I'd about had it with that kind of shit.

I spun in a tight arc so that we were almost nose to nose. I slid my hand inside his holster and snatched out the ill-fitted Sig Sauer. He'd left the safety off. I backed up three steps so I could keep an eye on all four of them.

"Thanks for the escort, boys, but I think I can handle it from here."

"We see you again, you're dead," one soldier said.

"I had a lot of good times here as a kid," I told him, "but I guess everything comes to an end eventually." I motioned them away. "Go inside. Shut the door. In five seconds I'm putting two shots through it, so back the hell off."

"My piece!" Chico cried.

"I'm keeping it."

I extended my arm and drew a bead on each one of them in turn. I just needed a few seconds to disappear up the alley to where the Challenger was parked. They retreated to the back door of the Fifth. Chico stood there like an angry kid who didn't want to go to bed. I waved him in. He pushed out his bottom lip in anger. I backed up for a five count and put two bullets into the base of the door. My going-away present, I supposed. I'd left my mark.

I held on to the Sig Sauer as I ran. The way things were going, I might need a piece again soon. I got to the Challenger, jumped in, and ripped out of there.

But I didn't go far. I parked again about a quarter mile up. I reached into my pocket and drew out the wallet and cell I'd lifted from Danny when I let him smack me in the mouth. I turned on the dome light and spent five minutes on the cell. It didn't have any names, initials, scheduling, apps, or anything else that looked like it could help.

I tried the wallet. He didn't carry much cash around, only eighty bucks. It was another sign that he wasn't right for the job. You head a family you always flash the green, even if you have to tax your lieutenants extra to make up for it.

A gold credit card. A photo of his father. And a small sheet of folded paper with backward phone numbers and corresponding initials written on it. Reversing the number and being one letter off on both initials was about as complicated a code as Danny and his mob were likely to use.

There was also a hastily scrawled message: *FX@CH Sn@8*.

FX was actually WE. Walton Endicott? CH? CH would be the meeting place. I didn't know any meeting places with the initials HC, but Danny might have used the code only for the names of people, not places. I thought I knew where he meant.

Tomorrow, Sunday, eight P.M., at Chez Hilliker. It was a small, fancy restaurant nestled back in Port Jackson. Route 25A sliced through the heart of town. Wide front and back parking lots shared with some neighboring businesses. At least three exits, probably a fourth out behind the kitchen. Noted for its demure atmosphere. The kind of place where a torpedo might call a meeting.

I wondered if Endicott would put one in Danny's eye if he ever found out Danny walked around with so much information stuck in his wallet.

I drove back to the Fifth, popped the back door on Danny's limo, left the wallet and phone wedged prominently in the cushion. He might buy it. Danny didn't need his wallet or phone much. He had right-hand men and left-hand men for that. I relocked the door. I sped home, the rain starting and stopping, flaring across the windshield, the smeared moon following.

Kimmy had said she was going to her mother's, but after her father died, her mom must've sold the place. In the morning I found that a young couple with a lot of dogs lived there now. The dogs rushed in and out of the pet door at the side entrance, ran each other ragged in the wet grass, and took up on the patio furniture.

I remembered where her aunt lived and drove over. Like I thought, Kimmy's mom was staying there now. I watched the three of them chasing Scooter across the living room floor. The gutters were clogged. Sheets of water ran down the bay windows, warping the warm light of hanging lamps and the shifting gray illumination of changing scenes on the television. I didn't see anybody else around. No feds, no hitters, no trouble that I could make out. I circled the block. I kept the Sig Sauer prepped under the center console. I practiced reaching up under the dash and snatching it free. I got the move down cold.

I phoned her.

"Did you find him yet?" she asked.

"I'm still looking."

"It does have something to do with that bank, doesn't it? I've been watching the news. There's a manhunt on. The FBI are involved. Did he have something to do with—"

"He didn't have anything to do with it, Kimmy, but he's had to go to ground. He's smart. Wherever he is, he's safe. I'll find him and help him clear this all up."

"Please, Terry—"

"Try not to worry. I'll call again soon."

I spent the afternoon at All Hallows' Eve, keeping an eye on Blake and Nox and sitting in on the making of *No Boundaries*. I tried to get a line on my uncle Will and my grandfather. I wanted to learn what I could about them. I wanted to see their business alive and in motion without them.

There was nothing suspenseful about the flick. It all seemed poorly acted and extremely fake. I wondered what that said about the Crowes. I wondered what that said about the movie-going public. Blake shouted out things like, "More blood! Stick her again! Stab her again!" I kept flashing on Collie's spree. The camera guy kept bustling around. Lights were reset and props moved. Nobody seemed to be enjoying themselves much. A couple of the cannon fodder women ran around topless. It wasn't erotic. I was glad Dale wasn't around to see any of this bullshit. I tried to believe that Los Angeles would be higher class than a warehouse horror movie set in Islip.

Blake tried to keep the energy level high with encouraging comments. He framed one shot with the shadows of the raindrops on the window falling over bodies. The whole thing bored the hell out of me within twenty minutes.

It took me that long to realize that Blake was wearing makeup. He had a shiner and a split lip and the on-set makeup girl must've worked a little magic on him this morning. He gave me wary looks on occasion. He had something to say but didn't want to say it.

Nox kept a close watch. The massive tower of muscle stood at my right side and never wandered very far. I'd inherited him as my bodyguard.

I said, "Blake mixed it up with somebody. What went down?"

"I don't know."

"I thought you two were a team."

"I do what he says. That's not exactly a team. He doesn't always invite me in when it counts."

"Did it have to do with the meth?"

"Maybe. Like I said—"

I phoned Darla and told her if she wanted to check out a horror movie set to come down and meet me. She said she'd close up the store and be right over.

There was a large table of catered goods. I had to keep reminding myself to eat. I threw down a Perc and made myself a roast beef sandwich and sat there quietly munching as folks stepped on and off the set.

In between takes Nox introduced me around to the crew and the actors. He called me boss. I worried about getting suckered for a while but then I realized he was just playing the cards he'd been dealt. He and Blake had their drug business to consider, and they had already made a lot of money, and they were still in the moviemaking game. I hadn't kicked them loose or killed them like Perry wanted. I hadn't told Danny Thompson about the money they owed him. Any way you looked at it, I was being generous. Blake continued to shout orders. All in all, nobody had much to complain about.

The next time the cameraman and lighting folks were resetting for a shot, I called Blake into the office.

"What happened?" I asked.

"What do you mean?"

"Someone gave you trouble."

"It was nothing."

"Who was it?"

He peered at me, considered me in total. His eyes flashed with scenarios, and he didn't seem to like any that he came up with. "You don't want to know."

"I do. That's why I'm asking."

"No, you really don't."

"Did it have to do with the crank?" I asked.

He looked cornered. He wanted to run. He was being pressured from all sides, and I was one of them.

"Tell me and maybe I can help," I said.

His voice hardened. "You're going to help?"

"Maybe I can help."

"Look, you wanted to steal this show, and now it's yours. You got the money. You're sitting in the big chair. The rest, you gave to me to run for Perry just like old times. So let me handle things in my own way."

"Sure. Was Perry in on the crank deal?"

"Jesus, you're a pesky bastard."

I kept checking my watch. At eight o'clock I was going to show up at Chez Hilliker's and try not to catch a stiletto in the brainpan.

Nox walked in. "You find out what was the matter with him, boss?"

"No," I told him.

"This movie's going to make a lot of money for you."

"Is it?"

"Well, you and your family. Sure. The lady there, that's June August. She retired twenty, twenty-five years ago, one of the original scream queens. But the Blade got her to come back to do this one scene. Paid her a hundred g's for it." He saw the look on my face. "Don't worry, boss, it'll be worth it."

"It's a fucking stupid B-grade horror flick."

"Barely any overhead on these things, so all the downloads, all the rentals, all the Blu-rays and DVDs, it's all profit, you know?"

I noticed six guys coming in and raiding the food. Like thugs, actors seemed to look a lot like each other. They had similar builds, projected the same confidence, appeared equally blasé. They were cannon fodder on the screen. I wondered what that did to their sense of self-worth out in the world.

Darla walked in. The six guys perked up. She exuded real eroticism, and the fact that she wasn't naked made her a mystery. They all showed interest. She spotted me and started to walk over. The guys descended on her like she was the one chick at a bad cocktail party.

Nox was actually fawning. He lumbered over, pushed his way through the guys, and smiled kindly at her. He was eager to help. "I'm sorry, I don't recognize you. Are you here for the sorority house possession scene?"

"My," Darla said. "No, I don't think so."

She ran a hand through her shag. It was hot and muggy in the studio thanks to the rain and the intense lighting. She put the rest of the cast to shame. She grinned in my direction and my chest loosened.

Darla glanced over at the current scene being shot. She swayed her hips and clasped my hand.

"So this is Hollywood?"

"This is Islip. But I'm guessing things are essentially the same here as there."

Her eyes were bright, enthusiastic, and a touch anxious. "And how exactly does a professional thief steal an entire horror film company?"

"More like I inherited it."

"From who?"

"My uncle and my grandfather. They've fallen on hard times and came to rely on its profit margin more and more. They let a meth dealer named Blake run it and I blackmailed Blake into sort of turning it over to me. Then I blackmailed my grandfather into letting me keep it."

"Why?"

"Because I hate the old prick."

"Ah." She glanced about. "Well. It looks very . . . profitable," she said.

"Maybe. Who knows. There's a lot of drugs around. And Blake was skimming and stealing digital masters and selling them to another company. It's kind of a big mess, but I expect it'll be a while before the roof caves in. If you wanted to pursue an acting career, this might be your way in. If you want it."

"I'm not sure that I do."

"Think about it."

She held me and kissed me. It was passionate and made me start to burn.

"You are different," she said. "Yes, you are."

"We've pretty much established that already, haven't we?"

"We have."

I pressed her back step by step into the office. A couple of secretaries or assistants or who-the-hell-knew-what-their-jobs-were-people were at a few of the desks. I liked wielding power. I liked not giving a shit if this place made millions or burned to the ground. I wasn't here to make money. I didn't like making money. If I couldn't steal it I didn't want it.

"Take an early lunch," I told them.

"We just got back from lunch."

"Take an early dinner then. Get out."

They skedaddled. I pushed Darla down into Blake's chair. My chair.

I hooked my arms beneath her knees and pulled her legs apart. She unbuttoned her blouse for my easy access. She undid my pants. I slid her panties aside and entered her. I kept my lips on hers, seeking closeness. We made an abrupt love. My resolve was focused. I hoped if things with Endicott went bad tonight she would mourn me.

Afterward I lay on top of her panting hard and drawing in her breath. I hid my face against the side of her neck, nipping, trying not to speak and ruin everything. She clasped me tightly to her. I felt strong and fast again. I wondered if I'd be strong and fast enough to stop Endicott, assuming he showed tonight. Assuming he hadn't already aced Chub. Assuming Danny hadn't already sent him after me just because I'd pissed him off last night. I was a little surprised and amazed at how many assumptions I needed to make just to get through the day.

We still didn't move. We were precariously balanced on the chair and each other. I stared into her eyes and wondered if I could love her and if she might actually want my love. She kissed my brow. Her lips worked down my face. They sought mine. She put her hands against my shoulders and pushed me off gently. I stood and we straightened our clothes.

"What aren't you telling me?" she said.

"What do you mean?" I asked.

"You're worried about something."

"I'm always worried about something. I'm a very uptight person. You haven't picked up on that yet?"

"In fact, I have. But there's something specific right now, isn't there?"

She always made me want to talk. It was a dangerous but perhaps necessary thing. I'd been bottled too long. I thought about Gramp being unable to make any contact with the outside world.

I opened the window and let the rain fill my cupped hand. I washed my face. "I've got to go see if I can find a pro hit man who kills people with a needle and stop him from murdering my former best friend Chub."

The tip of her tongue drew itself around her lips. "Say that again, slowly."

I said it again, slowly.

She frowned and sipped air in between her teeth. "A needle?"

"That's what they say."

"What kind of needle?"

"I have no idea."

"Don't." She put her arms around me. "Just . . . don't. Don't go find a man like that, don't aggravate him, don't stir up that kind of trouble."

"I have to."

"How close a friend is this Chub to you?"

"He hates my guts."

"Then what the hell, Terry!"

There was a knock at the door. Nox called, "Boss? You okay in there? The staff, they don't know whether they should leave for the day or if you're gonna clear the office soon."

"I'll be out in a minute, Nox."

"Right."

She gave an exasperated gasp that almost got me turned on again. "You have a way of discussing important matters as if they didn't matter much at all, Terrier."

"Criminals tend to do that."

"So I've noticed. I think we should talk more about this needle guy."

"He's got nothing against me," I explained. "I'm just going to ask him nicely if he'll—"

"Not kill the friend who hates you?" she said. "Do needle guys not mind talking to strangers about their . . . enterprise?"

"It'll be in a public place. A restaurant."

"A needle inserted in the spine might leave you paralyzed and lying in your soup."

I tried to picture someone using a sewing needle or an acupuncturist's pin to cripple someone else. I really hoped I could block a move like that.

"Stay with me instead," she said, stroking my face.

"I can't."

I kissed her palm. I told her I'd call her later. I walked out. Nox was eating a ham sandwich. Blake was drinking a tall glass of orange juice, still giving me looks like he had a lot on his mind and wasn't sure if he could trust me with any of it. I'd made the offer, the rest was up to him. A few of the girls were topless and sitting around relaxing between shoots, rubber wounds gaping on their chests and throats and bellies. A couple of them called me boss too. My spine felt itchy. I hit the door on the fly and walked through the rain to the Challenger.

I went and drove to the cemetery. I pocketed the Sig Sauer. I stood at my brother's grave in the storm. Someone had straightened the headstone. Someone had cleaned the graffiti off it. I imagined it might have been Dale, but maybe that was a stretch. I grasped the gun in my jacket pocket hoping it would feel right. I looked down at the muddy earth and the rage was on me. I despised my brother. I despised Lick 87. I pulled the gun and fired a bullet straight down into the ground. I ran back to the car and ripped along the slick roads.

At seven, Haggert's Caddy was parked in front of the Fifth Amendment. Danny and Haggert were eating, drinking, and smoking together. Wes hung close at a nearby table but appeared busy with paperwork. Things seemed calm. Maybe Danny had bowed out of the meeting. Maybe I'd misinterpreted the code. I drove over to the restaurant to see whatever I could see.

It was a seafood place on the South Shore, fancy but not pure ritz. I sat in the parking lot weighing whether I should pack the Sig Sauer or leave it under the dashboard. I imagined a wild ricochet pinging some kid. My throat got thick. I left the gun in the Challenger and stepped inside Chez Hilliker's.

I was underdressed, but so was a large percentage of patrons. It looked like a lot of late season Fire Island tourists had taken the final ferry home and stopped in just to get out of the rain.

There were three exits. The front door, the back kitchen door, and another one that led to the large closed deck on the water. Some of the sections of the restaurant offered a simple escape strategy to one or two exits. Only the far back section to the right lent itself to all three. I figured Endicott would be in there.

The hostess was a buxom redhead with a gracious smile, wearing a red dress that was nearly an evening gown. Bee-stung lips and a perceptive glance. She looked up warmly and pegged me instantly as potential trouble. My poker face was for shit lately.

"I'm Daniel Thompson," I said. "Dining with Mr. Endicott."

I expected her to direct me to follow her. I planned to make an excuse that I wanted to stop at the bar first and just have her point out

Endicott's table. I wanted to circumnavigate the area and decide on the best approach.

Instead she threw me a curve. "I don't have a Mr. Thompson listed tonight. Mr. Endicott is currently waiting for a Mr. Terrier Rand to dine with."

I'd been sloppy. Danny knew I'd picked his pocket. I'd been too edgy, I'd dropped my cool. I should've kept the wallet and kept him guessing. I'd underestimated him again. It was the kind of mistake that got you killed. I had to stop making it.

He'd figured out one other thing too. He knew I'd gotten Endicott's name from Wes. There was no other way for him to add up the info.

Endicott would be watching and waiting. If he wanted me dead I'd already have a needle in my ear. So we were going to be friends, at least for a while.

I stepped away and phoned Wes.

He answered by saying, "Not the best time."

"I think Danny figured out that you gave me Endicott's name. Will that cause trouble for you?"

"The fact that Mr. Thompson's hired Endicott isn't a secret. He's proud of the fact. He spreads the news around himself. If he's got a problem with me telling you specifically, he hasn't shown it yet. He seems to be in a really good mood. "

"That's because he knows I'm here at Chez Hilliker's about to meet with Endicott."

Wes took a three count and said, very slowly, enunciating very carefully, "Why in the fuck are you doing that?"

"I'll tell you at your place later tonight."

"Unless you get a syringe of poison stabbed into your heart."

"I'm going to try to avoid it."

"Jesus Christ, get the hell out of there. Stay away from him. Run."

I disconnected and returned to the hostess, who continued to eye me like bad news. I said, "Sorry about that. A little mix-up. Alzheimer's runs in my family. I forgot who I was for a minute. I'm Terrier Rand."

"Follow me, Mr. Rand."

She led me to the back area I suspected Endicott would be seated at. Eyes averted, she found the table, laid a menu across an empty plate, tried to smile and failed, and muttered, "Enjoy."

Walton Endicott glanced up at me, smiled, and said, "Hi."

He looked like the lead in every sixties surfer movie from *The Endless Summer* on. Blond, tan, handsome, pleased, with the world in his hip pocket. He had high cheekbones and cheerful blue eyes.

He sat at the far side of a large half-moon table with his back to the wall, facing a large window that offered a view of the deck and the bay beyond, eating filet mignon loudly, rapturously.

It was hard to get a read on his height since he was sitting, but I could tell he was lean, tall, trim, fit, maybe six feet one. He wore a charcoal suit, gray shirt, and bright yellow power tie. I checked for a tiepin, thinking maybe that was his needle, but there wasn't one. The wrists that broke from his cuffs were abnormally thick, knotted with veins.

I didn't see any hardware on him. His jacket was open. He didn't wear a holster on his belt or his shoulder. There were no blade sheaths anywhere on his person. My gaze skittered over him.

He looked me up and down and took me in entirely. He said, "Please, join me, grab a seat." There was a hint of laughter in his voice, but no derision. It was genuine amusement, interest. He took a sip of red wine. He glanced back down at his meal and took another bite with the same eagerness and enjoyment.

Endicott continued with his meal even as my shadow fell across him. He swallowed, hummed enthusiastically, laid his silverware in an X across his plate, and looked up again.

I stood before him and said, "You know who I am."

"Yes, I do," he said. "I know who you are and just why you're here, Mr. Rand. And you know my name as well. Please, sit. Relax."

I sat. I didn't relax.

"Would you like something to drink? Or may I order you some dinner? The late menu is first-rate. Don't be shy. For a restaurant known for its seafood their steaks are out of sight."

So much for introductions. "No, thank you," I said.

"Do you mind if I finish while we talk?"

"Not at all."

"I appreciate that."

A young and oblivious waitress came to take my order. I declined. Endicott asked for a second bottle of wine. She brought it and poured a small amount into a clean glass. He tasted it, grinned, and found it acceptable. He thanked her and kept on with his meal.

I used the time to study him more carefully. He either shaved very closely, perhaps twice a day, or he could only grow peach fuzz and rarely had to shave at all. His cheeks, chin, and upper lip were smooth, unlined without stubble.

He'd never been a brawler. His face and hands were unscarred and unmarked, nails perfectly manicured.

When he finished his food he wiped his mouth with the linen napkin, pushed his plate away from him with both hands, and sighed contentedly. He appraised me and smiled beatifically.

"That was perfect," he said.

Endicott laid his left hand on the table, palm up. It was a gesture with a touch of romance to it. It's what you did when you reached over on a date in an effort to hold hands with your girl. It's what I'd done when asking Kimmy to marry me. He waited. I thought, Holy shit. I still didn't want to make him mad. I also didn't want to give him any peculiar ideas. He waited. He didn't insist but we apparently weren't going to get anywhere unless I placed my hand in his. I wondered if this was the beginning of the thing that hit the switch.

I cocked my head and met his intense gaze and tried to prepare for the worst, even though there wasn't much I could do. I reached forward and took his hand.

There was nothing homoerotic about it. Or maybe there was. He was a pretty man. I wondered if he was purposefully trying to unsettle me, if this was a tactic he used on his hits. But his touch was warm, gentle, accessible. Nothing sexual or particularly sensual about it. It was simply the touch of a friend showing concern.

He beamed like a child.

"You've come to argue on your friend's behalf," he said. "That's admirable. Really. You don't see that much. You've got guts. You're loyal. There's a great deal of value in that." He searched my eyes. "But you've got to realize there's no point in it. It's already done. You can't do a damn thing about it. Like everybody, Chub Wright made his own choices. He called the tune, he brought the consequences to his own door. We're all in charge of our own fate. He and his colleagues adopted this one for themselves. We can't deny them that."

"Deny them?"

"That's right. We can't deny them. It wouldn't be fair. It wouldn't be just. And I believe in justice, Mr. Rand. It's the only abstraction I do believe in."

"You're hunting him because you were paid to do it. Not because you believe it's justified."

He tightened his grip somewhat. There was a fire and a violence to it, a strength and passion, like he really cared what I thought. As though making contact with me, physically and emotionally, mattered greatly to him. "Wrong. In this case, I was paid but I do believe that he took his course in order to meet me."

"Meet you?"

"That's right. Otherwise, why would I be here? I'd be looking for someone else."

I had nothing to say to that and so we sat there, clenching hands, feeling the depths of our own beliefs. His eyes were still gleeful, but they blazed.

"I took a contract and can't break it. This is what I do. This is all I do. I find virtue and worth in it."

I watched his other hand. It didn't stray toward any of his pockets. If it did, I wondered if I'd have the time and fortitude to grab his steak knife and stuff it between his ribs.

"Chub is only an addendum to the contract," I said. "I'm guessing you were hired to chase down the crew who knocked over the bank and killed the guards. Chub didn't. He made bad choices, but he wasn't there."

"How do you know?"

"I know him. He helps plan. He sells cars. He doesn't go on the jobs. The choices made on that day had nothing to do with him."

"He helped to found those decisions," Endicott said. "He offered advice, guidance, direction, and aid. More practically, he has as much to lose as any of the members of this particular crew. He has as much to gain in turning over evidence if the FBI capture him. He is equally guilty. My employer and many others will be betrayed and proffered for leniency. More and more men will be drawn into this fiasco. I'm stanching the flow of blood. I'm saving lives. Can you see that? Do you understand that, Terrier? Pardon me. May I call you Terrier?"

He still held my hand firmly in the center of the table. I supposed we were well beyond the point of using first names. But he waited for me to respond. His handsome face was filled with the question.

"Sure," I said.

"Thank you. And I am Walton."

"All right, Walton."

The rain whipped against the glass like it wanted at us. Endicott took his time formulating his next thought. It clearly meant a great deal to him. He looked at me deeply. A lot of people had gone deep within me, seeking out answers, responses, truth, love, even hate. But nobody had gone quite as deep as this, in this way.

Number eight. The expression on the face of the beautiful man who is holding your hand.

"Do you know what the downfall of society is due to primarily, Terrier?"

It seemed a big jump from what we'd been talking about, but maybe my perspective was skewed. Endicott tightened his grip just a hint. Twenty minutes ago I would've laughed at the question. But twenty minutes ago wasn't now.

I took the question seriously. I set my soul against it.

"The dissolution of the nuclear family?" I said.

His eyes flared with joy. "Oh, very good. That's most certainly a part of it. I'm glad you took the question seriously. Some men I talk to, they don't think it's worth answering. But you, you had, in fact, an answer already prepared, because you dwell on these types of matters too. Because these issues, they have significance. They're not merely rhetoric. They hold weight for us and have meaning. These beliefs give us purpose."

My family included killers of children and women. Our dissolution had begun long before I was born.

"We're getting off point."

"No, Terrier, we're not," he said, and finally he released my hand. I'd been so overtaken by his odd vehemence that I was almost upset when he broke contact. I drew my hand back and rubbed it. The waitress appeared again. Endicott ordered tiramisu for dessert and asked if I wanted anything. She mentioned the cheesecake was yummy. I shook my head.

Endicott flashed teeth too perfect to be real. They didn't look like crowns or bridges, but a full set of dentures. I suspected he changed his teeth as a way of accessorizing. Not only couldn't he be identified by them, but certain teeth might be better in certain social settings. The beach barbecue teeth. The Lincoln Center teeth. The dinner at Chez Hilliker's teeth.

"The degeneration of our society is due primarily to our willingness to accept failure. It's the lowered quality of our work that leads to the lower quality of life. It induces the collapse of personal dignity. Without personal pride and confidence in our capabilities we have little to offer the rest of the world. We have to find grace and nobility in ourselves first, you see? And not for ourselves but for those we love. For those we honor. For those we respect. We care about what we do because we care for them. So far as I'm concerned, this is capacity. This is dignity. This, everything I've just said, is real love."

"You're already quite aware of your own capabilities. You know—"

"Walton."

"You know that you do *distinguished* work, Walton. Passing one target by shouldn't shake your or anybody else's faith in you."

"That's accurate, Terrier, in a manner of speaking. But we always know when we are shirking our responsibilities, don't we? We know when we're failing ourselves and those we love. It shakes us. It makes us guilty. It corrupts us. We understand when we're not serving our own cause. These failures, we can't allow them. They only serve to haunt us. They destroy us in the end."

He was telling his truth as he saw it, but I vibed he was shaping his responses to get the greatest emotional acknowledgment from me. He was intelligent and perceptive. He had incredible acumen, but he didn't even need it in this case.

"What if I could get the contract lifted?" I asked.

He smiled affably and laughed some more. It was a contagious laugh. In other circumstances, it would make me want to laugh too. "That's not something that often happens in this business. My services have been paid for up front. And I'm sure you'll understand when I say I don't give refunds."

I tried to return the smile. "But if I could get it lifted on Chub Wright would you feel compelled to continue on and kill him just to accommodate your pride?"

"Maybe you've missed my point, Terrier. My pride isn't what drives me. Money doesn't either. I do what I do because fate chose me specifically to do it. I love what I do." He leaned forward, his lips moist, his beauty radiant. "I love. Oh God, how I love."

I realized then what I had known from the beginning. I wasn't going to be able to stop him. I could plead as much as I wanted, and hold hands with him, and stare into his golden glowing magnificence and false teeth, and in the end he'd continue forward like the driven killer he was. There was no help for it. I couldn't stop his needle, wherever it was, whatever it was. His love was stronger than mine.

"Do you know where your friend is currently hiding?" he asked.

"No."

"Do you have any information on where I can find the killing crew?"

"No."

He appraised me again. He overlooked my defects. He found some worth in whatever was left. "I believe you, Terrier."

He reached into his pocket and I held my breath, already too late if he was going for a gun or blade or stickpin. Then he slid a business card across the table to me. It was blank except for a phone number.

"I've truly enjoyed our talk," he said. "And I do hope you don't hold it against me when I kill your friend. Perhaps we'll meet again soon under more pleasant circumstances. Please call me whenever you like. I think I would enjoy spending more time with you."

I felt the devil.

The storm roared on. The bay crested the ca-
nals. I had trouble seeing and crawled through flooded roads and
highways. Headlights splintered in the burning white raindrops. I
kept looking at the hand that Endicott had held as if it had betrayed
me. I rubbed my fingers as if my circulation had gone bad.

Washed-out cars lined the Sagtikos Parkway down to the South-
ern State as I headed to Wes's place. I jockeyed around them like they
were traffic cones without slowing. The Challenger handled the desperate conditions perfectly. I kept pushing the pedal. Small whitecaps
crossed three lanes and washed into the woods bordering the parkway. The wind reared. I turned the radio on and spun the volume
until the speakers were pulsing.

I pulled up outside of Wes's house as the storm reached its peak.
The rain slammed down so hard that there was no way to even reach
his front door. The waves burst over the pylons and swept across his
lawn.

I made a dash for his door. The water was mid-calf deep. We
could've talked on the phone but I felt the need to speak to him directly when discussing Walton Endicott. I slid on the walk and nearly
went down. There was a very good chance that if I fell I'd skid right
into the bay.

Em opened the front door as I hit the first stair of the stoop. She
asked, "Are you all right, Terry?"

"Yeah."

"Who were you talking to?"

"I wasn't talking to anybody."

"I thought I heard your voice."

"How could you hear anything over this storm?" I asked.

"You were really loud."

"It was the wind. Or that creaking dock. It sounds like a crying woman."

"No, it was you—"

I was dripping on the floor. Wes stepped out of the bathroom with three fluffy fancy guest towels. I knew I was breaking social convention again. You never use the nice fluffy fancy guest towels. My mother would have a fit if any of us ever tried. I was hesitant to take them at first as Wes thrust them at me. They were pink. I did my best to wipe myself down.

He said, "You look half-past dead. You starting to pick up on the fact that you're taking too many risks?"

"What else am I going to do? Work on my stamp collection?"

Em asked, "Coffee or hot chocolate?"

"Hot chocolate, baby," Wes answered.

"Mini marshmallows?"

Wes looked at her like it was an insane question. "Of course."

I folded one of the towels up and laid it on the leather couch and sat on it so I wouldn't ruin the furniture. Wes sat across from me. I realized just how much I'd come to rely on him for friendship, guidance, advice, loyalty, all the things that he was supposed to be giving the Thompson syndicate boss.

"I met Endicott," I told him.

Wes flung his arms up. "Jesus, I told you to stay away from that psycho. You met him? Really met him, face-to-face? Or met him, like you crept around behind him from a very safe distance?"

"We sat together at Hilliker's. He held my hand."

"Held your . . . ? What do you mean?"

"I mean he held my hand."

Wes couldn't get his head around it. "Like . . . like . . ."

"Yeah."

"Like couples do? Romantic couples do?"

"Yeah."

"Wait." Wes made a stop motion. "He held your hand in the restaurant?"

"Yeah."

Wes drew his chin in. He looked over his shoulder for Em so he could share his disbelief, but she wasn't there. "Why the fuck did he hold your hand?"

"I don't really know. I think he likes me."

"He likes you?"

"I think so."

"He's a mechanic. A total machine. He doesn't like anybody."

"And you were wrong. He talks. He talks plenty."

"You talked to him and held his hand?"

"I didn't think I had much choice in the matter."

"Fuck no, you didn't, not if it's what he wanted. Why did you go after him? I told you to let it go."

"I couldn't. Kimmy asked me to save Chub. I promised her I would. I promised her."

"You shouldn't have," Wes said.

Em entered with the cocoa and a dish of cookies on a tray. She put it down in front of me. She sat beside me and handed me a cup and helped me to raise it to my mouth to take a sip. I hadn't realized I was trembling so badly from the cold.

I leaned forward over the table in case I spilled. She took one of the towels and dried my hair with it. Then she combed through my curls with her fingernails to make me presentable again.

She put a hand to my back and rubbed in semicircles, shushing me gently. "It's okay, Terry. It's all right. You're fine now."

I sipped and began to loosen.

"You're safe now," she said.

"I know."

"He put the shits up you," Wes said.

"I guess he did," I admitted. "Not so much at the time, at the table, but the more I think of the guy, the more weirded out I feel."

"You've never met anyone like that before. A real iceman."

I shook my head. "It wasn't that. Well, maybe it was that, but it was more. It's how accessible he was. Just sitting there having dinner. Unimposing. More than that. He–"

"What?"

"He makes you want to like him."

"That's bad, Terry. That's really bad."

"I know."

"But you knew," Em said. "You knew all the while he could kill you whenever he wanted. And there was nothing you could do about it."

"Yes."

I drank my cocoa. There were a ton of tiny marshmallows. She'd overloaded the cup the way my mother used to when I was a kid.

"And what did he say when you asked him not to kill Chub?" Wes asked.

"We discussed the downfall of society."

"Uh-huh," Wes said. "That's what you talked about?"

"Among other things."

"You'd rather take fifty goombahs on than a nut like that."

"You're right," I admitted.

"How did it leave off?"

"He gave me his phone number. He asked me to call him any-time. He hopes we meet again under more pleasant circumstances."

It got a bark of incredulous laughter from Wes. "Like what? Going to the fucking circus? Taking a Caribbean cruise? You guys going to take in a ball game? For the love of Christ stay away from him."

"I intend to."

Wes went to the kitchen, came back with a bottle of Dewar's, and poured a little into both of our cups.

"He's not the only hitter out there, Terry. It's getting sort of crazy. The feds are flipping out chasing their own tails, all the snitches are ratting each other out hoping to turn up something on the crew, and the cops are running everybody ragged."

"Anybody got anything on them yet?"

"Feds got their names. It was only a matter of time before the dead driver led the feebs back to accomplices."

It was bound to happen. "Do you remember what they are?"

"I didn't recognize any of them. Driver was McCann. The three others were . . . Dunbar, Edwardson, and Wagstaff. No records. They're old school, been off the grid their whole careers."

"Off the grid and out of prison. They've never been nabbed."

"No. They're that good. Like you."

"Not like me."

I'd spent overnight in lockup. I'd been fingerprinted. I had a jacket. These guys, though, they were ghosts.

"Do the feebs know Chub was involved in any way?"

"Not that I've heard. But who knows with those tricky sons-abitches?"

"Right."

We stared at each other and I could almost hear him saying what he'd told me the other day, that if I just let things go their natural way Kimmy could be mine again. It was my worst secret thought that wasn't a secret at all. The underneath wanted to draw me down to that dark happiness, and I didn't even have to do anything but stop fighting and just go with it. I could lie back and achieve my own awful ends.

I looked around at the framed photos propped on the tables and hanging on the walls. Em continued to rub my back with careless strokes. I spotted Wes and Em together in various poses, in gardens, standing before ruins, on beaches. They'd done a lot in the last two months, gone to a lot of different places. They had a habit of making funny faces at the camera. Em grinning a touch wackily, or her lips pursed, kissy kissy, tilting her head. Wes wearing shades in a lot of the pictures, guffawing. It was a touch too cute, but they had a right to be annoyingly adorable. As much of a right as anybody.

I said, "I've been so wrapped up in my own action I never asked how the two of you met."

Em checked Wes, a little bemused, silently asking permission to tell the tale. Her hand withdrew and she reached for her cigarettes. She snatched one from the pack but didn't light it. I thought she must do it out of habit, the same as Haggert with his cigar. Wes appeared uncomfortable. Em turned to me. She found a wild curl on my head and flipped it back into place with her fingers. "They sent him to break my legs."

"Not exactly," Wes said. "More like fracture. Hairline fracture."

"Can you believe it?" she asked. "A thug like him? Beating up a sweet little thing like me?"

"I'm an imposing figure," Wes said. "Not a thug. Not anymore. I've been promoted. Besides, I wouldn't have actually had to smack you around much. That's the whole point of sending someone like me in the first place." He sipped and added more whiskey. He met my eyes. "She has a bit of a gambling problem."

"I'm a junkie," she said. There was no shame in her voice. "Used to work as a dealer on the gambling boat off Orient Point. They'd sail into international waters and we'd do sixteen-hour tours at a time."

"And the Thompson family takes its slice," I said.

The cigarette Em hadn't lit hissed. The tip was ember red. I looked more closely. It wasn't a cigarette at all. It was one of those fake mechanical smokes where the tip lights up and it makes a sound just like you were taking in a draw. It even released a puff of white vapor that had a flavored smell to it. This one was minty.

"You ever go on one, Terry? A gambling cruise?"

"No," I said. "My uncles used to hit them on occasion and pick up some pocket change. But being trapped out at sea scared them too much to make any big plays."

"Big Dan practically started that run," Wes said.

"And you were skimming, Em?" I asked.

She held her fingers up about a half inch apart. "Just a pinch." Her smile dropped. She sucked at the faux cigarette again, and the thing hissed, the smoke poofed. "At first. Then a bit more. And a little more. I couldn't stop. And it wasn't just about the money."

"It was the excitement of getting away with it."

"Yes. I'm in recovery now, but–" With a wag her golden tousled hair swayed and framed her face. "You know all about that."

"I don't get too excited about stealing. Not like it's fun. It's just what I do. But if I don't do it for a while I feel an edge coming on."

"You don't get juiced?" she asked. "Not even a little?"

"Maybe a little," I said.

"Well, that's all it takes for some of us." Her eyes swirled with need. Just talking about it was getting her back in the mood for risk, for the bad dare. "For me it's all about pushing the limit. My limit, their limit, any limit. I nudge and prod, and I keep right on pushing until I crash. There's no other way for it to end. I'm hardwired to it, even in small ways. Like . . . I hardly ever fill the car with gas. I love watching the needle pointing toward E. I get a buzz when the 'low fuel' gauge light goes on. Because it's then that I realize *I'm there,* pressing my luck. Every gas station I pass I think, Can I make it just another half mile farther down the road? Can I win this game? I think–"

"Talk about it in group, Em," Wes said. "That's where you're supposed to go over it all. Not here at home. That's borderline obsessive. You've got to retrain your brain."

I looked at him. Retrain your brain. He had the therapy talk down. He sat in with her at Gamblers Anonymous or couples shrink sessions or wherever it was she was in rehab. It wasn't just about playing house. He'd made an impressive commitment to her.

"So you didn't break her legs," I said. "Instead, you covered her losses."

"Yeah. Sixty large."

The number made Em wince. I didn't blame her. It was a lot of cash to steal from the mob. But it proved she was a damn good card sharp to get away with ripping off that kind of money for so long. I figured she must've had a partner somewhere along the way who helped her. Another dealer or a shill out front at the tables.

"Don't you think he knew you'd do that?" I asked.

Wes didn't have any idea what I was talking about. "What do you mean?"

"Don't you think Danny knew from the start that you'd never hurt a woman? He's got fifty legbreakers for that purpose alone. He could've sent any one of them instead if he just wanted to kneecap her. But he knew you'd cover the debt. It was all about getting his money back. He'd just as soon get it from you as anyone."

"Mr. Thompson wouldn't do that to me."

"Would Haggert?"

Wes's features went stony, and the flush returned to his cheeks. It wasn't a pink glow this time, but a serious mean heat. He shot a hard glance at Em and she shrugged.

"He was making a point," I added.

"What point?"

"That you weren't the best right-hand man anymore in his new reorganization of the business. It was the start of him pushing you out."

Wes raised his chin and stared straight ahead. He said, "Huh." He couldn't be too pissed that he'd been given the job that had brought him together with his true love. But it had finally dawned on him just how far he'd been eased out of the mob that had been his home since he was sixteen years old. And he'd been taken for a chump while it was happening. He let out a flat humorless laugh. Way down at the bottom of that laugh I could hear real indignation. "Huh. Those pricks."

Em stood and moved to his side, slid against him and kissed his throat. He kept staring straight ahead, seeing and not seeing.

"It doesn't matter," she whispered to him. "It brought us together. That's the important thing."

"It is," he agreed.

"It's all for the best. You want out."

"I do," he said, but he didn't sound convinced.

"Maybe this just proves that they're letting you out. That they're letting you go."

"Maybe," he said.

I got to my feet. I'd botched another chance at being a part of a normal social setting. I'd hurt my friend. Em was holding his free hand. In the other he held the Dewar's now. He drank from the bottle. I wanted to tell Wes not to confront Danny and Haggert, that there wasn't any percentage in it. I wanted to say sorry for ruining their night. I wanted to tell him and Em that I'd make it up to them somehow. It was a lie but I was a liar. I wanted to thank them for a lovely evening the way normal folks would. I imagined myself holding a Bundt cake and a bag of exotic dry roast coffee. I thought I'd easily give sixty grand to have the love of my life in my arms.

It took over an hour to get across town. Most of the traffic lights were out or blinking yellow. Emergency crews were set up in camps on roadsides, waiting until the winds died down before climbing up into the tree line. I kept the pedal down halfway, gliding like a street shark through the dark waters, knowing that if any car could make it through the storm it would be one that Chub had worked on.

I pulled into our driveway and noticed a couple of toppled trees at the edge of the woods. I'd have to clear them out early before my father got it in his mind to do the same. I didn't want him anywhere near that brush.

I walked through the house checking on everyone. My father was in bed asleep next to my mother. I was glad for it. I wanted him home and safe. I wanted us all together. Dale had fallen asleep reading *Tiny Alice*. I liked the work of Albee but didn't particularly understand that play either. She had a penchant for esoterica. I wondered how that would affect her career, if she ever managed to carve one out for herself.

I sat in front of my laptop and checked out the *ROGUES* site. There were no new videos of Dale running wild with the punks. I watched them piss on my brother's grave again. I hit replay. The rage rose, passed through me, and hung in the night. I fell into bed and dreamed a black dream of my brother's victims. I saw topless women running from the Blade. I woke covered in a chill sweat and the sun drying my brow.

It was after six. That was late for me.

I drove to Darla's. As I moved up the stairs to her apartment, my hand skimming the handrail, I spotted something down on the street that pushed a button. I didn't know what it was, but I flattened myself against the stairwell wall.

I eased back down to the ground floor and scanned the area again. I felt the same pressure of memory but nothing more came into focus. I didn't see anyone. I moved back up the stairs and knocked on her door.

The television was on low, but it seemed to be a horror movie, with screams. There was a scuffling of activity within. I heard Darla murmur. It sounded pained. I tried the door and it was locked. It would take me twenty seconds to pop the lock. I took a step back, set myself, and kicked the door in.

Darla was slipping into her robe, tying the belt loosely around her waist, one breast out.

She stared at me and said, "What's the matter? Are you all right?"

I took a quick inventory. Her hair was a mess. I had to remind myself it was early. The breast was beautiful but slightly reddened and marked, as if pawed at, pinched. I hadn't done that. But her concern was genuine.

"Are you?" I asked.

The Blade was naked in her bed. He used the interruption to take a hit off a line of crystal stretched out on a coffee table book about the history of European castles. Dressed only in a pair of black boxers Nox sat in a nearby chair drinking a caffe latte, one foot in a little basket where he was kneading a pile of red yarn with his toes. He appeared a little hungover and had that look about him that thieves got after a good score. He and Blake must've gotten rid of the ten pounds of meth and made a serious bundle.

I realized what had caught my attention out on the street. Blake's red Taurus was parked at the curb.

Nox said, "Hey boss."

Blake glanced around, spotted me, and hurled a hard look I

couldn't register. He pulled out his cell and began texting someone. In between responses he grabbed his pants and put them on. His eyes smoldered like the bottom of a three-day-old fire pit.

One of AHE's movies was playing in the DVD. The stink of the acidifying paper was now married to the aroma of sex and burning crank. I stared at her gorgeous breast knowing who had made those marks.

She said, "You're upset."

"Just a little surprised."

"Why?" she asked. She tried to lead me deeper into the small apartment. I held my ground at the door. I forced myself not to look over at the other two guys who'd just slept with Darla. The noises on the TV were quiet but insistent. She was beautiful and I wanted her badly. I wanted to love her badly. I knew she'd kick the two doofuses out if I wanted, but oddly enough I felt like that was some kind of cheat. I didn't want to cheat. It might've been the first time in my life I didn't want to cheat at something.

"Listen—"

"Would you rather I was picking up strangers in the Elbow Room?"

"No. Yes. Maybe. But—"

Darla covered her exposed breast. She looked up at me with her eyes dark and hurt. "You just wanted me to be here for you whenever you wanted me. And I am here for you. But I have a life too. And interests and fascinations and inclinations. I thought you understood that. I thought that's why we got along so well. It's why I decided to take a couple of minor roles for upcoming films at All Hallows' Eve."

"Hey, boss, you ain't mad, are you?" Nox said.

"No."

"You sound mad."

"I'm not."

"You kinda sound it."

Blake continued texting. He snorted another bump of meth. His pipe was lying on the nightstand, along with a lighter. His makeup had been worn off and his black eye was ugly and swollen and the split lip had become worse.

"It's all right, Terry," Darla said. "It's okay." My breathing hitched hard. I'd delivered her into their hands. I'd probably done it out of fear of intimacy and to keep a dying dream alive. I wasn't sure. I thought of Scooter stumbling her way through the children's section of Darla's store. I imagined her picking out books and holding them up to me, calling, *"Da."*

Nox asked, "You want a hit of this?" I turned for the door, aware that I was the clever architect of my own ruin.

I took a step and Nox screamed, "Hey!" and Darla shouted, "No!" and Blake let out a yawp of viciousness and was on me with a four-inch hooked knife.

The curve of the knife missed me by a full inch as it whistled past. Blake tried to take another swipe, drawing the blade back in reverse, but I blocked his wrist with my forearm, ducked, and gave him a left-handed jab to the mouth, same as the other guy who had beat him up. He let out a startled sound but he was too high to really notice. Nox was still tweaking too, and got up to either join in or help me, but his foot was stuck in a bunch of yarn and he tripped over himself.

Darla shouted, "Erik, no! Stop! What are you doing?"

What he was doing was stabbing up at me with an underhand thrust. He was pretty good with the knife, either because he practiced and tried to live up to his "Blade" nickname, or just because the meth was giving him a surge of lunatic strength and speed. He still wasn't talking, which was irritating as hell. Usually people who were trying to kill you liked to explain why they were doing it.

"What's this about, Blade?" I asked.

"You should've stayed away. I warned you."

"No, you didn't."

He kept lunging. I kept diverting his attack and punching him in the face. His nose and mouth were bleeding. A mouse had formed under the non-black eye. It was going to be a nice shiner, much better than the other.

"I told you!"

"No, you didn't."

The knife flashed again and I backed up and while I was pulling away he dropped his shoulders and bulled into me. I went over a stack of books and the two of us rolled out the door. We hit the far side of the small vestibule at the top of the steps hard enough to rattle my teeth and make the back of my skull sing. Darla tried to follow us out but there wasn't enough room. Our gazes met.

She said, "Kill him if you have to, Terry."

It was nice that she supported me anyway, but I really wished all these people would quit telling me to murder others on a whim. I didn't need to ice this mook to stop him.

As I was thinking that he punched me square in the bad ribs and the pain ignited my head and made me cry out and I threw a wild punch that carried me over his shoulder and knocked the two of us down the flight of stairs together.

We tumbled and bounced into the walls and railing, flipping over each other. The best thing for me would've been to try to get on top of him and ride him down like a surfboard. But I really didn't want to kill him. I made an effort to control our plunge, shifting so that we each took about half the brunt of the fall. I had him in a headlock and my shoulder cushioned his neck. I reached for the railing with my other hand but couldn't get a grip as we zigged and zagged. Finally we came to a stop at the front entrance to the shop and my fist closed around the railing in time to keep us from both going headfirst out the glass security door.

The back of Blake's head bled across the foyer floor and I was beside him with my shoulder wedged into the corner, my arm still around him like I was looking for a cuddle. My hand was smeared with his blood. His eyes slowly spun toward a stop. Darla appeared above us.

"Are you all right?" she asked me.

"I'll let you know."

"Erik? Erik?"

"Yes, Darla," he said.

"What in the fuck is wrong with you?"

"I hurt my head."

"I mean, why did you attack Terrier with a knife?"

"I can't tell you that."

I got to my feet and my knees were shaky. My ribs screamed and I let out a groan and Darla said, "Your ribs?"

"Yeah."

"I have more Percocet."

"Get them."

"Come upstairs with me."

"Not right now."

"Will you be okay?"

"We'll be fine."

She turned and climbed the stairs two at a time. Blake looked at me and said, "I hurt my head."

"You came at me with a hooked blade. You're lucky I don't beat your brains out against that bottom stair."

I grabbed his knife and stuck it in my back pocket. He held his hand up like a child who wants Dad to give him a piggyback ride. I took his hand and helped him to his feet. The top of his scalp had been split open and blood ran into his hair and poured down his back and leaked out down his face. Nox had finally disentangled himself and came plodding down the steps. When he got in front of Blake, Blake smiled goofily and passed out in Nox's arms.

"He might need an ambulance," I said.

"It's not his head, it's the meth. He always acts like this after snorting a few lines. I mean, it takes him a while to come out of it. He gets a little crazy sometimes."

"Wonderful. Carry him upstairs and put him to bed. Get some ice on his crown, patch him up a little, try to keep him awake. He might have a concussion."

Nox checked the wound. He seemed to have a lot of experience with wounds of all kinds. "Nah, he'll be fine."

Nox carried the deadweight of Blake easily up the stairwell. I followed them back to Darla's apartment and watched him lay Blake down in her bed. She stood there with the bottle of Percocet and a glass of water. She handed me the pills and I drank the glass down.

"Why are you taking so many Percs?" I asked.

"I use them for sleeping pills. They relax me."

I nodded. We stood as if to embrace but neither of us made the next move. Neither of us would ever make the next move again.

I turned and Nox was getting ice cubes out of the freezer tray. He dumped them into a kitchen towel and put it to the back of Blake's head. Blake's eyes opened at the sting and he said, "Sorry," to nobody in particular and then shut his eyes again.

"What's it all about, Nox?" I asked.

"I don't know."

I checked Blake's pocket and got out his phone. "He cleared the number of whoever he was texting with."

"Maybe Sal's pissed."

That got me focused. "Sal Domingo? Guy who runs Fireshot?"

"Yeah."

"Why would he be pissed? Didn't you sell the stolen films to him?"

"Yeah."

"Then he made extra money with no investment, he ought to be happy, right?"

"Yeah."

"What happened to the drugs, Nox?"

"We sold them too."

"Okay. To who?"

He shrugged. "I don't know. The Blade runs all of that side of the thing."

"How much did you make?"

"Our cut was almost three grand."

That shocked me. "That's all? I thought you guys were running that operation?"

"No way, we're just middlemen. Bottom middlemen, boss. We just watched over the crank while it was stashed at AHE."

"Stashed by who?"

He gestured at Blake. "He doesn't tell me much."

"Christ."

I ran through it a few times. Everyone should be happy. Old Crowe got his leverage back, and most of his money. Blake was still running things at the company. Sal Domingo had a few extra horror movies to distribute. The meth manufacturers were doing their thing and making a big profit off these lunkheads. It worked out across the board.

"Oh," I said.

"What's that, boss?"

"Nothing. I made a mistake along the way."

"What mistake?"

I took one last look around and moved to the door. I brushed past Darla and she put a hand out but the hand didn't touch me and I didn't reach back. Maybe I was a hypocrite and maybe I was just following her advice about not falling in love. She gave a sad smile and I returned it, and then I went and met the rain.

Part IV

A DUSTIING
OF SNOW

I could've knocked. I could've rung the bell. But my mother was right: I was absolutely the kind of person who wanted to start up dramatics.

It took a long eight minutes to circumvent the security and get in through the back door. The overhang kept the rain off me. No one walked past. I didn't have to worry about servants because there weren't any anymore. Those days were gone.

I stepped inside. I felt as uncomfortable as the last time. I had exactly the same sense of exile as before.

I found him in the den again, this time seated at the huge maple desk, lost in thought. The weak glow of gray sunlight slipping in through the windows slid across the dark cherry paneling, draining color wherever it touched.

I entered his field of vision. He looked up.

He motioned to the portable bar and the top shelf liquor. "Drink?" he asked.

"It's not even eight in the morning."

"Can you pour me a bourbon?"

I poured the bourbon. "Ice or water?"

"Both," he said.

I mixed in both, returned to where he sat, stood in front of his desk, and hurled the drink in his face.

He gasped and shot to his feet like he might take a poke at me. I came around the desk because I really wanted to see that. He thought better of it. He sat again. He pulled out a clean handkerchief and mopped his face. After he was done he looked at me and chuckled quietly.

He didn't ask what I was doing there and he didn't ask why I'd tossed the bourbon. His silence proved I was right.

Now I knew why my uncle Will hadn't wanted me to listen to old Crowe and help him out with any absurd favors.

It was Will who ran the crank trade. He stole the films and undercut All Hallows' Eve. He ripped off his own father and went into competition against him and used the money to finance his own dealings while the old man lay slowly dying.

I remembered Blake saying, *How much do you know about your people? You have any idea what you're getting into?*

And my naive retort. *I think I'll get the hang of it.*

Will and old Crowe were both scrambling to save their own careers, to gain back their fallen empires. Together they might've done it easily, but they'd had their hands in each other's pockets.

We've only recently ascertained that Blake's been liquidating assets for months, old Crowe had said. *Perhaps as much as a quarter million.*

Crowe had thought Blake was stealing his and Will's profits. But Blake and Nox were just the middlemen, the bottom middlemen on a much longer chain. Crowe was too close to see that at the other side of the chain stood his own son.

I leaned back on the corner of the desk. I stared at the brother of my mother and said, "You ordered Blake to kill me."

"I did no such thing," Will said. "I told him to scare you off."

"He tried to stab me with a hooked knife."

"He's a damn fool."

"He's your damn fool. Maybe you should've waited until he wasn't high on meth before you gave him orders to try to get rid of me."

My uncle Will looked appropriately remorseful. It didn't do anything to make me want to kick the hell out of him any less.

"I'm sorry things got out of hand. But it's only because you interfered. First, you listened to my father, although I practically begged you not to. Then you inserted yourself into our business. And then you tried to take over."

"It was a lark."

"You should've known better."

"Maybe I should have," I admitted.

The seven Emmys shined. The celebrity faces in the photos shaking Will's hand attested to the kind of strata he'd reached, the kind of sphere he'd once moved in. Lost pride and the past made men do incredibly stupid things. It made them gamble with their lives. It twisted and hardened and turned them into shadows of their former selves.

"Blake wasn't skimming at all," I said. "You just made it seem that way. You were robbing AHE, stealing profits from your own old man, and using them to finance your own little drug trade."

"Not enormous, but hardly little. It's just business. Like any business."

"It's eight to ten in Sing. It's a bitch move, is what it is, fucking your family like that. Perry was so worried about things that he asked me to kill Blake and Nox."

"He's a bloodthirsty prick."

"So are you."

My uncle came up out of his chair, his solid frame hovering over me, his fists clenched. "Maybe so, but what gives you the right to judge? You stole from us. You allowed the product to continue moving. You suggested Blake take our undistributed films and sell them to competitors. You ripped off twenty grand of my money."

"Actually, that was my fee for ripping off a hundred g's."

"Your whole life has been crooked. And you find me reprehensible?"

He stormed around me and went and poured himself that bourbon. He sat in his fancy leather chair like he was trying to calm himself with the posturing of better days. He reached for a cigar, pulled it out of its tube, but didn't light it and didn't put it in his mouth. He sat there drinking and holding his cigar, imagining past conversations when his voice shook the foundation of a city.

"Don't you get the feeling all of this is a little beneath you?" I asked.

"Of course I do. But after spending most of my life succeeding and winning accolades for my work I've been expunged. Unlike you, I wasn't born to this. I do it out of necessity. I don't have any choices left."

"It's only necessary because, like your old man, you burned all your bridges."

"I overestimated my inherent value," Will said with real emotion. "It's easy to do. You think you're irreplaceable, you believe you have friends, protégés, benefactors. But you don't. You think you can count on family. But you can't." He glared at me, driving his words home with the depth of anger in his eyes.

"And with all these profits you still haven't made a new film," I said. "You still haven't gotten back out to Hollywood. You're comfortable with churning out the cheap horror fare and turning a quick profit on the films and making the big bucks on the crank. You haven't even helped your own son with his career. "

"John doesn't need any help."

"No matter how much cash comes in off the meth, you'll still never make another movie. You were never very sophisticated to begin with, betting forty bucks on a drag race with a wallet stuffed with C-notes and your chest puffed out. You were petty and gaudy and boring. You people wouldn't let my father in the front door because you thought he was sordid and inferior. You turned your backs on my mother. You turned your backs on each other. In the end you're more conniving and corrupt than any Rand ever was."

The Crowes were bent in ways I'd never quite seen before. Or maybe it just looked that way because there wasn't any reason for it.

They weren't sick. They had plenty of assets. They were offered and afforded every chance. I thought of the dying old man upstairs who couldn't take a deep breath without hacking up clots of his black soul. I thought of the old woman who was so bored and tired that she prayed for murder and death. I thought of this house where my mother had been shamed and sent away. I'd imagined she'd made a mistake. I'd believed she would have been better off in Hollywood being wooed by her father's false friends than among the Rand clan's criminal and futile efforts.

Now all I wanted to do was thank Christ that she'd been set free from this nest of crows and snakes. I looked at Will and realized I could keep hurting him. I could follow through on the threat I'd made to Blake. I could tell Danny that he was being cheated out of his full tax. But he was my uncle, he was my family, he was my blood. It meant something. It still had to mean something. If it didn't, then I was the one who was lost, not him.

I left him there, grateful I'd been taught by other, more principled, thieves.

Dale, cousin John, and my father were having breakfast in the kitchen. John sat in Collie's chair, looking like Collie, full of Collie's gestures, while my mother cooked pancakes at the stove. She didn't turn when I entered. She was as silent and self-aware as her own mother was when cooking for us.

Despite her attitude, the mood was light. Dale and John were gabby as children. He was telling stories about TV show sets, actors he'd met, the foibles of his grandfather. Old Crowe had made some real stinkers in his day. A family film about a wrestling grizzly, a circus pony, and a deaf seeing-eye dog that go on a journey of self-discovery over the Swiss Alps before being adopted by a professional yodeler. Perry had paid over a mill for the script. It turned into one of the biggest critical bombs in decades and old Crowe paid another wad of cash to have his name taken off the credits.

Dale said, "I'm renting that tonight."

John told her, "You can't, it's never been released on video or DVD."

"You don't have a copy?"

"I might have a bootleg someplace."

My father seemed pleased by Perry's losses. He chuckled and drank green tea.

I'd never known him to drink tea. I'd never known him to drink much of anything besides beer. He was making an effort to fight off the onslaught of Alzheimer's. I should be drinking that shit myself. He glanced up at me and raised his cup in a kind of toast.

He said, "Hey, come on and sit and join us."

I did. Dale and John discussed the audition process. She wanted to know more about SAG. He name-dropped and talked about face time on screen, walk-ons, cameos, Foley gigs. I was surprised that my father showed such interest. He asked questions about stunt work. He said he once considered trying to be a stunt driver. I'd never heard such a thing before.

So Dale had broached the subject of moving to L.A. My ma put a plate of pancakes in front of me. She didn't wait for me to say thank you before she returned to the stove and started to clean. She hadn't said a word yet. The others kept conversing. I ate and watched. My mother didn't know about *ROGUES* but she could tell that Dale was hitting those seriously troublesome teen years that would mark the rest of her life. It was easy for a Rand to make major mistakes during this period. We were designed for it.

My mother put down side dishes of bacon, toast, hash browns. It was a long-standing fact that whenever she was upset she cooked and served. I couldn't shake the double image of my grandmother doing the same thing. I ate what I could.

My old man watched John jabber and nodded along with him. I wondered if my father was getting even half of whatever John was talking about. I wasn't. Dale met my eyes. They said, I spilled the beans. Thank you for helping me.

I wondered what John would think if I explained who and what the Crowes really were. He might not even be surprised. He might know a lot of it already, working with Blake. But I just couldn't see it.

There was finally a pause in the conversation. John turned to me and said, "We probably should have had that dinner. The whole family, I mean."

"Breakfast is just as good."

"Sure, but I mean, us. All of us. My dad too. He wants to see Uncle Pinscher."

"Why?"

"I don't know."

My father slurped his tea. His Adam's apple bobbed almost dramatically. His gracious grin held very little of him in it. My mother cracked eggs.

"Perry's taken a turn for the worse," John said.

"Another turn for the worse," I said. "A worse turn for the worse."

"Right. Another one. But this one was bad. Pretty bad. The docs want him in the hospital, but he's too stubborn. He wants to die at home. My dad spends all his time with him. They're working on a script together. First one they've ever collaborated on. My father thinks it's his shot back into the Hollywood elite. He was never really a superstar, but he was moderately successful, more than moderately, really, when you get down to it, and out there that counts for a lot."

"What's it about?" I asked. "The screenplay?"

"I don't know, he hasn't let me read it."

I wondered if there was one. I could see them writing together, scratching out ideas in a notebook, throwing names around, trying to regain their action and cool, while Will collected cash and crank, and sent drugs up and down the chain. Another family drama, this time about a pair of swans that lead a brother and sister into a magical land on the other side of a golf course pond. The title: *Double Birdie*.

My mother refilled everyone's glasses of juice, milk, my old man's tea. She still hadn't looked at me. She still hadn't said anything. She smiled absently, emptily. She soaked dishes and ran the scouring pad across them.

"I think I've got a place," John said. "I looked at pictures of it on the Web. Looks nice. Right on a nice stretch of Sunset. One of those old mansions that was originally owned by one of those crazy stars in the twenties. Now it's been converted into affordable housing."

"So long as it's near a college with a good night class," I put in. I sounded like my high school guidance counselor.

John said that it was. Dale said, "He showed me the area online.

It's a perfect location. And if it doesn't work out, I can always come home again, right?"

"Right."

"First thing we do," she went on, "I want to see the stupid sign. Get it out of the way at the start so I don't have to worry about it again."

"The Hollywood sign," John said. "Sure."

"You know where it is."

"Of course. Beachwood Canyon, off Franklin Ave. I had to go see the stupid thing too."

"Fancy spot?"

"Total pits, but every tourist has to do it."

I said, "Terrific meal, Ma."

I headed for the living room. JFK followed. Old Shep watched his cartoons. I had an overwhelming desire to push him in his wheelchair all over town. I probably would've at least gone around the block with him if the streets weren't still backed up.

I caught my father's silhouette framed in the morning light of the front door. The screen slammed as he went to sit on the porch. My mother was already beside me.

She laid a plate of food on the coffee table and tied a bib around Gramp's neck. I was about to open my mouth and say I'd feed Shep when she gripped my jaw firmly in her left hand. She dug her fingers into the nerve ganglia beneath my left ear. It was a nice move and hurt like hell.

"Who do you think you are practically moving your sister to Los Angeles without saying a word to me?" she whispered vehemently.

I tried to answer but she really had a hold on me. She loosened her grip enough for me to speak.

"I didn't," I said.

"Don't you lie to me, Terrier, don't you dare."

"I told her she had to stay in school until the end of the year, and she had to get your permission if she wanted to go to the West Coast."

"Oh, what a load of horseshit," she said. It stunned me. I had never heard my mother curse. She squeezed me tighter and the pain sliced up the sides of my face. "You got my lousy father to pull some strings. He offered her everything short of a seven-year studio contract. Clearly this had something to do with the score he had you pull."

"Ma—" I managed to groan.

"You think because I'm the only one in this family who's not running some kind of scam that I'm an idiot?"

"No!"

"Now you've gotten your cousin to move his entire life back there to Hollywood. He already came limping back home once, and now you're sending him out there again. We hardly know him, and here you've given him responsibility over my daughter? You think I trust him? I don't. And you shouldn't either. Not yet. You think I trust anyone when it comes to my children? My family?"

"Ma!"

She released me and I stood there massaging my cheeks. I took a breath to say something and she cut me off. "You made promises to Airedale. You paved the way and made it easy for a sixteen-year-old girl to run off to pursue some half-baked dreams."

"She's a good actress," I said. "You've seen—"

"Oh, stop!" my mother hissed. "We've seen a young girl in some high school plays. By giving her such an easy road in, you've clinched her getting her heart broken. Don't you see that? Don't you understand? If she'd fought for it, worked hard for it, step by step, she would have learned about self-confidence and conquering self-doubt. But now, you've virtually promised to make her a star. There isn't a sixteen-year-old girl alive who isn't already an ingenue. What happens if the doors start slamming in her face? Are you going to teach her how to pick herself up again?"

"I'll—"

"You don't get to make the important choices in someone else's life. Not when it comes to my daughter, Terry. You've made enough poor decisions on your own. You'd better just damn well hope she doesn't get hurt. You'd better hope John does right by her. If he doesn't, I'll settle with him, and then I'll settle with you too, my son."

With that she trumped any kind of comeback I might've been preparing. I shut up and rubbed my jaw. She sat and began to feed Gramp his breakfast while I drifted back into the kitchen.

Holy fuck, I thought.

Dale tugged at my sleeve and whispered, "We couldn't hear what she was saying, but it seemed pretty bad. She was really going at you."

"Sorry," I told her. "That didn't go as well as I'd hoped. Ma might stonewall you leaving now. I fragged the whole deal."

"Oh, she's letting me go," Dale said. "I talked it out with them both last night. I promised them the same as I promised you. That I'd finish out this year of school, get my G.E.D., and then take college night classes. John's going to help me with all of that too."

"I did the same thing my first time around L.A.," John said. "My father didn't care, of course, but I thought it was something I should do."

"I don't know why she gave you the beat-down you got," Dale said.

But my mother was right. I hadn't thought things through.

I'd entrusted my sister to a man I didn't know, maybe because I could shove him around in the way I could never settle the score with my own brother. John finished his milk and smiled at me.

My father's cup of half-finished tea sat there like a memento of my own unspoken future.

I rattled cages. I showed up at bookmaker joints, mob-owned pizza parlors, and bowling alleys where illegal gun deals were being made between games. It was a last-ditch effort and a risky move, but it was the only one I had left. I had to show myself. I had to be found out. I had to be seen by all the wrong people. Asking about Chub was just going to get all the snitches interested in me. When the feebs asked if they'd heard anything they could all say, *This guy came around asking—*

I kept pushing, working the circuit, moving from one crook to another. Nobody had anything to tell me, but they all made note of me. Some acted like it was a reunion, others glared and told me to fuck off. I got a few free slices of pizza, a couple of sure bets to put down on fixed games, and one outright death threat from a twitchy little Bolivian bastard who was trying to push through a major new coke distribution channel. He looked me up and down and said, "I keel you and drop you in the ocean I see you again."

Finally I made my way to Shelby. He was a third-rate fence I used to work with back when I was a full-time second-story man. He barely dipped his toe into stolen goods but he had a sharp eye for jewelry and easily moveable items. A quick turnover kept me that much more removed from the hot merchandise.

But more than that, he was a guy who kept his ear to the ground. He plucked information out of the air and made money off it where he could. He wasn't involved with heisters and never went in on major scores, not even to back them, but I was running out of options.

I walked into Shelby's pawnshop on 25A in Smithtown at around closing time. He had cameras in every corner and small guns stashed all over the store. He had a carry permit and wore a popgun .22 on his belt, but his arms were so gangly I couldn't imagine him actually drawing the thing if he ever got into trouble.

Shelby stood tall, six feet five, painfully thin, with a quick smile and speedy walk. He liked to rush around the aisles, different angles reminding him of different jobs around the shop. He'd zip and zag, a bottle of glass cleaner in one hand and a rag in the other. He had the neatest pawnshop I'd ever seen. Despite having no employees and a million different items on display—everything from musical instruments to high-end computers, stereo equipment, vintage wear, figurines, a wall of vinyl records—the place sparkled. You couldn't find a trace of dust anywhere. Shelby was what you might delicately call a type A personality.

He crouched in front of the cases putting out collectibles. He was humming Sinatra. He had old-school tastes, a lot like me. He caught my reflection in the clean glass, turned, saw me coming, and then looked away. I could see the sudden tension rise in his shoulders as he straighened, closed, and locked the case.

He sort of propped himself against the counter, stretched his arms along the length of the edge, his huge hands and long fingers spread like hawk's wings. He didn't smile at all. He looked scared. He watched me warily. The .22 on his belt was extremely clean and shined in its holster.

"Hey, Shel," I said.

"Terry."

So, no small talk. Right to it.

"What have you heard about Chub and the crew of bank robbers?" I asked.

"The cop killers?"

"Yeah."

"Nothing."

That stopped me. Shelby never admitted that he didn't know anything. First he'd suss out a fish, see how much the information might be worth. Then he'd keep the mark on the hook for as long as he could, see if he could find the information from another source and make some cash along the way. The thing he never did was tell someone that he didn't know anything.

"Shelby—"

"I told you, Terry, I don't know anything."

"I know what you said. But everything about how you say it makes me think I shouldn't believe you."

His jaw muscles throbbed as he gritted his teeth. He gave himself a five count before he responded. "I can't help that."

"Sure you can. Tell me the truth."

"Or what?" he asked.

"Or what?"

"Right. Or what?"

I thought about it. I didn't have a good answer. I liked Shelby. I didn't want to strong-arm him. I didn't need more heat or trouble coming down. If I went after him, I'd have to steal his digital recording equipment. Chances were that I wouldn't be tech savvy enough to delete myself off it.

"I don't know, Shel," I admitted. "How about if we don't go down that road and you just tell me what it is you so obviously know."

He dropped his right hand so that his long fingers hovered near his holster. "I'd like to see your hands, Terry."

"You'd like to see my hands?"

"Yes."

I showed him my hands.

"You're not going to give me any trouble, are you?" he asked.

"Have I ever?"

"No, but I haven't seen you in years, and the Rands . . . well, let's just say your family has picked up a lot of baggage the last little while."

"None of it's mine," I said.

"That's a matter of opinion."

"Is it?"

"Yes. A lot of talk circulates about you, Terry. About your old man. Mal's murder. Grey's grift. Collie's execution. Your pal Chub Wright. Your pal Wes Zek. You get way more attention than any criminal feels comfortable with. Nobody wants to be around you. I don't want to be around you."

"You're not, Shel."

"I am today. I am right now. You're standing right here. What comes down on you might wind up hitting me. So let's not have any misunderstanding here. I don't want whatever you're bringing to my doorstep. Life is rough enough."

I still had my hands up. I felt like a dope but I'd decided to ride the situation out.

"I haven't brought anything. I just wanted to ask what you've heard about Chub."

He took his time answering. He had something to say. He had a subject to broach. He didn't know what I might do but I wasn't giving him any trouble and that was good for a few more minutes of half-hearted trust.

"I heard you sold out Chub," Shelby said.

"What?"

"That it was you who set him up."

"Set him up?"

"Because you wanted his wife."

"Oh Christ—"

"But now that he's gone on the run you're hunting him down, trying to fix the mistake."

Danny Thompson or Haggert had spread the word. It was a good way to throw me into the deep end, get me on the feebs' radar or get me looking bad to my former colleagues and compatriot crooks while still giving me enough rope to lead them to Chub or just hang myself.

No wonder I'd had a couple of bad run-ins with guys in the bent life. They thought I wanted Chub dead and that I was hoping they'd sell him to me. They wouldn't mind turning him over to the feebs for reward cash, a free pass, or to keep from getting their teeth handed to them, but giving him up to me was just bad business.

"None of that's true, Shel."

"So you say."

"That's right, so I say."

"Nobody believes you, Terry."

"Can I put my hands down?"

"Yeah."

I did. I grabbed my cigarettes and Shel shouted, "Not in the store. Come on! What's the matter with you!"

I left the pack in my pocket. I could imagine Danny and Haggert having a laugh at my expense. It was a cheap ploy, letting me wreck myself like that, but I should've expected it. I really hated for Danny to outfox me. I wanted to lash out. All the delicate items in the shop called for me to cut loose. The underneath wanted me to panic and rage. I held back. I glared at Shelby and he unsnapped his holster.

"Don't get stupid," he said.

"Too late." I let the Sinatra tune that he'd been humming go through my mind.

I approached and he said, "Careful."

"I just want to leave you my number."

"I really don't want your number, Terry."

"I got that from the top, Shel, but take it anyway."

He didn't want to fight me badly enough on the point. He moved back out of arm's length and I found a pen and pad on his counter and wrote out my cell number.

"Okay, I'm going to be leaving now."

Shelby nodded. "I think that's a good idea."

"It won't make any difference, but if you get a chance, put it out there that I didn't rat on Chub and I'm only looking for him so I can help him."

"You're right, it won't matter," Shelby said. "You're a thief and a liar. Just like I am. Just like they all are. Let it go, Terry. If you wanted to help him it's way too late for that. He's dead. And if you actually set him up to take the fall, then don't look so grim, because your plan worked. Now go nab his old lady while you can. I got a feeling the hammer's coming down on you soon."

My mother phoned, her voice hard and brittle as shale. "How far away are you?"

"Five minutes."

"Get back here."

"What's the matter?"

"That kid Dale is dating. They're parked out in front of the house in his truck. Arguing."

"That's what teenagers do. You forgot?"

"This is different. He's shouting. Crying."

"She's probably telling him it's over."

"He's shaking her by the shoulders. He's reacting badly. If your father sees that he'll kill the boy."

"Ma—"

"If I have to go out there it's going to be bad. I'm thinking about calling the police."

"Don't call the cops. We don't call the cops."

"I know that."

"I'll take care of it."

"That's why I phoned you."

I floored it. As I pulled up in front of our house, Dale was sitting with Tony in his 4x4, parked at the curb. She spoke animatedly. She kissed him with two powerful pecks to the lips. She smiled. He didn't. Tony didn't look at me as I climbed out of the Challenger. He was crying but from what I could see he wasn't sobbing from heartbreak. He looked nervous, wild, scared.

The windows were rolled up and I couldn't make out what they were saying despite their voices being loud. A single word managed to cut through. *Ketch*. I saw a blur of motion and then a spurt of red. I heard his low, powerful voice slicing through the gray day. I ran to the truck just as Dale managed to get the door open. She fell out of the 4x4 backward as Tony stood on the gas pedal and gunned it. The tires skidded on the slick road surface, sent up a cloud of greasy smoke, and caught traction. Dale hit the front lawn on her back. The truck jumped forward and the passenger door slammed shut. I saw the red spurt of her blood running down the inside of the glass.

Dale's mouth bled. She stared up at the sky and said, "Terry?"

"I'm here."

"I don't know what happened. I told him I was leaving in a few weeks and he went crazy. He slapped me."

"He's a punk."

"It was more than that."

The gray smoke wafted over her and into my face. When it passed I picked her up and put her back on her feet. "Where's he live, Dale?"

"He has his own place."

"Where?"

"Don't kill him."

"I'm not going to kill him. Why would you think I'd kill him?"

"You've got that look."

"What look?"

"The look that says you want to kill him."

"Where's he live?"

She gave me the address. She gave me a few alternative spots where he liked to hang out. I asked about Simon Ketch. She said she still didn't know if he was a real person or not. But whoever he was, if he was anyone at all, Tony seemed scared of him.

"Was Tony one of the Rogues who pissed on Collie's grave?"

"Yes."

"He's Lick 87?"

"Yes."

"You need to stop dating assholes."

I got in the Challenger and tried his apartment first. It was a nice place in West Islip, much classier than a punk should be able to afford on his own. Simon Ketch paid well for low-end felonies. I wondered what else Tony was doing for Ketch. I let myself in. Tony had a number of roommates or maybe his place was the one where everyone else crashed. I looked around trying to get a line on the Rogues or Ketch. I didn't come up with anything.

I hit Tony's other hot spots that Dale had given me. She said that the House Blend was a bar, but I knew it was a topless place. Turned out that they served a dinner buffet right there at the edge of the stage. The girls moved languorously and tried not to step into the chicken wings. I didn't know how hungry you had to be to eat a buffet at a topless place, but the idea of it incited my gag reflex.

Tony was in the corner drinking a mug of beer and brooding. I took up perch at the bar, where I had a perfect line of sight to keep watch of him. He didn't look at the girls. He talked to himself and argued with himself. He had a loud head and the quarrel spilled outside of himself. I know what it's like. I tend to do the same thing. Every so often I could see his lips frame a curse. He hissed words, swallowed them, spit them, growled them. He never glanced toward me and even if he had he wouldn't have seen me.

He spent his money on beer and big tips for the waitresses. I spent mine on overpriced drinks for the dancers after their sets. They floated up to the bar and engaged me in trivial conversation. I tried to be polite. I did what I was supposed to do. I ogled them in their see-through gossamer robes and let them rip me off for expensive glasses of champagne that were really cheap sparkling wine. They asked if I wanted to go in the back room for a private dance. Only five bills. Visa and Mastercard accepted.

Tony kept checking his phone. He was either screening calls or receiving texts. Every time he looked at the cell he'd start talking to himself again. The guy was scared and not handling the pressure well.

After an hour I'd had one glass of seltzer and was down two hundred and fifty bucks. I hoped Tony would make a break soon. I didn't have enough cash to hang around here much longer. He had a couple of quick shots and chasers, settled his bill, finally rallied himself to his feet, and moved out the door.

In the parking lot I came up behind him at his truck, threw a cheap shot into his kidneys, and watched as he dropped to his knees and puked up the beer. It took a while. I knew how painful it could be.

When he was done he wiped his mouth, glanced up at me, and said, "Oh shit."

I said, "Take me to Ketch."

Tony swore he didn't know where Simon Ketch
lived. He said Ketch had so much money that he moved from hotel to
hotel, taking out the largest suite or sometimes an entire floor for days
or weeks on end. There were constant parties. Liquor, drugs, endless
amounts of amazing women. *ROGUES* wasn't his only Web show. He
had others, including one featuring drunk chicks on spring break
going fucking nuts. He always had the cameras rolling.

"Where is he now?" I asked.

"I'm not sure," Tony said. "The past few days he's been in the
Hilton Garden Inn out by MacArthur Airport. He's got a couple of
private planes."

"A couple of them?"

"Yeah."

"Who needs more than one private plane?"

"If you've got the money you buy shit like that, right? He's always
flying off someplace. Chicago. Los Angeles. Bermuda. Mexico. He
sometimes stays in hotels out in Islandia, Ronkonkoma, Bohemia. Or
farther east."

"Where's he been flying off to lately?"

"So far as I know, noplace. But I'm not in his inner circle."

"Who is?"

"I have no idea. Man, shit, my kidneys. That really hurt. You
didn't have to do that, Terry. I'll be pissing blood for days." He
crouched down but that would only hurt worse. I helped him to his
feet.

"How do you find out where the latest party is?"

"Leave me alone, Terry, please."

"How do you find the latest party?"

"The word gets out and somebody texts me."

"Who?"

"Somebody. Anybody. He surrounds himself with a lot of people, I told you."

I leaned back against the 4x4, lit a cigarette, and stood there smoking.

Tony asked, "We done?"

"No."

"Oh God. What else do you want?"

I finished my cigarette. Drunks moved in and out of the doors of the House Blend, laughing. Some were escorted out by the bouncers. Some were arm and arm with the girls, whom they walked to their cars and climbed in the backseat with. A few minutes later the girls returned to the joint. Everyone was lonely, everybody was out to make a buck, and everybody needed to be held and lied to for a couple of minutes.

"Why'd you hit my sister?" I asked.

In the glare of the parking lot lights I saw that Tony had enough character to look embarrassed.

"That was a mistake," he admitted.

"I know it was. Why did you hit her?"

"I was scared, man."

"Scared of what?"

"Ketch. If there's one thing you do not do, it's disappoint Simon Ketch."

I kept staring at him. I wondered if the sight of her blood would haunt him forever.

"She really liked you."

"Terry, oh man, I like her. I might even love her. I mean, I'm not like this. I don't do that. I don't hit girls. I never hit girls! Never!"

"Except you did."

The realization meant something to him. "Yeah," he grunted. "Yeah, I did. He told me to do what I could to keep her on. Ketch has a thing for her. He really digs her. She's the face of *ROGUES*. He doesn't want to lose her."

"So what?"

"What do you mean so what?"

"So you make her bleed because of him?"

"You don't understand, Terry," Tony said, his hands working uselessly in the air. "He gets what he wants. He's got serious coin. He's got people."

"People?"

"Yeah, people. Guys he hires to take care of things for him. You know what I'm talking about?"

"Strong-arms."

"Strong-arms with guns. He's got a bunch of attorneys who handle his business in court but you can bet that a lot of the charges against him don't go through because his people pay folks a visit."

I imagined a short little tough in black Armani with slicked-back hair and a smarmy smile. No wallet, just a wad of C-notes in a gold money clip with diamond initials, and he never stopped peeling bills off.

"What's he look like?"

"I don't know how to describe him."

"Try."

"He's average. I mean, you know. He sort of looks like you. He always wears a nice suit. Vintage. That's his thing. He wears a suit and a fedora. I don't know what color his hair is, or if he has any hair at all. He's always got the hat on. He's got style. Presence. What else is there to say? Are you through? I've got nothing left to say, really."

I had another question. "Is *ROGUES* real?"

"What do you mean real?"

"I mean real, Tony. Pay attention. Are you assholes really breaking into houses and filming what goes on?"

"Of course. That's the whole idea. That's what the show is. That's why it's such a hit. Didn't you know that?"

"Was it you who got Dale involved?"

He leaned over again, his kidneys aching. "I showed her some of the earliest episodes, when I first started with them last summer. She wanted to be involved. She asked me to set something up with Ketch. She wanted to be a part of a viral show. She's got big dreams. Broadway, Hollywood. She thought it would help her acting career. And it has. She's big. She's sexy, she's beautiful. People are interested."

I kept seeing the spurt of blood running down the passenger window. I kept seeing the punks in the graveyard.

"You pissed on my brother's grave."

"Look, man—"

To his credit he knew what was coming so he got the first shot in. He swung on me and brushed my chin. I dodged and he didn't want to follow up with another punch. He looked left and right wanting to run or shout for help. The lot was empty. He grunted with frustration.

He held his hands up submissively and said, "Please, Terry, I don't—"

I wanted to hurt him. I very much wanted to hurt him and make him bleed and leave a scar so that he would never forget. And then I realized he was just a stupid scared punk who let his fear and emotions run away with him. The underneath had called to him too, and I had a chance to help him from it instead of pushing him down farther beneath the waves.

I dropped my fist to my side.

I said, "Come on."

I walked him over to the Challenger and held the passenger door open for him.

"Oh man," he whimpered, "please. Don't do this."

"What's the difference? If you show up you're just joining in on the party, right?"

"You don't need me. Just go up to their biggest luxury suite. His functions are always top floor."

I didn't really want the punk along, but I also didn't want him alerting anybody that I'd be coming to cause trouble. I didn't need to fight my way through five strong-arms or have Ketch skipping out.

I drove over to the Hilton Garden Inn with Tony brooding again. He sat like a kid who hadn't gotten the right X-mas presents. You showed your true colors when you showed your face. With his face hidden on the show he whooped and laughed and tore through houses having fun, terrifying families and robbing shit right out from under their noses. Without anonymity he couldn't do anything but glare and tremble and take his beating.

We walked across the lobby of the Hilton straight for the elevators. I punched the button for the top floor.

Tony said, "What do you think this is going to accomplish?"

I had no real idea. I didn't know what I wanted to do to Simon Ketch except get him to back off of my sister. Maybe he would be reasonable, but in my experience men with money never saw reason unless you forced them to see it, up close, with their noses down in the dirt.

Ketch's men were obvious. They were thugs and looked like thugs and smiled like thugs and wore their violent tendencies and entitlement like thugs. They wandered the party, sticking their barrel chests out, occasionally chatting up the girls, drinking, even dancing. They compromised their hands, holding drinks, holding hands with the ladies, smoking cigars. That meant they weren't pros and were easily distracted.

Only one mook wore a gun so far as I could tell. The others were intent on getting drunk and laid. I looked for someone wearing a fedora. Nobody wore fedoras anymore. I checked for a vintage suit and didn't spot Ketch anywhere.

"He's not here," Tony said.

"Keep looking."

"I don't need to look anymore, he's not here. The bedroom doors are open. If he's not in the main suite and not in the bedrooms, then he's not here."

"Maybe the bathroom."

"I don't think so."

"Ask somebody."

"You ask somebody. Nobody's going to answer me that wouldn't answer you."

"Just ask."

Tony went and asked a couple of girls. He threaded his way through the throng and the atmosphere started to get good to him. He talked to people. He got himself a drink. He almost forgot I was there. I moved in closer. I gave him the dead eye. I kept him moving along. He asked the guy with the gun. The guy with the gun gave him the same dead eye as I had. They exchanged a few words. Tony slunk off.

"He said it's still too early for Simon to show up. He won't be here until later."

"Later when?"

"Later when? How the hell should I know later when? Later."

My breathing hitched and my head got a little light and my vision grew red along the edges. "Tony, I'd really consider it a personal favor if you were just a touch more helpful when I'm asking you questions. It would go a long way toward my not kicking the shit out of you."

"You already did, man."

"Not hardly."

He appeared abashed. He felt his kidney area tenderly. He thought of my sister's blood the same way I did. He licked his lips and glanced around one last time. "I'm leaving, Terry. I did everything you wanted me to do. I'll catch a ride back to the House Blend and get my car. You and Ketch . . . well, you do whatever you've got to do. Me, I'm—"

"You'll stay away from my sister," I said.

"Listen. Just tell her . . . just tell her I'm sorry. You'll never know how sorry I am that I did that. I . . . just tell her—"

"Sure," I said. "I understand. We'll call it a wash. You walk away and you stay away. Don't ever cause me or my family any more trouble, Tony. Don't ever come near us again. Or I'll bury you."

"What?"

"I'll bury you in my own brother's grave."

He believed me. And he should have.

I hung around at the party for another hour. I was used to boredom. I could case a house for days. I could hide under a bed while folks were screwing around on top of it. I had my cool when I needed it. But this kind of action wore me down. I didn't want to talk to chicks. I didn't want to constantly be needled to do some crank or blow or crushed Ritalin. The open bar kept the power drinkers happy and loud.

I asked the thug with the gun when Simon might be around.

"Later," he said.

"Can you narrow that time frame down a little?"

"No."

"How about giving me his number?"

He frowned at me. "Who the hell are you?"

"A fan."

"Then stick around and enjoy yourself. That's what Simon wants. It's still early."

I checked my watch. It wasn't even eleven yet. Maybe he'd put in an appearance for the break-of-dawn crowd.

I drove home. I scanned the yard pooling with mercurial moonlight. The trees swept toward me, bowing and gesturing in the night wind. I ate a few leftovers. I drank some of the awful green tea. I didn't know how my father did it. I thought I'd never get used to it.

I went up to my room and hadn't even crossed the threshold when I heard a creaking downstairs. It wouldn't be my silent old man coming in or going out. I thought it might be one of the crooks I'd seen today, somebody who might've decided to come brace me for asking about Chub and the crew. Someone hired by Danny. Someone who wanted to bring me hog-tied to the feebs.

The last person who'd tried to boost the Rand house had had his jugular torn out by JFK. I wondered if the little Bolivian bastard was making a play.

"Terry, I know what—!"

At the bottom of the stairway my grandfather sat in his wheelchair staring up at me. His eyes were bright, his face composed. Despite my mother's best efforts to keep him trimmed and clean and shaved his bright white hair was a bit wild, leonine. His stubble glinted in the downstairs night-light. Beside him sat JFK, who stared in puzzlement from the elderly man to me and back again.

Old Shep appeared alert and clearheaded. He watched me closely, with the smallest grimace plying his lips.

"Gramp—" I said.

His eyes met mine.

"It's not your fault. I was there. I helped, remember? I did what I had to do. You did the same. Don't let it eat away at you. I see what's been happening to you, Terrier, to you and Dale."

"Jesus, Gramp—"

"You tell her what I said, even if she doesn't believe you. You did nothing wrong helping her get out of here, no matter what your mother says. You made the right choices, you hear me?"

"Shepherd—"

I stepped off the top stair and he held his hand up, motioning for me to stay put. Whatever was going on inside his head, the fight for clarity was costing him a lot and he couldn't afford the distraction. The hand began to flutter. His eyes grew unfocused. "I helped kill my own boy. It had to be done. It had to be done. But—"

A sound escaped him halfway between a moan and a whine. JFK let loose with a similar whimper. I had once heard a horse sucked down a river bleat the same way. I could jump six steps at a time and be at Gramp's side in less than a second. I wanted to see him while he was still there. I had a million things to ask him.

"But–" he repeated. "But–"

He was stuck on the word, trying to get over the hump.

"But what?" I asked.

"But . . . *why did you bury him so close by?*"

I didn't want to dump my uncle Grey in the ocean, his feet wrapped in chains and cinder blocks, alone in the endless darkness. I couldn't chop him to pieces and scatter him across the island. I needed to keep him near. I could kill him but I couldn't abandon him. I opened my mouth to respond.

Gramp's head tilted down. His mouth went slack. JFK turned away. I rushed down the stairs but I was too late. He was gone again, imprisoned within himself. I told him thanks. I told him other things I could never say aloud to anyone else.

I pushed the wheelchair to the living room. I put in a DVD of his cartoons and poised his chair in front of the television and prayed that his mind had ebbed into the distance just enough and he wasn't still aware.

He watched the vibrant screen come alive with leaping colors.

When the DVD finished Old Shep's chin dropped to his chest like his throat had been cut. He took a deep breath and whispered, "He's out there. My son, he's crying."

As I moved through the muddy woods I heard weeping.

I broke into the small clearing where dead tree limbs and half a ton of leaves lay scattered.

My father stood in moonlight, bathed in silver, shivering in the night. His eyes, except for tears, were as empty as the darkness. He was caught in the throes of the underneath. He had forgotten where he was.

You couldn't see a hint of Grey's shallow grave. I'd covered it over well. But my father knew exactly where it was, and if he knew that, then he knew what had happened.

Dale and I had proven ourselves unstoppable creatures for hiding the truth, but my father wasn't stupid. He'd figured it out. I'd left minor clues, no doubt. I was a relentless, inflexible engine of concealing secrets, but I might have talked in my sleep. I had a death wish. I might want my father to pit himself against me. It was genetic. It went back generations. It went back a hundred thousand years.

Now I knew where my father had been spending his nights when he wasn't following me. He hadn't been out cheating on my ma. He hadn't been boosting houses or scoring antiques shops.

"Dad," I said.

I took off my coat and put it around his shoulders. He didn't resist. His face was blank. He appeared childlike and wanting. The wetness on his cheeks and chin caught the moon and turned it into drops of mother's milk. He looked like one of his figurines. Weeping boy in dark woods.

"Dad."

Number nine. The expression on the face of the shadow of your father.

Finally he fell out of his trance. An acknowledgment of anger mixed with confusion and embarrassment. It was hard to get a full read with only the moon to see by. His personality began to fill the empty vessel of himself. I watched it happening, second by second, as my father returned from the underneath to his body.

He turned away from me. He cleared his throat. He turned back and he was my old man again.

I hated him in that moment. I hated him because he knew the thing I didn't want him to know. And he had known for a while, and he had never said a word, not even to curse me. I had been oblivious.

"Tell me everything," he said.

"No."

I spun to return to the house. In an instant he was on me with those powerful arms. He pressed me backward against the trunk of a dead oak. He held me rigidly in place. "You did what you had to do," he said. "I understand that. But it's been hard. I want to hear you explain it."

"I can't." I tried to fight my way out of his grasp, but for a little guy he was much stronger than me. "I can't do that."

"You can," my old man said. "And you're going to, Terrier. You're going to tell me everything. Right now."

So I told him everything. As the words poured out of me my father's clench shifted until he was sort of hugging me in an effort toward encouragement. When I was done he was still holding me while I stood stonily.

"You're having more trouble remembering, aren't you?" I said. "How about if you tell me everything now, Dad?"

"You already know most of it, don't you? I fade in and out. I'm on medication, a stricter diet that's supposed to help. Doing mental memory tests that make me feel like an idiot."

We sat together side by side on the log. I lit a cigarette. I blew smoke into the breeze. When I was ready to toss it he said, "Let me take the last puff." I handed him the butt and he took a single drag, then flicked it into the dark. He put his arm around me.

"You shouldn't have buried him here, Terry. That was stupid."

"I know."

"I moved the body."

It rocked me like a right hook under the heart. "What?"

"Don't ask me where. I won't tell you. It's better that you don't know. But he's gone."

"And still you come out here?"

"Like I said, I have a little trouble remembering."

I thought of my old man digging up the decomposing body of his brother, packing it into a canvas bag, dragging it through our yard, and tossing it into the back of his car. I pictured him driving and depositing the corpse. Reburying it somewhere. Down by Sheepshead Bay. Behind Kennedy Airport. Stealing a boat and taking it out to Orient Point, letting it drift into international waters behind the gambling boats. Like he said, it was the smarter move to make.

When I was done my father was gone and my coat was folded beside me. He'd vanished without a sound.

I sat in the Challenger parked in the driveway, the engine running and the heater fan blowing. I stared at my house and wondered if I was being haunted there or if I was doing the haunting. My cell rang.

"Terry? It's Shelby."

"I didn't think I'd hear from you ever again, Shel, considering how things went in your shop."

"I'm taking a chance on you."

"How so?"

"Just by talking to you."

"Okay. What do you have for me?"

He paused. The pause grew. It lengthened until I would've asked if he was still there, except I could hear him breathing. I let him take his time. I turned the fan up another notch. I aimed the vent at my throat. I couldn't lose my chill. I could feel my father staring from his bedroom window.

"Maybe you already know," Shelby said.

"Know what?"

"Danny Thompson's dead. Or as good as dead."

I shut my eyes against the night. There are deaths that, when you learn of them, you can't help but acknowledge your own. You know the name, and for a moment you think it's your own.

"What happened?"

"He was found lying in front of his house. At first they thought a stroke or brain aneurism. Turns out someone stuck a needle through his tear duct into his brain. He was lobotomized."

My Christ, I thought.

Haggert.

Haggert had had it done. So he could take over.

It wasn't until Shelby responded that I realized I'd spoken aloud.

"Haggert's always been a number-two man, it's where he's comfortable," Shelby said. "Looks like your pal Wes Zek is going to try running the family all on his own."

"What?"

"Yeah. He's already got me putting together a big card game of captains from Chi and L.A. He's flying them in on his dime. Lots of big action. Whores, drugs, good food, the usual. They're going to rent a party boat and set sail off Orient Point. It's his coming-out party. If he ever asks, you didn't hear any of this from me."

Shelby disconnected.

I snapped my phone closed. Then I opened it again and dialed a number. My call was answered before the end of the first ring.

"Hello?"

"Hello, Walton. I hope I didn't wake you."

"Terrier, my new friend. It's so nice to hear your voice. How are you?" He sounded genuinely pleased to hear from me. I thought of his charmer's smile, the handsome glowing face, the devil's beauty.

"To be sure, Walton, I've been better."

"That saddens me. Is there anything I can do to help?"

"Maybe," I said. "I have a question."

I imagined him drinking wine. I saw his red-stained lips. I felt the touch of his hand. "Certainly. Don't stand on ceremony. Ask."

The wind kicked up and rocked the car a little. I kept looking at the house, thinking of my lost father wandering inside its halls, waiting for me to somehow lead him back to wherever he needed to be. I pressed down on the gas to hear the engine hum.

"Did Haggert hire you to do away with Danny Thompson?" I asked. "Or was it Wes Zek?"

"I don't know what you've heard, Terrier, but to the best of my knowledge Danny Thompson remains alive."

Even the iceman hitter of a hundred men sought refuge in semantics when it served his purpose. "But he's been done away with nonetheless."

"Yes," Endicott responded. "Don't tell me that bothers you."

"It does, as a matter of fact."

"It was what he needed to happen. It's what was called for. No more or less."

"You haven't answered my question."

"No, I haven't. I'm sorry, Terrier, but you must realize I can't reveal my employers."

Danny and I had both been ready to kill one another at least a couple of times over the last few months. Maybe push would've come to shove eventually. Maybe I was only alive now because Danny had been targeted for something much worse than being slabbed. I pinched my nostrils together and tried not to picture a needle being jammed up my sinuses.

"You know what another factor is in the downfall of society, Walton?" I asked. "The lack of trust. It's hard to believe anyone nowadays. There's always a chance somebody is just trying to advance their own agenda."

"Yes," he said. "I know exactly what you mean."

I told the truth. "But I'd believe you, Walton. Of everyone I have in my life I think I would trust you more than all of them. More than my father. More than my best friend. Even my girl. The girl who was once my girl."

"That makes me sad," Endicott said, his voice low, calm, but still with that timbre of amiability. "I feel sorry for you, Terrier, for saying such a thing. You must lead a cold existence. But I think I understand. You really want me to find and kill your friend, don't you? He's married to your former lover, isn't he?" Those fake teeth shining. His talking on the cell phone teeth. His lobotomizer teeth. "You can serve us both if you just tell me where he is."

"I still don't know."

"And I accept that. You see, we truly do share a belief in each other."

"Another question, Walton, if I may?"

"Please."

My fingers were freezing. I switched hands and held the phone with my left. I jammed my right in front of the heater. Numb as it was I was still reminded of his touch.

"I don't know much about lobotomies. Why did you do it that way? Why don't you just kill them?"

"I usually do. My employer in this case specified a particularly cold-blooded form of . . . compensation."

"It's sadistic."

"It was someone else's sadism. They initiated. I was only the instrument. Do you understand the difference?"

"I understand your need to apply a differentiation."

"But you don't agree."

"No, but I'm not a hitter."

"But you are a killer, Terrier," he said. "I don't know who you've murdered but I could see its taint on you. You're my kind. We know about the disappeared, you and I. We know where the vanished are hidden. We understand these things. We share a particular perspective. We are knowledgeable."

Endicott's eyes would now be full of forbearance and comprehension. Maybe nearly as much as Collie's when he'd stared at me through the glass as they gave him his hot shot, and he watched my face full of all my love and hate for him, and he silently urged me to realize that I was on the same path.

"If that's all, my friend," Endicott said, "then I'll wish you a safe and good night. I hope to see you soon."

I drove past MacArthur Airport and watched the red-eyes coming in. I pulled back into the Hilton Garden Inn and walked across the lobby. The girl at the desk asked if she could help me and I told her no and took the elevator up to Simon Ketch's suite.

Only a couple of hours had gone by but the place had cleared out. Maybe the party had moved on to another happening spot, or the hotel dicks had crashed it, or the gang was off on a coke run. A few folks dawdled or lay half conscious on the couches. They watched me like they weren't sure I was real or a hallucination. They didn't care if I was actually there. They did a few more lines, shuffled around, and left.

Both bedroom doors were shut. The bodyguard/bouncer/thug with the gun met me with a huge hand to my chest.

He said, "Party's over."

"I noticed. You told me to come back later."

"Now you're too late."

"Is Simon here?"

"That doesn't matter. You have to go."

"Okay. Mind if I just get a quick drink first?"

"Make it fast."

He walked me to the bar. The bartender was gone.

I said, "You want anything?"

"No."

I picked up a bottle of JD and swung it into his stomach. The air in his lungs exploded out of him like a hurricane and blew my hair back. He made a painful *eep* sound and went to his knees. He showed me the sweet spot on his crown. If I hit him in the head with the JD bottle it might cave his skull in. He gasped and tried to grab me. I slid the bottle back onto the counter and spun my hips, got my weight behind my fist, threw a roundhouse right, and laid him out flat. I got his pistol out of his holster and put it in my jacket pocket. It was a 9mm.

I tried the first bedroom.

In it was a seriously stoned couple on the bed making love. I knew they were stoned because they were two feet away from each other on the mattress and facing in opposite directions. I suspected they were never going to get around to grabbing each other but that didn't seem to slow them up in any way.

I opened the other bedroom door.

Ketch was alone, seated at the desk before his laptop, tearing away at the keypad. I heard teenagers laughing and the screen showed blurs of activity inside a shaky cam shot. Maybe he was watching *ROGUES*. Maybe his *Crazy Chicks* show. He hadn't noticed me yet. He had his jacket hanging off the back of his chair. The fedora and the charcoal vintage suit couldn't help but snag your attention. The suit was a throwback to the forties. I didn't know if it was actually vintage or if it was just supposed to look that way.

The window was open. An icy breeze blew the draperies over the back of a divan, making them whirl as if the dead were hiding behind the curtains. I walked up and Simon Ketch turned and saw me coming. His eyes grew alive with a dark excitement, perhaps a reflection of my own.

He smiled at me.

"Heya," Ketch said. "I'm glad you found us."

"So am I."

"Help yourself to a drink."

"I'm good."

"Crank?"

"No."

"There are some girls still around, I think."

"No."

I couldn't help myself. I reached out and tugged the hat off his head.

I don't know how to describe him, Tony had said. *He sort of looks like you.*

He did look like me, right down to the white streak in his hair.

My cousin John said, "You want to know what it's all about, right?"

I remembered the poster of Bogie on his editing room wall. If you were going to have another identity, you might as well make it one of your heroes.

"No," I said. "I already know what it's all about."

"Can I tell you my story?"

"No, John, I don't want to hear your story right now."

John doesn't need any help.

My uncle Will had been right. John didn't need any help at all. He knew how to make money. He knew how to ride cultural phenoms. He knew how to use people. He understood how to control and deceive others, his own family, his own blood.

I had gone deep into him. I had stared into his eyes and sent myself into him and I still had missed the fact that I was looking at two people.

This guy wasn't an act. That was the real John and this was the real Simon Ketch. He was both men, the same way that old Crowe was a classy old-world cool cat and a sordid hustler, the same way Will was all style and top-shelf bourbon and drug-selling horror-flick-king rip-off artist.

"Why'd you tell Tony not to let Dale leave the show?" I asked.

"I told you I was obsessed. I couldn't have her abandoning me. *ROGUES* needs her. I need her."

"You need her?"

"I found her. I made her. I sought her out. I saw the draw she had. Just in the news reports about Collie when the journalists were camping out in front of your house, whenever the camera got a piece of her, whenever she flashed her smile or said a word, I saw the thing in her that made her different. I sent Tony after her to bring her in, to set her up and make her the face of the show."

A wave of nausea passed over me. I had practically gift-wrapped my own sister for him. "I trusted you."

"Did you really think I would move back to L.A. on a whim? You think you can make that kind of a decision for a grown man?" He went deep into *me* this time, peering into my eyes, seeing what was inside, my guts strung out for him. "You know nothing about people, Terry. You think that's how the world works? All you do is overstep your bounds."

He was right. I tried to respond but nothing managed to find its way out.

"And you gave me a pitiful ten grand to help you." It got him laughing humorlessly. It corkscrewed into my temple and I had to grit my teeth. "I told you I had money. But you didn't believe me. You really think I want back into Hollywood? That hellhole? Spend all my time beating my brains out making documentaries? You know how much money I have? Do you want to know how much I'm worth?"

"I know exactly how much you're worth, John."

He smiled. "Two hundred million. And it's only the beginning. I'm just starting to come into my own. I've been siphoning funds from my father and grandfather for years. From All Hallows' Eve, from Fireshot, the crank, and the money pours in from *ROGUES*, Terrier. In advertising revenue alone I clear—"

"I don't care."

"Yes, you do. You're a thief. You want money. That's all you want.

You don't want to have it. You just want to take it. You want what's mine. What belongs to the Crowes."

He was feeling the connection, knowing me, understanding me, like we were partners now, down in the double helix, our fates entwined. I felt it too.

Protecting your family was a Pyrrhic victory. Even if you could save them they'd just turn on you and set fire to you in the end.

"Do you know what I'm going to do to Dale?"

"John—"

"I'm going to make her a star. You're going to be proud. You just wait."

My breath started to come in bites.

"You want to kill me, don't you?" he asked.

"No," I said. "Why would you think I'd want to kill you?"

"You look like you want to kill everybody all the time, Terry."

Someone moved behind me. I almost pulled the 9mm, but a familiar voice spoke quietly in my ear and said, "It's all right."

I turned and my parents were standing there.

My father in his black cat burglar outfit. My mother, wearing her everyday clothes. I could see that my father wasn't entirely here. He looked at me without any recognition. My mother had brought him along, had aimed him, and had used his skills to keep tabs on me. He didn't need me to lead him to wherever he needed to be, after all. He had my mother for that.

She was holding the Sig Sauer.

"Oh, Ma," I said. "What are you doing?"

"Did you really think I was going to let anyone take my baby girl away without my knowing everything about him? Without my checking? Without my learning all their secrets?"

"Ma—"

"You tricked us," she said to John.

"No, I didn't. I told you the truth. I just didn't tell you every-thing. Why are you so mad?"

"I heard what you said—"

John had no idea what was going on with my dad. "Uncle Pin-scher?"

"—about being obsessive. So am I. I'm obsessive about protecting my family."

"What's the matter with Uncle Pinscher?"

"I'm dedicated to it, John."

She slashed him twice across the nose with the barrel of the gun. "Did you think I'd let any of you Crowes harm anyone in my fam-ily?"

"I am your family!"

"You're nothing to me."

He moaned and doubled over and spit blood. He reached into his pocket and I grabbed his wrist. He was going for a handkerchief. He dabbed his face. He had a wide cut on the bridge of his nose, and his nose was broken. It leaked blood badly. "I didn't harm anyone. I'm going to make her a star."

"You had her running around with a bunch of little felons while they performed illegal acts."

"Why should that bother you? You're all a bunch of crooks!"

"You hire henchmen and stooges. You hide behind a fake name. You play dangerous games."

"I'm a businessman. I'm an artist."

"You're going to go away," my mother said. "You'll go back to doing or being whatever it is you are. I don't ever want to see you again. And just in case you think I might be just pretending, that this might just be an act of some kind—"

She took a step forward. He flung up his arms to protect himself and let out a yelp of terror that almost sounded like "Ma," a wild cry for mother, which will be the sound we all make at the moment of our greatest horror, when the underneath drags us all down. My mother grabbed a satin pillow off the divan, took two steps to her nephew, the guy who looked like her father, who looked like her brother, who looked like her oldest son, who looked like me, pressed the pillow to his thigh, jammed the barrel tightly against it, and shot him twice in the leg. He shrieked and she stuffed the barrel in his mouth.

"Do you understand me, John? Nod your head."

Tears rippled down his cheeks. He nodded.

"I don't care how much money you have, or how many people you hire, or if you try to tug at my heartstrings again. If you don't stay away from us we'll have to hurt you even more. I'll set my son against you. I'll set my husband against you. And I'll be against you. You won't survive."

I picked up the hotel phone and dialed the desk. I told the girl on duty that Mr. Ketch had been in an accident and we needed an ambulance.

My mother and father left the bedroom. I followed them out. The thug I'd nailed with the JD bottle was starting to come around. He tried to make a grab for me again as I passed by. My parents and I walked out of the suite and down the opposite hall toward the freight elevator. My old man was still way out of it.

My mother hadn't brought her purse but she'd hidden the Sig Sauer someplace on her person. We got into the freight elevator and took it down to the first floor. It let us off someplace near the kitchen, which was closed. The nearest exit was only a few feet away. I stepped in front of them and went out the door first to make sure no surprises were waiting. There weren't any. We turned the corner of the building and my father's car was parked next to the Challenger.

"Why'd you follow me?" I asked her.

"I saw that boy Tony hit Dale."

"I made him pay for that," I said.

"I thought you would. I asked Dale about him. She was upset and didn't want to talk but I was relentless. I told her I wouldn't let her drop out of school and move to L.A. She was furious but she eventually explained about *ROGUES*. Why didn't you tell me?"

"I was hoping she was done with it and she could put the mistake behind her."

"You still should have told me, Terry. You know our mistakes are never very far behind us."

"I was wrong, Ma, I'm sorry."

"I thought you might have gotten an address on Ketch from Tony. I knew you would send a message but I thought it was important that I signed my name to it as well."

"Jesus Christ, Ma, when did you get like this?"

"I've been a Rand for thirty years. Longer than you. Before that I was a Crowe. I've always been like this, Terrier."

I looked at my father hoping he'd be back inside himself again, but he just stood there, glass-eyed, his chin down on his chest exactly the way Gramp's usually was in between cartoons.

"He knew something was wrong," my mother said. "He was watching you sitting out in the driveway."

"I know."

"When you pulled away he left the house. I went after him and we tailed you. Terry, you should always try to shake a tail, even if you don't know one is on you, even if there isn't one at all. Always act like there is."

"I'm starting to realize you're right."

"Yes, I am."

"How often does he get this bad?" I asked.

"More and more often, at night. When it's very dark. He stares into the darkness and disappears inside himself. It takes a few hours for him to come out of it again."

"What do the doctors say?"

"They have explanations for everything, but they can't help much.

He's on some new medication. Maybe it will slow the advancement. I need for you to pick it up for me tomorrow at Schlagel's."

In twenty-five years I'd be a night crawler, drained of personality, creeping beneath the moon, full of silence and skill, without words, values, or purpose. I only hoped I'd have a woman like my mother to help guide and watch over me.

"We don't ever talk about this, Terrier. This is the thing we do not talk about."

"I have a lot of things I don't talk about, Ma. I understand."

"Not a word."

"Never," I agreed.

She handed me the Sig Sauer and said, "Get rid of this. You shouldn't have a gun anyway."

"I left it under the dash. You're the one who pulled it. How'd you even know it was there?"

"You were practicing your draw in the driveway earlier."

"I was?"

"Yes. Throw it into the ocean."

I watched her get behind the wheel of my old man's car. He was strapped into the passenger seat like a child. My father came out of his fugue, looked at me, and said, "I just wish I could figure out what the hell the whole thing was about. I couldn't wrap my head around it. It was very . . . very . . ." He fought for the proper description.

It took me a second to realize where he was in his mind.

"French," I offered.

"Yeah. Exactly."

They drove off. It hadn't started to fall yet, but I tasted snow in the air.

I wanted to see Will and Perry. I wanted to tell them the truth about each other. I wanted to let them know what John was, in case they weren't fully aware. I wanted them to understand that while they were jamming each other up for tens of thousands, cousin John was sitting on top of two hundred million and two private planes.

I wanted to raid their home. Shelby would know how to fence the Emmys. I crept their house again. I went through John's cutting room and got my hands on *The Maltese Falcon* poster, yanked it out of its frame, and shredded it. I left the bald mutant cannibal from *The Hills Have Eyes* peering in the shadows, waiting for John to get home from the hospital. Bogie was my hero too.

I checked the bedrooms. Will wasn't in his. I imagined him at All Hallows' Eve or Fireshot, sitting in a hot tub with horror actresses, or worse, with Darla. I wondered if John, the cops, or the hospital had called and he was now in the waiting room with his boy. I couldn't see it but I couldn't see a lot of things.

I stepped into old Crowe's bedroom.

He was dead on the bed. My grandmother was still hanging on, lying beside him, her face turned to his throat in a mockery of romance, breathing rapidly, her eyes open.

She had fed him an overdose of his meds. I could see that he had fought with his strong hands, but she was stronger still. She had really wanted his ass dead.

I remembered thinking that it was things like that tinkling bell that drove people to murder or suicide.

"Oh Christ," I whispered. I snapped open my phone and dialed 911.

I climbed onto the bed and asked her, "What did you take?"

She was drowsy but willful. She refused to answer.

I gave 911 the address and told them the situation. I read the labels off the prescription bottles. They told me to shut any pets into a closed room and make sure the front door was unlocked.

I put my arms around her. I tried to haul her out of bed and onto her feet. Old Crowe's corpse lolled back and forth as I jounced the mattress. He still had something to say to me. His mouth was open, his eyes slitted. He semisneered. He'd vomited on himself but she'd kept stuffing the pills down his throat.

"There's still time," I shouted at her. "Get up."

She began to cry. "There's nothing left for me. I've failed at everything."

"You've got my mother. You can talk to my mother again. A real talk. You can have a real relationship with her again."

"This house is cursed."

"It's not the house," I said.

"The people in it."

"The people in every house are cursed. Now get up, lady!"

I overpowered her and got her on her feet. I slung her arm around my shoulder and walked her to the bathroom. I pried her mouth open and stuck my index finger down her throat as far as it could go and she threw up in the sink. I wet a towel with cold water and washed her down. She woke up a little more. I stood her back up and we walked through the house.

"Go. Just go."

"Don't die," I pleaded.

"Why not?"

"I don't want you to."

"Why?"

"You're my grandmother."

EMS and a couple of firemen arrived. They asked me a hundred questions about her that I didn't have the answers to. They worked on Perry for a ridiculously long time. The fucker would never be any more dead. They asked me point-blank if she had killed him. I said no, he'd killed himself after a painful struggle with infirmity following several strokes. Let them prove different.

They got her on a gurney. My grandmother held her hand out toward me and I took it. I walked alongside the EMTs until they put her in the back of an ambulance. I went to climb in with her but they told me I'd have to follow behind. She kept her eyes on me until they slammed the doors and pulled away.

I asked someone, "What are her chances?"

He responded, "She's old."

I could feel Chub dying out there somewhere. I parked in front of Kimmy's aunt's place again. It was two in the morning. I sat and watched the dark house for over an hour. My breath froze. It was turning colder. I had to run the engine to stay warm. I lit cigarettes and cracked the window. I thought about Danny Thompson in the hospital with only the barest brain function. I could see him sitting at a long-term care facility in a white day room, his chin covered in drool, his wife feeding him baby food.

A light went on in the house. Kimmy stood framed in the bay window. She'd made me.

I climbed out of the Challenger. I went to the side door. Kimmy unlocked it. She moved out of my way. I eased inside.

We stood face-to-face, alone in the shadows thrown from a single low-level light left on over the sink, her mother sleeping somewhere in the house, just like the old days. I had the same mixture of excitement, lust, expectation, and vague dread I always had when I was in her presence. Only when you're with someone who means the world to you do you fear being destroyed if they should ever be taken away.

She turned her face up toward mine as if waiting for a kiss. I could lunge forward and steal one and spend the rest of my life apologizing for it. It would be worth it to feel her lips again.

But some measure of self-control I didn't know I had took over and I stepped away. She turned on the kitchen light and signaled for me to sit.

"I was waiting for you," she said.

"How did you know I was coming by tonight?"

"I've been waiting for you every night. I've seen you parked out there, watching over us. Usually you only stay a few minutes. Tonight you didn't leave."

She waited for me to respond. I said nothing.

"Do you want coffee? Caffeine never used to bother you no matter how late you drank it."

"Sure."

She made a pot. She checked on Scooter. When she returned she poured us two cups, set one in front of me, and took the far seat. She didn't bother with milk or sugar. She sipped. She had dark smudges under her eyes. I bet she hadn't slept for more than three hours straight since this thing started. We stared at each other over a centerpiece of plastic sunflowers.

On the floor in the corner was one of those toy ovens with knobs that turn and ding. There were little toy pots, frying pans, and cutlery, alongside cans of soup and plastic pieces of steak, ham, turkey legs, eggs, and vegetables. I imagined Scooter standing there pretending to cook alongside her mother.

Kimmy waited for me to explain myself as the mood between us thickened. I could feel the tension inside her fighting to get out. I don't know where she got the strength to hold it all in without so much as a grimace. I sat there with my chin tucked in waiting like a frightened child to take a well-deserved punishment.

"Have you found my husband?" she asked.

"No," I said.

"Can you tell me what's going on, Terry? Does it have to do with that big bank robbery?"

"It has nothing to do with the bank robbery. The rest of it, I'll let him tell you when he comes home."

"And will he? Will he ever come home to me?"

"Of course, Kimmy."

"Then why is he on the run? What trouble has he gotten into?"

"No real trouble. Stop worrying. It's just a misunderstanding and it'll be cleared up soon."

"Then why can't I go back to my house?"

"I told you, it's just a precaution."

"You're a bad liar, Terry. You're worse now than ever."

"I'm not lying."

"You don't even put any effort into it. And you don't even realize you're doing such a terrible job. It's because of your family. You all lie to each other so often, so indifferently, so . . . frivolously that you've all simply come to accept it. You don't ever question one another, so you don't think anyone will ever question you."

Maybe she was right. It felt like she was right. But some things, even when you imagine they might be true, you can't bring yourself to agree with out loud. I finished my coffee. I tried not to lie. I stood and went for the door.

She sensed my reaction and stepped in front of me. Her body language distilled our history. She crossed her arms over her chest and let her head dip back like she offered her body to me, her lips, her throat. The moment began to shift into something else.

I could make love to her. I could have her again, if only for an hour. It might be enough, it might never be enough. She would allow it. She might even return some of my intensity. I had my words prepared already. They were soothing. They were wanting. They were rough. They were honest. They were bullshit. I knew a few extra moves I didn't know five years ago. Darla had taught me a couple more recently. I couldn't help thinking that Kimmy would be impressed. She moved closer to me. The muscles of her forearms touched my chest. The electric thrill was still there inside of me. I watched her eyes. She felt nothing but heartache and the barest hope that I might help her without exacting a debasing payment.

A page from a coloring book was up on the refrigerator, held in place by magnets. A crooked house, window with four panes, sun in the upper corner with a few lines showing it was shining, a tree with a knothole in the trunk. Scooter had scribbled wildly across the picture, big zigzags of red, blue, and yellow crayons, just trying to brighten the thing up. I tugged it off. I wanted it. I always took what I wanted.

Beneath was another picture of a house, this time seen from the back. This time with people. Mommy, Daddy, little girl, and a dog, all standing in descending order of height, all smiling with big funky teeth, even the dog. More zigzags of orange, green, yellow.

The chord struck like the last note of a song I'd been listening to for most of my life but had somehow forgotten.

"She misses her father," Kimmy said. "And don't tell me that she's too young and she doesn't know who he is because you'd be wrong."

"I'd never say such a stupid thing."

"Just so you know. Just so you understand what it's been like these last few days. I'm scared, Terry. I'm scared and I'm angry. I can't sleep. I can't go home. I can't do anything. I'm helpless. And I see you sitting out there. So tell me, tell me again, what are you doing to find Chub? What are you doing to fix this, whatever it is?"

"I'll call you later."

"Terry, what—"

"He'll be home soon. I promise."

All my promises were lies told for my own benefit. I said whatever I needed to say to get to the end of any situation and free again. So long as I made it away with the cash and my skin, I'd tell anybody any old shit.

But this time, looking into her eyes, I meant it. This time, I thought proudly, I would save her and Chub at the cost of my own heart. I didn't have to steal everything, all the time, from everyone who mattered. I could give Scooter her father back, and with him bring the hope for a house of chaotic colors and tremendous smiles.

Number ten. The expression on the face of your lost love when you've made another promise you should not have made.

I returned to Wright's Garage. I got that same feeling of someone watching me once more. I sensed death in the air. I could practically smell it.

I packed the Sig Sauer. I grabbed a flashlight out of Chub's office and wandered the lot. It was a big lot. Chub had a bunch of restored cars. Others were in various states of disrepair, some that needed new engines, some that would necessitate serious bodywork. In back, lined up against a distant fence topped by loops of barbed wire, were dozens of total junkers.

Five wouldn't fit in the fastback.

They hadn't carjacked some old lady and held her hostage in her station wagon.

There'd been two getaway cars. When the driver wiped out, the crew piled into the second car. With a second driver. Someone who knew the route. Someone who was sharp behind the wheel.

Those scrapped cars were laid out in heaps. Piles of bumpers, engines, crankshafts, undercarriages, hoods, doors, stacks of tires. Cairns of spare parts rose up all around me. I drifted among them, scanning the roofs of the houses that backed up to the lot. Cheap A-frames, saltboxes, and double-wide trailers. It took me a while of meandering before I could see a pattern emerging to the maze. Another route through the lot came into focus. It led to a well-hidden little alcove shored by gutted, topless convertibles covered in bird shit. Inside the niche was a tarp-covered vehicle.

I untied the tarp and pulled it off. Beneath was a '62 Crown Vic with a battered body and a souped engine. It was big enough for all five of them, but Chub would've wanted to go his own way afterward.

That's why the two cars. The tight four-man crew heads off in one direction, Chub speeds off on his own. But after the botched bank job, and the driver breaking his neck, Chub got stuck taking the rest of the heisters out of there and babysitting them until the heat was off. Except with all those dead ex-cops the heat would never be off.

Thank you, Scooter. Two pictures of houses, one hidden behind the other, helped to point the way.

Last time I was here I thought about how Chub would have land, a house, or a pad already prepared. Maybe out of state, maybe upstate.

Or maybe right behind the garage.

Just like hiding a second safe beneath the first. I could see him being brazen enough to buy a hole-up space within spitting distance of his own place of business. It was ballsy as hell. Maybe it was smart too, I wasn't sure.

There would be a well-hidden locked gate somewhere nearby. I didn't bother with searching for it. I took out the passenger-side car mat of the Crown Vic and tossed it over my shoulder. The ten-foot fence had metal slats like Venetian blinds woven through the chain links for privacy. It made it hard for me to get a grip as I jumped onto the hood of the Vic. I reached, clung to the fence, and started to climb. When I got to the top I finagled the car mat over the barbed wire topping and managed to scurry over without tearing my flesh or my clothes. I leaped down and found myself in the small grassless yard of a dark saltbox.

It didn't matter. I knew someone from the crew would be patrolling and watching, just like he had that night I staked out the garage. There was a reason I'd felt eyes on me.

I stood there and lit a cigarette. I smoked in the cold air and said, "I want to see Chub."

The guy was careful. It took him a couple of minutes to work around and sneak up behind me. He pressed the barrel of a gun into my ear. "You didn't learn the first time you ran up against us?"

"I wasn't running up against you then or now, even though every-body else in the world is. I just want to talk to Chub."

"You're packing. Lose the piece."

"No."

"Then I'll shoot you in the head right now."

I took another drag on the cigarette and flicked it away. "It's al-most four o'clock in the morning. You'll wake up a lot of people. This might not be the best neighborhood on the island, but I bet a .44 going off nearby would still get a few folks dialing 911."

"Let's go."

I led him toward the back door of the saltbox. The door was unlocked. I walked in and lights were on. The place had been blacked out like a London apartment during the Blitz. The window shades were made of an especially thick material and were pinned in place.

The other two crew members stood there in a kitchen empty of furniture. Empty beer bottles had been carefully restocked inside the cardboard case containers. I smelled recently overcooked meat. Plates, glasses, and silverware had all been washed and stacked in the drain-board. Like me, they'd probably heard a lot of the same stories of guys on the run who'd wiped down all the prints from some hideout, for-getting about the dirty dishes. They weren't going to make such a dipshit mistake.

The other two held their hardware on me as well. All three of them were carrying .44s. Without their little black wool caps on and their coats zipped to the collar, they still looked similar, cut from the same cloth, but I could pick them out of a lineup now.

I knew their names. "Dunbar, Edwardson, Wagstaff. Which is which?"

"That shouldn't matter to you."

It didn't. I applied the names just to keep the three of them straight in my head.

"He's carrying," Dunbar, the guy who'd been roving the area, told them.

"How about if you lose the piece," Wagstaff said, emphasizing his words by pointing his gun at my face. I removed the Sig Sauer from my pocket and Dunbar shoved the barrel of his .44 a little harder against the back of my head, reached over my shoulder, and snatched the pistol from my hand. He jammed it into his own coat pocket.

"Didn't we make our point well enough last time, little doggy?" Wagstaff asked.

"That was before you guys turned a score into a bloodbath and lost your driver."

"He wants to see Chub," Dunbar told them.

Edwardson and Wagstaff shared a weighty look and then Edwardson shrugged and Wagstaff nodded. "Let him."

Dunbar pushed me forward into the next room. Calling it a living room would've been gracious. The walls were empty. A small television had been set up in the far corner. At one window sat a chair. On the sill was a pair of binoculars. A slit had been made in the shade. Chub had it worked out that he could look into his office window from here and check on cops, feebs, or hitters who wandered into the garage. I guessed that some of the metal slats in the fence had been removed in certain places so the crew could take turns checking on anybody nosing around. That's who I'd felt watching me.

Chub was on a brown Naugahyde couch with orange throw pillows, and he was dying. One look told me he wouldn't last another hour. He lay half covered by a too-small comforter, coughing and shuddering with his shirt off, his chest much whiter than the seeping bandages wrapped around his stomach, lathered in a viscous ashen sweat. His lips and nostrils were caked with blood.

He gave me a cockeyed grin.

He said, "Hey."

My mind was filled with so much that I wasn't thinking about anything anymore. I held my ground for a second. Dunbar crowded me and I fell back against him. He shoved me off. Scooter's smiling dog ran past in my mind, and in my mind I named him FDR.

I kneeled at Chub's side, peeled his bandages back while he moaned, and tried not to vomit at the smell. The bullet had torn a jagged chunk from his lower belly, leaving a runny hole the size of my fist. It was badly infected and oozing pus and bile. There was no exit wound. They'd found him some bent doctor, but the butcher must've been like most underworld docs: disgraced, drunk, and ambivalent. There were hesitation cuts. The incisions were amateurish. Some halfhearted attempt at suturing had been made but the stitches had pulled. Chub's skin had started to go citrus yellow.

"Which one of these pricks shot you?" I asked him.

Wagstaff said, "Us? We didn't do it. A trigger-happy armored car guard pulled his pistol and started the ball rolling."

I hissed at Chub, "Why for fuck's sake did you go on the job?"

"I wanted a bigger cut."

"Why?"

He grinned stupidly. It seemed a point of pride with him not to answer me.

"The doc wasn't sure if the bullet nicked his liver," Edwardson said. "We're pretty sure now."

"Antibiotics?" I asked.

"He's taken them all."

"You guys couldn't have broken into a pharmacy and picked him up something else to try to hold off infection?"

"We couldn't leave. That was the whole point of locking down in here."

"You could've called me."

"We wanted to," Wagstaff said, which surprised the hell out of me. "But he told us no. He's a stubborn son of a bitch, same as you."

That made Chub chuckle a little, followed by a wave of agony rolling through him. He shuddered and tried to keep from screaming. The concern on my face made him laugh even more, which caused him greater distress. He leaned aside and spit red-flaked phlegm into a wastebasket set near his head. He huffed for air but couldn't seem to catch his breath. I put my hand on his bare back and rubbed and patted.

"The doc gave him something for the pain," Edwardson said.

"Where?"

"End table."

The freshly polished tabletop smelled of pine. They probably cleaned every couple of hours to sweep prints and strands of hair away. They weren't just pros, they were fastidious, obsessive fuckers who'd been crawling all over each other for days. I looked for prescription bottles. It took me a second to realize that wasn't the kind of painkiller he'd been given.

"Jesus Christ," I said, lifting a baggie of white powder. "This is heroin."

"It's done the job," Dunbar said. "He's not feeling much. Don't let him have any more right now or he'll OD."

I pulled out my phone and all three of them said, "No," and pointed their .44s loosely at me. They were starting to look exactly alike again. I drew the Sig Sauer. I'd plucked it from Dunbar when I'd fallen against him. I pointed it at Edwardson's chest because he happened to be standing in the middle of the trio.

"You let me call," I said, "or this situation goes into meltdown."

"Then that's what happens," Wagstaff told me. "Give up the phone and the piece."

"No."

I was close. I was on the edge. I'd been there for a while. The underneath called to me and begged me to fire, to murder, to die. It promised me the end of anguish and a proper understanding of purpose.

Chub said, "Terry, don't be a moron." He giggled. The H had

him out of his head, but it didn't seem to be helping much with his pain. He held his hand out to me but I was standing just beyond his reach. He tried to grab me again. "Forget it."

"You need a hospital."

"No hospital." His voice was barely a whisper.

"Now's not the time to be obstinate, you asshole."

"Would you go?"

I would go. I would run. I would push little old ladies out of the way. I wouldn't die on Naugahyde, coughing up my yellow guts. But I didn't have a wife and child to share in my stupidity and terror and humiliation. If I did, I'd probably die quietly alone like Chub wanted to, if I could find the courage.

I snapped my phone shut. The three of them jammed their guns in my face and grabbed the phone and the Sig Sauer. This time Dunbar sneered and tucked the piece in his inside pocket.

They saw in my eyes that I wasn't going to do anything else. That there wasn't anything else to do.

"You should pack faster," I said. "You need to get out of here now."

"Why is that?" Dunbar asked.

"Some very bad people are after you. If I can find you, so can they."

"We'll be gone in fifteen minutes."

"Go faster."

They left me there with Chub and gave the place one last quick spiff job, wiping all surfaces down, before heading to the bedrooms to pack up. The hideout was blown. Even if they killed me, what were they going to do? Hide both our bodies in the bathtub? Bury us in a back lawn that didn't even have grass or leaf cover? The crew gathered their guns and satchels and luggage.

I sat on the edge of the couch and took Chub's hand.

"You watched me come and go," I said.

"They saw you and told me."

I grabbed a pillow, tore off the outer lining, and ripped it into rags. I soaked them in the sink and washed his face down. I dabbed his forehead and wiped his mouth. "Why didn't you talk to me?"

"I wasn't sure if you would help or not."

I couldn't blame him for that. "So why was my number in your phone?"

His organs and nerve endings were shutting down. The pain seemed to ease. He spoke more clearly. "In case anything happened to me, Kim would give you a call and you'd look out for her."

The crew came out carrying their bundles. They paused in the doorway but had nothing to say. Chub gave a nod in their direction.

"Watch out for a handsome guy with perfect teeth," I said. "He'll ice you with a needle, if you're lucky. If you're not, he'll just scramble your prefrontal lobe."

"What the hell are you talking about?" Wagstaff asked.

"Just keep an eye out for him."

Then they were gone. I didn't know where they had stashed a new car, but they'd have one. I didn't hear them walk away. I didn't hear a car engine start. They stepped into the darkness and disappeared along the path of their plan, one that Chub had helped set up. He had organized a hundred escape routes before, but now when he needed only one more, there weren't any left for him.

Not even thirty seconds later, a sound. I heard a heavy, blunt noise like a wet cough. It was a grunt of pain. It was the unmistakable sound of instant, traumatic death.

Then, from the doorway. "Terrier?"

"Hello, Walton."

He stepped into the living room. He stood there being beautiful and merciless, with three more lives added to his score sheet. His hands were in his pockets. I still didn't see the needle, wherever it was, whatever it was. He beamed at me.

"Who's this?" Chub whispered.

Endicott said, "I was hired to kill you."

"Too late."

"I see that. I can smell the sepsis from here. I'm sorry."

"If you were just going to kill me anyway then why are you sorry?"

"I would have made it painless. I would've answered your call. I would have fulfilled your purpose."

"My call?" Chub asked. "My purpose?" He looked at me.

"Walton talks like that," I said.

"Oh."

Endicott watched me, smiling, his brash good looks almost daring me to jump forward and meet my own death head-on, his will drawing the mongoose forward to the serpent. Except he wasn't the fulfillment to my purpose and he wasn't getting paid to dispose of me.

"Who hired you to kill Danny? Was it Haggert or Wes Zek?"

"I hope we meet again soon, Terrier."

"Pardon me if I say that I hope we don't."

He smiled at me once more and was gone.

"Weird," Chub whispered.

I fought to keep my voice steady. I tried not to let the rage out. But just as with all the times it had counted before, I couldn't control myself when it mattered most.

"What the hell were you doing?" I asked. "Why did you go with them on the score? And a bank heist? An armored car heist? Why?"

His teeth and lips were red but he managed another laugh. "It sounds so stupid when I say it out loud. But I wanted to make one final big score."

"Why? You didn't need it. You had plenty stashed. The garage was doing good business. I saw your books. Both sets of them. You could've given your family everything. What did you want more for?"

He sucked air and just looked at me. "I had to keep my girls."

"They're your girls."

"And I had to keep them." He sank deeper into the couch. I mopped his face. "It's always been you, Terry. She still loves you."

"You ass. I ran out on her. I abandoned her during the worst time of her life. She hates my guts."

"You've always had your head screwed on wrong. She loves you. She's always loved you. It's always been you. When you came back . . . the clock started. It was just a matter of time before she went back to you. I had to make one good score. I had to sell the shop. I had to move her away someplace safe. I needed to give her whatever she wanted."

"All she wants is you, Chub."

His own insecurities has been growing worse since I came home. I wasn't the only one who was jealous and defensive. All this time I'd thought I was protecting him, saving him, and instead I'd been pushing him into making the biggest mistake of his life.

"You are not laying this on me, you selfish prick."

"My cut's in the back bedroom, top of the closet, stashed in a kind of vent. Get it to Kim." He tried to grab the bag of heroin, but he couldn't reach it. "Here, give me another tap of that."

I handed it to him. He took a pinch, raised his fingers to his nostrils, and had a snort. "Never tried it before," he said. "Think I could develop a taste." His eyes started to roll. He swallowed thickly. He cleared his throat. He was panting heavily. "Open a window, would you?"

I did. An icy breeze hurtled across the room.

"Is it snowing yet?" he asked.

"No."

"Feels like it. Got that heaviness in the air, you know?"

"Yes."

"You always liked the cold more than me."

We looked at each other across a gulf of love and shame. The distance continued to grow even as the rest of the world fell away. All my lingering ghosts crowded alongside me in the room. I pictured my girls on the beach at Montauk, the three of us wandering the dunes and watching porpoises on the rocks in the distance. Kimmy took my right arm and Scooter grabbed the left. Chub held his yellow hand out to me and I clasped it. He repeated himself. *"She loves you. She's always loved you."* I wanted to argue the life back into him. I had so much left to say that I feared I would forget. Ice touched my cheek. I'd been wrong. It was snowing. Flakes sprinkled on the wind. FDR barked happily. Chub spoke my name. They were the words I wanted to hear most and the ones I didn't want to hear at all. He lifted his other hand and put it on my shoulder, like a fallen king offering grace to a knight. The dead can't offer redemption but the dying can. Yes, I liked the cold. Yes, I would've gone to the hospital. Yes, I would've spent the next twenty years in prison just so there was a chance to see my girl again. I'd learned that much being alone for five years. His breathing grew more labored. With each halting rise and fall of his chest I could feel myself drifting further away. I willed him to stay alive for my sake as much as his own. I asked him why he called her Kim instead of Kimmy. I would never be able to face her again. I would never be able to press my forehead to Scooter's again. His eyelids fluttered open and he focused on me. He gave me a tender smile. He made a last effort to speak but nothing came of it. His eyes closed and his head fell to one side. The snow dappled his face and melted on his cooling skin. The last whisper in the dark. *She loves you. She's always loved you.* The final minutes of night withdrew like a broken fever. I cried too because with him went my only dream into the unknowable borders of dawn.

About the Author

TOM PICCIRILLI, author of over twenty novels, has won the International Thriller Writers Award and four Bram Stoker Awards, as well as having been nominated for the Edgar, the World Fantasy Award, the Macavity, and le Grand Prix de l'Imaginaire.

About the Type

This book was set in Garamond, a typeface originally designed by the Parisian type cutter Claude Garamond (1480–1561). This version of Garamond was modeled on a 1592 specimen sheet from the Egenolff-Berner foundry, which was produced from types assumed to have been brought to Frankfurt by the punch cutter Jacques Sabon (d. 1580).

Claude Garamond's distinguished romans and italics first appeared in *Opera Ciceronis* in 1543–44. The Garamond types are clear, open, and elegant.